NO GLOVE NO LOVE

Ron Shillingford

First published April 2000 by BuzzWord UK
1st Floor, Supreme House
Stour Wharf, Stour Road,
London E3 2NT.
Project Manager: John Hughes
Tel: 0171 702 8012 Fax: 0171 791 3572
email: jhughes176@aol.com

Copyright: Ron Shillingford

ISBN 1-902544-00-5

A CIP record for this title is available from the
British Library

Cover photography: Black Ink Photographic
Tel/Fax: 020 7923 1980   020 7377 5365

Cover design: Inderpal S Patti
Design Gurus. email: indypatti@hotmail.com

Design and layout: Burhan Ahmad
Diehard Design. email: burhan@diehard.co.uk

Printed by Cox & Wyman Ltd
Reading, Berks. UK

This book will be available on the worldwideweb in French,
Portuguese, Spanish and Italian to be downloaded at a
small cost. The first book on the WWW in four languages.
WWW.noglovenolove.co.uk

Distribution by: Central Books, 99 Wallis Road, London E9 5LN.
Tel: 020 8986 4854 Fax: 020 8533 5821
email: orders@centbks.demon.co.uk

RON SHILLINGFORD
THE WORLD'S LONGEST APPRENTICESHIP

Ron Shillingford has been a sports writer since 1982 and is currently the sports editor of the *New Nation*, a weekly black newspaper in the UK. An exclusive Frank Bruno double-page interview in December 1996 in *New Nation* was bought by *The Observer* and *Daily Mirror*.

His last big exclusive was an interview with Mike Tyson in *New Nation* when Iron Mike made his British debut in Manchester.

Other exclusives have included interviews with Muhammad Ali, Bruno (in Uganda), John Barnes (in Jamaica), Brian Lara, George Weah (in Jamaica) and Lennox Lewis (in Ghana). He covered the Mike Tyson rape trial in Indianapolis and has travelled throughout America, Europe and the Caribbean on assignments.

He has worked in television, as an assistant producer with *Trans World Sport* and sub-edited for *The Times* and *The Observer*.

His articles have appeared in most of the national newspapers and he also contributed to a weekly sports slot on BBC GLR radio. London-born of Dominican parents, he is married with one child and lives in Dollis Hill, north-west London. He was an amateur boxer at the Hogarth Club in Chiswick and has run the London Marathon twice.

No Glove No Love is his debut novel.

ACKNOWLEDGEMENTS

I want to thank all these people for providing help and inspiration: Seltzer 'Nasty Love' Cole for his guidance. Eddie Nestor and Robbie Gee for making me laugh. Ross Slater for support. Delphine Lath and Aisha Bank who made me believe it was worth carrying on.

Tony Fairweather for his connections. Sarwar Ahmed for being a thoroughly good geezer. Lloyd Bradley, Janis Elie, Adam Licudi, Patsy Antoine, Unal Rauf and Angela Hart for their editing skills.

Michael Eboda, the best editor I've worked with. Gillian Joseph for TV contacts, John Fashanu for remembering his roots. Tania Follett for giving me an extra chapter. Al Hamilton for limitless encouragement.

And for various reasons:
Rodney Hinds, Carole Pyke, Leone Ross, Ambrose Mendy, Frank Bruno, Frank Maloney, Lennox and Dennis Lewis, Ade Ogun, Llewella Gideon, Colin Hart, Brenda Emmanus, Mike Best, Jonathan Hicks, Anthea 'Love' Lee, Justin Onyeka, Karl George, Dotun and Diran Adebayo, Henry Bonsu, Steve Pope, Steve Bunce, Senanu Mortty, the Lule posse, Ken 'Decorum' Barnes, Wayne Alexander, Valerie John, Anne-Marie Hudson, Tony Attille, Gaby Jesson, Trish Adudu, Steve Lillis, Anne-Marie Parris, Cecilia Marquis, Wilton Hansel at Millennium Sports Management, Nick Awde, all at EMG, The Voice massive past and present, St Theresa and Jerry Shillingford.

Roger Dow - we're going to Vegas mate!

John Hughes - thanks for steering me through the maze, geezer.

Liz and Jasmin - this one's for you.

CHAPTERS

CHAPTER 1

CHASE DAT CRAZY BALDHEAD

Tiger swerved but his car still hit the drunken man in the street. It was a sickening thud like the time Tiger was in his uncle's car when he accidentally drove into a dog in the street and killed it.

The rain lashed down in the cold night air, making visibility as bad as you would expect on a windswept December night. It was not Tiger's fault but who would believe him? The man had appeared from nowhere.

Tiger felt the rear side of the car hit the man's legs, heard a muffled scream and imagined how he had rolled over and over until he hit the kerb on the other side of the road.

For a split-second Tiger slowed down, thinking of stopping to see if the man was alright. Through his rear-view window he could see him rising and breathed a sigh of relief, assumed he was not that badly hurt and decided to drive on. He was in a stolen car and already on probation for a number of juvenile offences and could not face another brush with the police.

Dis time I'd go down forever.

So he carried on driving the Cosworth carefully through the streets of south London, worried that someone had seen him and had taken his registration number or that the police would be pulling him up at any second.

He parked in a quiet road near the Elephant and Castle Shopping Centre and decided to walk the few miles home to Brixton Hill, avoiding the main roads in the process in case the cops pulled him up. Tiger made sure he did not walk past the scene of the accident on the Brixton Road, passing through Stockwell instead.

On the way home he passed a boxing gym where he occasionally trained, but for once paid no attention to it. This was no time for dreaming about one day being a world champion. His mind was still racing.

Dat guy was crazy getting in my way like dat. What happened to Junior in his car? Must have given up racing me.

He quietly turned the key to his mother's flat, crept into his bedroom, ensuring not to wake his mother and brother, pulled off his clothes and jumped into bed.

He could not sleep. Did not even try. The thought of the accident too vivid to allow any other thoughts or actions.

As the morning light crept into his bedroom, he switched on his TV to see if the accident had made the news. There was no mention on the Newsroom Southeast bulletin, but just for his peace of mind, he looked up the local news on Teletext.

'BRIXTON MAN KILLED IN HIT AND RUN' screamed the headline. Tiger sat down on the end of his bed suddenly woozy. A feeling of nausea surged from his stomach to the back of his throat.

I've killed a man...I've killed a man...I've killed him....It was me, the murderer....killed him....dead...

~

Dale Harrison could feel the steady trickle of blood running from his nose and into his mouth. The force of Tiger's punches numbed his senses and he felt a terrible nagging pain on the right side of his head from pounding left hooks.

This was the third round of their sparring session and the whole gym had stopped to watch Dale, the best known boxer from the recently defunct Streatham Hill Boxing Club, take on Tiger Crawford, the Champion Gloves' best. Tiger was a vicious fighter and malevolently asserted his superiority over this newcomer with ease.

Coach Nelson, barked: 'Stick ya jab out, Dale, if ya wanna keep him at bay. Jab, son, go on, jab!'

By now Dale's resistance was virtually non-existent. He pawed feebly with a tired left glove to fend off the swarming punches, but pain and exhaustion enveloped his every limb.

'Twenty seconds left!' shouted Nelson. 'Hands up, Dale.'

A weary Dale was determined to last the course.

I've got to keep going otherwise everybody'll think I'm a pussy.

Wham! Another thudding left hook rammed against his swollen right eye.

'Ten seconds!' shouted Nelson. 'Jab and move, Dale!'

Blood and snot combined in a gory mess over his handsome features, partially limiting his view of a sneering Tiger, evidently enjoying the session as he breathed heavily through a black gumshield, fierce eyes raging inside his headguard.

The ring bell finally tolled and the thirty-odd spectators now congregated around the ring apron applauded spontaneously as Dale stumbled to the corner for Nelson to remove his gumshield and headguard.

'Well done, kid,' said Nelson in his New York drawl. 'I'm proud ah ya. I know Tiger is rough but I needed to see what ya made of.'

'Thanks coach,' whispered a panting Dale between swollen lips. 'I did alright.'

Tiger approached. 'Respec', Dale,' he muttered, slapping him on the backside grudgingly. Tiger paused and looking

11

directly into Dale's bruised face and ignoring Nelson's presence, added: 'But don't forget who's de raas-claat don in 'ere. You get me?'

Tiger rarely complimented anyone. He viewed anyone entering the gym as a potential arch-rival and since Dale's arrival a fortnight earlier he had watched him train with undisguised hostility. Tiger preferred playing Bob Marley on the gym stereo as he trained and his favourite track was 'Crazy Baldheads'. He would grunt along whilst hitting the heavy bag: 'We're gonna chase dem crazy baldheads outta town...'

The gym, a vast converted derelict church, with bare wooden floorboards, desperately needed decorating. The smell of liniment and stale sweat hung heavily in the air. There was an elevated ring in one corner and eight punch bags suspended on chains in another. Posters and photos of champion fighters adorned the red brick walls.

Fly posters of championship fights, professional and amateur, broke up the monotony of dozens of black and white images of boxers in fight poses.

Tiger, the multi-titled champion since winning his first schoolboy title, aged thirteen, was the Champion Gloves' most accomplished fighter. A moody, scowling youth, he was especially grumpy as the tension mounted two weeks before the Junior Amateur Boxing Association championships.

Eighty wins against only seven losses in his career stood him up as one of the best welterweights in the country. Had it not been for a flash of anger when he argued with an ABA coach over training techniques while on an England squad session, he would have earned more than the two international vests proudly mounted on his bedroom wall. The coach threw him out of the squad for dissent.

'You're strong but you've got to learn to control that goddamn temper of yours, kid,' coach Nelson, an ex-New Jersey
policeman, told him. 'Otherwise you're gonna find your argumentative butt nailed to the floor. Remember the England
business?'

'Coach, de man was ignorant and his methods belonged in
de stone age. Jack Johnson had more modern moves dan 'im.'

'Jack Johnson died seventy years ago.'

'Dat's what I mean.'

They laughed.

'Anyway, Tiger, you shouldn't be upsetting the England
coach. It hasn't done your international career any good, has
it? Sometimes you've got to show some respect to people in
authority. It ain't that difficult. If you wanna get on in life,
you've got to eat humble pie now and then. You've got to kiss
some butt before you can kick it.'

Tiger walked away sullenly. He was not in the mood for one
of Nelson's sermons about respecting authority.

A surly, aggressive youth, a product of the Brixton Grange
council estate, from an early age Tiger had come to know only
violence as the most eloquent form of expression.

As a child, his parents' arguing often woke him up when his
father returned to their tiny two-bedroom flat after a Saturday
night's drinking session.

Milton was basically a good man, but life was tough in
London and had a debilitating effect, drawing him to drink
heavily at weekends. Far from the bouncy, outgoing personality he was in Jamaica, he had become increasingly morose.
Little things triggered off flashes of anger. Like Tiger mashing
up his shoes playing football and having to find money for
repairs or a new pair on the meagre family income.

In the poor districts of Kingston they did not have much money either and there was no welfare system in Jamaica, but the sense of community pulled everyone together. There was an abundance of fresh fruit and vegetables so nobody starved. People living on the street, aka the sufferers, could literally pick mangoes off the trees if needs be. Anyway, such was the community spirit, kindly strangers always made sure the real poverty-stricken and destitute were always fed, especially mothers with babies and small children. Milton and Iris missed that sense of togetherness.

Entertainment was not a problem either in Jamaica. Men played cards and draughts or drank the local rum in ramshackle bars. Occasionally arguments broke out and sometimes the frustration of life in the ghetto boiled over into vicious fights with knives, bottles and even machetes. Worryingly, guns were becoming more regular arbiters of conflict.

The natural disposition of Jamaicans and Caribbeans generally, ensured that a peaceful, law-abiding atmosphere reigned even in the most impoverished areas. The perpetual sunshine, lush vegetation and relaxed way of life was a different world to the harsh realities of south London.

When he could get work in Jamaica, Milton was a building-site labourer. He enjoyed the physical side of it, even in ninety-degree heat. Best part of the day was enjoying a few Dragon Stouts with his workmates, as they tried to chirps the pretty women passing the bars in downtown Kingston.

Iris was a seamstress for an uptown haberdashery. She worked from home, earning the equivalent of a few pounds a week, knowing full well that the dresses she so meticulously and neatly sewed were sold for ten times her weekly wage to rich tourists.

She did not earn enough to enable her to move out of the concrete jungle, but enough to put some change in the church's collection box every Sunday where she lit candles and spent most of the day thanking the Lord for their modest blessings.

Eventually, they scraped enough savings to move out of town to rent a tiny two-bedroom brick house in Bull Bay a few miles east of Kingston, near to a Rastafarian community. The smell of ganja always hung in the air. Iris detested it, but Milton, an occasional cigarette smoker did not object. She sometimes thought she could smell ganja on his breath but Milton always denied it with a glint in his eye.

~

Tiger had inherited his father's quick temper. Although neither of them was innately bad, it was more their circumstances that seemed to bring out the worst of their characters.

Milton was a strong believer in fate. 'If de Lord God deals you a bad hand den you gwan be at de bottom of de pack,' he would say to Iris.

Although short for his age, Tiger enjoyed bullying bigger and older kids. It gave him a thrill, a sense of purpose in this mad, antagonistic world. He knew he was just another delinquent statistic after getting caught by the law for looting during a street disturbance on Brixton's frontline.

The police were amazed that such a small boy could be lifting such a big television. He was very strong for his age and size. Tiger just shrugged off the warnings he was given. He saw criminal activity even at that early age as the sole option of gaining material things.

Look how hard modder and farder work and how little dey earn. Black people don't get any respec' in dis world, dad says. Might as well take what you can get, when and how you can get it. Dad says that Malcolm X used to say 'By any means necessary'. Malcolm was right.... So is dad. Always look after number one.

That was the motto his father always used before returning to Jamaica, a despondent man after years of working hard in the building trade, but always feeling like an alien in a hostile, racist Britain.

Milton remembered his first working day on a building site. It was a cold November morning and despite the thermal underwear and five layers of clothes he wore underneath his donkey jacket, he was shivering violently.

The foreman did not even bother to ask Milton his name. He just told him to reposition a pile of scaffolding poles from one side of the site to another. Milton had no gloves and the foreman did not offer him any. The poor man's fingers were so cold and inflamed from the freezing conditions that he felt they were going to fall off.

Bwoy me can't even feel dem.

Tea breaks in the canteen hut gave him some respite. And after eating his corned beef sandwiches for lunch on that first day, Milton promised himself he would buy a Thermos flask next day so that he could have something hot every day.

Iris's red pea soup will help warm up my poor col' body.

His white co-workers ignored him and the three Asian brickies said hello but were clearly not interested in conversation with him.

It took Milton a full two hours of sitting in front of the two bars of the electric fire in the living room before he thawed out. 'Dat foreman, don't like me at-tall, Iris. Me fingers feel like dem ah drop off yet 'im still mek me pick up dem poles. What a wicked man, eeh!'

Milton loved his family, but the free spirit in him made a return to his beloved Jamaica imperative. Iris, a round, bubbly woman with an indefatigable spirit, refused to even contemplate returning though. Despite the hardships, she liked London life where the boys were born and brought up.

The Crawfords arrived in south London in the mid-Sixties with high hopes for a better life. They already knew that things were tough from the stories friends and relatives told when they came back on holiday, and in letters from people in England who could not afford to visit Jamaica or were too ashamed to return to their homeland for good with nothing to show from years of hardship in the Mother Country.

The Crawfords soon learned that the streets were paved more with racist hate and resentment than anything else.

Tiger's older brother Cassius was named after Cassius Clay, aka Muhammad Ali, and his father hoped that he would turn out to be a boxing champion, but it was only Tiger who showed the boxing prowess. 'Him look like a champ to me,' Milton would say when Cassius was first born.

Cassius inherited his father's love for boxing but mother's gentle nature. He used to cry when his father put boxing gloves on him because it meant at least an hour of arm-aching training. If he protested or got tired too quickly, Milton would clip him around the ears. 'Always look after number one, son,' Milton used to say.

Thankfully for Cassius, Tiger took to boxing almost as soon as he could bunch his tiny fingers into a fist. Milton was delighted and instantly turned all his attention on him. Tiger was a hyperactive child and showed an aggressive streak even at playschool where disgruntled parents complained that he was assaulting their children.

He actually wanted to be liked, but was not articulate enough to hold his own in the banter with his peers, so violence was always the inevitable last resort.

Cassius loved his younger brother but could not stand his unruliness and preferred to watch boxing on TV rather than practise it. His real passion was drawing. Not arty stuff, mind. More technical drawing. He appreciated the outlines of buildings and bridges far more than a perfectly executed right-uppercut. His father felt he had a lost cause on his hands when Cassius began to talk of becoming a draughtsman or even an architect.

'Don' full up your 'ead wid dem grand ideas, son. T'ink of somet'ing more sensible, like being a carpenter like your farder.'

There was only two years between the boys so they often played together with the other children on the estate. Inevitably, when a dispute in a football or basketball match occurred, Tiger was in the thick of things. Cassius often had to help his troublesome brother keep away from confrontations.

'I love you to the bone, man,' Cassius would say, 'but you've got to stop losing your rag. One of these days somebody's gonna beat the shit out of you.'

'Shut your raas, Cass,' would come the terse reply. 'See me? I can handle myself. Dem bwoy deh ah fuckery.' From the earliest age Tiger preferred to talk in Jamaican patois, picked up from the times as a boy he was sent there by his parents to 'learn some manners an' respec'. He thought it gave him an edge in toughness and by the time he was a teenager talking

Yard-style was second nature. American and Cockney euphemisms were mixed into his hybrid street language.

No-one got the better of Tiger in a streetfight, despite Cassius's admonishing. Milton's boxing lessons, coupled with his natural aggression, put him in good stead.

By their early teens, Cassius and Tiger no longer moved in the same circles. Milton had long gone and Tiger was constantly in trouble with the police. Cassius had acquired an old drawing board and although not academically brilliant, he was one of the best at technical drawing. Iris was very proud of Cassius but resigned to having to cope with Tiger's constant brushes with the law.

Iris loved her job as a ticket collector at Victoria tube station and financially she was quite secure with the savings Milton had left her. Despite living five thousand miles apart, there was still a bond and no hint of a divorce.

Although he loved his mother, Tiger continued to distress her by attracting lots of attention from the local police.

Every time the door bell rang late at night and Tiger was still out, Iris assumed it was another policeman asking her to escort him to Brixton Station to retrieve her wayward son.

'Why you can't be more like Cassius, son? Him don't get in trouble,' was Iris's constant plea.

'Always look after number one,' Tiger often replied.

By his mid-teens Tiger had already accumulated an alarming criminal record. Thieving, vandalism, car-jacking, extortion of school-mates, possession of cannabis - the list had grown very quickly. Iris was distraught. It was a disturbing list but his love of cars was the most worrying aspect.

Tiger had been obsessed with driving from the time as a toddler he started watching Formula One motor racing.

'Mummy, I want to be a racing driver when I grow up.'

'Yes, son,' Iris would reply. 'One day you'll be a champion.'

He collected toy racing cars and fantasized about being the world champion. But as the years went by, he soon realised the probabilities of becoming any sort of racing driver was highly unlikely. It was far too costly and elitist, dominated by white boys whose fathers spent thousands on go-kart racing for them as kids. Formula One drivers had multi-million pound budgets behind them. It did not take long for Tiger to realise that he would never be part of that world.

I don't even see any black men wid de mechanics.

He started stealing cars instead to vicariously act out his fantasies.

Joyriding was better than straight thieving. Grabbing a pair of trainers in a West End shop and running out was all very well, but it could not beat the rush of adrenalin Tiger experienced in breaking into a car, starting it up with a bogus ignition key and the excitement of driving it around south London with his mates. He was an expert hot-wirer too which earned extra props from his peers.

Getting chased by the cops added to the thrill. He was too irresponsible to worry about jumping red lights or knocking little old ladies over at pedestrian crossings. Tiger was bad - and very, very lucky he never killed or maimed himself or anyone else.

The pleasure he got from passing his mates standing at bus stops was exhilarating. Sometimes he would stop to give them a lift, but if they were with their mothers he would just nod his head with pride if he caught their eye. Driving a stolen car was a symbol of manhood, and excitement. The element of danger at getting caught added to the buzz.

If he had to make a run for it, Tiger knew every getaway vantage point in the area to evade even the most enthusiastic cop. He used to enjoy gloating at a cop, bent up with exhaustion, puffing his lungs out as he threatened from the other side of a railing to catch Tiger next time and wring his 'little black neck'. Tiger would just shoot two fingers their way in comtempt.

He liked best driving to a dead end on a high-rise estate, jumping out and leaping over a wall to escape their clutches. It was great fun, a superb way of winding up the racist cops who tried to make his life hell anyway and a great opportunity to build up his reputation amongst his peers.

Tiger felt like a man when in a stolen car, usually a Ford Escort or Vauxhall Astra, two of the easiest wheels for even the most inept joy rider to get his hands on. Joyriding became Tiger's big passion. He started on Escorts, graduated to Rovers and ended up specialising in Beemers. But joyriding led to the terrible accident on the Bad Night, something that would haunt Tiger for the rest of his life.

The police found Tiger's fingerprints on the abandoned Cosworth's steering wheel. They matched the car's paintwork against the marks on the dead pedestrian's clothes. As they already had Tiger's fingerprints for other crimes, it was inevitable they would soon catch him. Tiger did not bother to even try to deny it. It came as a relief to him actually, as he had not been able to sleep properly in the three days it took the police to track him down.

The fatal accident caused an uproar when Tiger was sentenced to only four months youth custody and two years probation. As he was already on probation it looked as if his probation period would last until he was ready to draw a pension. He was only fifteen but as strong as a grown man with an attitude twice as vicious as a druggie's pit-bull.

But the short, sharp, shock treatment did not work. It made him worse, in fact. In borstal, Tiger learned how to become a better criminal. He was given tips on burglary, fraud, what to say when arrested and how best to conduct himself to gain sympathy and a more lenient punishment from magistrates.

One of Tiger's favourite films was *Scum*, the notorious portrayal of the worse aspects of borstal life. Tiger had experienced everything portrayed in the film. As the 'daddy' he was always the instigator of the worst abuses. Bullying, extortion, gang violence, dealing contraband... Everything except rape. 'Nobody ain't gonna trouble my batty,' he would declare in a packed canteen. 'Dey will have fe kill me firs'.' Not that anybody would consider taking him on. Even a gang would not succeed. One time, not even six wardens could subdue him after Tiger's argument with an inmate got out of hand over whose rightful turn it was to go on the pool table. A whole bunch of wardens from another wing had to be called to help drag him to solitary. They kicked the shit out of him for all the trouble he caused but Tiger still managed to knock a few teeth out and break someone's nose before being knocked unconscious. Like the police outside, the wardens had a grudging respect for his toughness. That was going to be a recurring theme of his life.

Apart from stealing cars, boxing was the only major interest in his life now. After serving his sentence Tiger joined a local club and instantly fell in love with it. Motor racing was a white man's sport; boxing had lots of black heroes. Apart from Ali, there was the Sugar Rays, Robinson and Leonard, Marvin Hagler... It gave him some sort of direction during his time in detention centres.

Tiger prided himself on his superior fitness over the other detainees and nobody dared take liberties with him, including the wardens, who knew that the penalty of losing privileges or even solitary confinement was no deterrent for the rugged youth.

Boxing was his salvation and Tiger bludgeoned his way through all the preliminary rounds to reach the national ABA finals at Wembley Arena. In the final he faced Welsh champion Gareth Williams. The result was a foregone conclusion and Williams was despatched in two brutal rounds.

Tiger was having his post-fight meal in a restaurant in the bowels of the arena when a big, smartly dressed man approached him in a black pin-striped suit, reeking of too much expensive aftershave. Tiger recognised him instantly as Archie Stretch, Europe's most successful boxing promoter.

'Well done, Tiger, me old mucker,' he said, holding out his hand to congratulate him. Tiger shook it then continued tucking into his steak and kidney pie and chips.

'Archie Stretch, professional manager and promoter,' Stretch said. 'Mind if I sit down, son?'

'Go ahead.'

'I liked the way you took care of Williams, Tiger. Nice style.'

'T'anks, Mr Stretch.'

'Call me Archie, mucker. Tiger, you're good, but you've got to remember to keep your hands up. If that Welsh boy had been able to punch you might have been in trouble.'

'Williams couldn't break an egg wid his powder puff shots.'

'Yes, but you've got to improve your defence, mucker. You've got an exciting style but in the pros someone will expose your lack of defence.'

'Bwoy, I'm not intending to go pro just yet, Archie.'

'Well if you do, here's my card. Please get in touch. I've got a fantastic gym in King's Cross and as you probably know, Bobo Hendricks and Jake Carson train there. You could train and spar with them, learn the ropes. Might even take you to Vegas for an undercard fight. I can see you being a champ within a couple of years. How old are you son?'

'Seventeen.'

'Bit young, but you've got a great style for the pros. Why not turn pro now and earn some money instead of just collecting trophies in the amateurs?'

'Maybe.'

Stretch spent the next ten minutes talking excitedly about his stable of fighters and how much they were earning, the venues they had fought at and the TV exposure they received.

Tiger was not impressed. Stretch had a reputation for exploiting his fighters, especially black ones.

That notion was confirmed when he said: 'If you signed with me I think I could find a little signing on fee. Say five grand.'

Tiger pretended to be excited, but he knew that Jimmy Banfield, the blond welterweight had just signed with Stretch and got a twenty thousand pound fee, a sponsored Rover and a kit deal with Adidas.

And Banfield ain't even the ABA champ. If he's worth dat, den I should get at least as much.

'T'anks, Archie, I'll t'ink about it.'

They shook hands and Stretch walked back into the arena, presumably to prey on another fighter he was looking to sign.

'How much did Stretch offer you to turn pro, Tiger?' coach Nelson asked him.

'Not enough, coach. De man's trying to tek steps wid me. But de vibes was dere. I'd love to test dem man dere in de pros. I'm fed up of de amateurs.'

'Whoa! What about the Olympics? Surely, you'd like to go next year?'

'But you know de crap wid de ABA officials, coach. Deh don't like me. And dey are more likely to pick one of dem white boys whose farders drink and socialise wid dem. We both know dat a lot of my losses were bogus. Blatant. I'm better off earning nuff, nuff dollars as a pro.'

'Okay, little man, think about it and make sure you look at all the options from all the managers.'

'Really and truly I've already made up my mind, star,' Tiger said slowly. 'Derek Coleman. You know, Colly, the manager in Lewisham who's got The Terminator and some udder wicked prospects? I've spoken to him a coupla times and he seems a safe bredda. Even if he's white!' He laughed.

'Don't treat you like a piece ah meat, him fighters say.'

'Colly sounds like a good choice, Tiger. He's a real cool hombre. Lonnie Baker's his trainer. Nice guy, Lonnie. Knows his stuff and both of them will look after you good. Well, if your mind's set I'd like to meet him. Your mother must give her permission too, you know that, of course.'

'Okay, coach. I saw Colly outside just now but if I don't see him again I'll give him a ring tomorrow.'

Tiger did not see Colly. Laying in bed that night he was beside himself with excitement. *ME A PRO! Gonna be a champion. De world champion. De don. Modder's excited too. She's glad dat I won de ABA title. Says de pro game should keep me outta trouble. Doesn't like seeing me take punches in de ring though. You can't win wit' modders. I'll see what Colly's got to offer.*

The next day Tiger was coming out of the First Choice bakery in Brixton when he bumped into Wayne Byrd, the notorious Cockney wide boy. Wayne, a lovable character with delusions of grandeur, would make even Walter Mitty look dull.

Wayne had been inside so often on fraud and deception charges, the standing joke was that the screws reserved his own suite in Brixton prison. And that his surname was the only one he could have because he was always doing bird! Dressed in a smart business suit and carrying a bogus Louis Vuitton briefcase, he certainly looked the part. Tiger knew Wayne had no-one in particular to see or nowhere to go but he was the sort of guy who always had to style it off.

He's probably on his way fe sign on.

'Easy, Tiger,' Wayne offered his fist in greetings. 'Saw you on TV last night winning the ABAs. Nuff respec' star.'

'T'anks Wayne. What you up to?'

'Oh, just duckin' and divin'. You know how it go! Actually, I'm doing a little boxing management now. Thought you might be interested in me handling you.'

'You don't have a manager's licence.'

'Aah. That don't mean shit, my friend. That's the rednecks' way of keeping the breddren down. You know that.'

Wayne reached into his jacket pocket and pulled out a business card. 'Give us a ring if you're interested. I was speaking to Don King last week and mentioned you to him and he said I should try to sign you up so that all us brothas could work together. Y'know?'

'I've got King's number, I t'ink I'll give him a ring tonight and sort it out direct,' Tiger thought he would meet Byrd's bluff with his own.

'Nah. Leave it to me, Tiger. Those guys don't have time for youths like you. Only I can get through to him.'

Then Wayne reached into his trouser pocket and pulled out two fifty pound notes.

'Here Tiger. As you're my bona fide breddren, I'm giving this to ya as an act of good faith. Even if you don't sign with me at least you know I have your interest at heart and maybe down the line we could do some runnings together.'

Tiger looked at the money in Byrd's hand but did not move.

'Go on, brotha. It's yours. No strings attached. Straight up.'

Tiger took it. 'Respec' Wayne. I can't promise I'll sign wid you but I will safe you up as soon as I can when my career takes off. BELIEVE!'

'Peace brotha. Peace. You will run t'ings, rude boy.'

They gave each other another fist and walked away.

Tiger was pleased with his windfall. He caught the tube to the West End and went into a sports shop. He found some top of the range Nike trainers and a couple of cotton T-shirts, total cost ninety-five pounds and handed the two fifties over. He was hungry and intended to spend the change in Burger King.

'I'm sorry sir, we can't accept these,' said the shop assistant.

'Why?'

'Because they are counterfeits.'

Tiger shook his head.

I shouldda known.

He ran out before the store's security men could grab him.

CHAPTER 2

DO IT WITH PRECISION

Whilst Tiger had been getting into trouble, Dale established himself as the second best welterweight in Britain. But he was still only the number two in the Champion Gloves gym. The rivalry with Tiger intensified when Dale was selected to represent Young England for the Commonwealth Games in Nigeria. Dale won a bronze medal in Lagos and when he returned to the gym received a hero's welcome from everybody. Everybody, that is, except the sullen Tiger.

Dale loved boxing although his parents detested it. He found the physical and mental challenge of the ring far more stimulating than his studies. Boxing gave him a certain celebrity status too and helped attract the prettiest girls at school.

Dale's father and two older brothers feared for Dale's future. Justin Harrison had always taught his sons to respect authority and education more than anything else. Curtis and Justin Junior had both got their degrees at the London School of Economics and become successful chartered accountants.

Dale seemed totally different to his brothers. Not only was he fairer in complexion and at six feet two inches, he was much taller than all three of them. Justin often wondered why this was but assumed Dale took after his mother, Charlene's, side of the family. In reality, Justin, a car mechanic at the time, did not know that Dale was the product of a brief affair Charlene had had whilst her husband was away in Canada, studying for an engineering degree. Dale was different for a very good reason.

Charlene was always amused when Justin boasted: 'Curtis and Junior have got my brains and Dale's inherited my looks.' Rumours abounded behind his back that Dale was the illicit son of a 'hit and run' lover.

Dale was a loner at the new comprehensive school, Beacon Manor, in Vauxhall. He was not particularly popular with the boys because he kept his distance, although he was an exceptional all-round sportsman. There was an aloof air about him they disliked. Even in team games he did not mix well. Nor did Dale endear himself by always winning at cards, usually fleecing his mates at poker. People suspected he cheated but no-one ever caught him.

Dale enjoyed the attention of girls and as a schoolboy had a pretty active sex life. He did not respect them though. Girls were strictly for waxing and nothing else, as far as Dale was concerned. If he couldn't get inside their panties he wasn't interested.

He didn't have many mates either. Just one special friend; Shane. They forged a friendship through feeling different to the other kids. Shane was considered weird because he was not into the usual teenage things. Artistic and intellectual, Shane's nickname was Solomon because he could quote from the Bible and Shakespeare and had an interest in philosophy. Dale and Shane did their homework together in the common room and often left school together.

The teachers noticed Dale's lack of popularity too. The story that everybody always mentioned about his coldness to his peers was the time when he scored the winning goal in the London Schools' Cup final. Dale was carried off the pitch on his team-mates' shoulders.

He attended the celebration party in the school hall the following Saturday evening, but left with his girlfriend, Belinda as soon as he received his Man of the Match award. To say everybody was slightly pissed off would be an understatement. One disgruntled teacher remarked: 'That kid is so single minded, he's bound to go far. He may not win popularity contests, but he'll get on in life.'

Dale was more interested in celebrating with Belinda at her parents' empty house in Norwood. He likened Belinda to a Page Three girl. He loved stroking her big titties which were the envy of her girlfriends and a source of amazement to the boys. Dale enjoyed doggie-style sex so that he could juggle her bouncing breasts at the same time.

'They're going away for the weekend and my sister's going to an all night party,' Belinda told Dale, excitedly earlier that week. 'Remember to bring your condoms, Dale.'

'Yeah, and I'll bring a bottle of Pink Lady too, the poor man's champagne. We'll have some Chinese takeaway and by then your sister should have gone out.'

'It's gonna be wicked,' she said enticingly.

His caramel skin, slightly pointed nose and long face gave him an almost European look which made him immensely popular with the girls, especially as he was tall. He had lost his virginity at fourteen with a girl two years older, during the summer holidays at her house, when her parents were at work.

'When he finishes with Belinda, I want to go out with him,' was often a remark in various cliques in the common room. 'Light-skinned boys like Dale are so much nicer than the dark ones.' They liked playing Buju Banton's record 'Browning' which praised the beauty of light-skinned Jamaican women over darker ones.

Belinda was one of the most attractive girls in the school. Tall and curvaceous with long blonde hair, even some of the teachers had lustful thoughts about her.

Dale only went out with white girls which caused some resentment amongst the black girls, but he did not worry too much about the sistas' attitude.

Who are they to tell me who I can and can't go out with, just because I prefer white girls. Don't they realise all the most beautiful women in the world are white? Black girls are too feisty, anyway. They're too bossy. And they make you pay before they give it up.

Belinda had been seeing John, a boy from another school, but when Dale started getting coverage in the South London Press for his boxing exploits, she began taking more notice of him. She had been having sex with Dale for two months, whenever their parents were out.

She was always telling him she loved him, but had to force him to say the same. 'Look, I'm not into all that lovey-dovey stuff, Belinda. We're just going out, right.'

Justin could not understand why an intelligent son of his with all the trappings of middle-class prosperity would want to become a boxer.

'I wish you'd put as much h'energy into your studies as you do in training, son,' he would often say.

'Why can't you be more like that nice boy down the road, Simon Brady? He wants to get ten GCSEs. His father was telling me at the golf club last week that he wants to be a doctor.'

'Dad, you know I never neglect my homework and always get good reports, so what's your problem? I haven't said I wanted to be a boxer, anyway. I just do it as a hobby.'

'Don't you talk back to me, young man. Do you know who you are talking to? Show some respec'. When I was a boy in Jamaica...' Dale never hung around long enough to hear the rest of the tirade as he knew it off pat by now.

The Harrisons lived in a grand six-bedroom Victorian house in a leafy road in Streatham, close to the common. Justin's engineering firm in nearby Thornton Heath had a healthy annual turnover of three million pounds. His twenty-odd workers called him Precision because his favourite statement was: 'You've got to do this with precision.'

Justin took his responsibilities as an employer, husband and father very seriously. Too seriously, many thought. He considered himself a respected member of the community but was more of a joke figure for being too pompous, too English in his ways and for the crass way he flaunted his wealth.

Like the fact that he would drive everywhere in whichever flash car he owned at the time, even to the newsagent's two minutes' walk around the corner. By the time he had started up his car, driven to the shop, found a place to park and got out, he could have been there and back on foot.

Justin loved to boast about exactly how many bottles of vintage champagne he kept in the cellar. One hundred and twelve at the last count. Dale thought he would never miss one when he took a bottle to impress a new girlfriend but had hell to pay a week later. Justin made Dale pay sixty-five pounds for it and promptly added a second padlock to the one already on the cellar door.

Becoming a local magistrate helped increase Justin's respectability and acceptance amongst his white colleagues and friends but did little to enhance his standing with the black folk.

Dale used to shake his head in shame at Justin's craving to be accepted by the bourgeoisie. He joined a golf club and encouraged his wife to attend wine tasting evenings and join various classes, including flower arranging, sculpting and interior design. Dale was disgusted by their delusions of grandeur. He hated his father's speaky-spokey English accent, dropping his aitches where he shouldn't and adding them where they didn't exist.

Dad's a coconut. Sucks up to the establishment and authority. He's always comparing us to the Cosby family. Hah. They're so creepy it's untrue. Sometimes I wish they were dead.

CHAPTER 3

GET STUCK IN, MUCKER

Much to his parents' dismay, Dale decided to forgo a university course to pursue a boxing career. Justin was beside himself with disappointment. Charlene just kept quiet. She wept quietly in the downstairs toilet the first time Dale announced that he would not be going to university like his brothers.

The tension between father and son was becoming unbearable for Charlene.

At the breakfast table one Saturday morning, Dale scooped up his last spoonful of cornflakes and chopped banana and got up to leave. Putting on his black puffa jacket and picking up his kit bag, he pecked his mother on the cheek and walked into the hallway. Justin's squat physique seemed to cover the whole of the front door.

Dale could tell his father was on his way to the golf club because his beloved clubs had been taken out of the stairs cupboard and parked right beside the front door. Justin looked the archetypal golfer in his brown slacks and beige polo shirt underneath a green Pringle V-neck sweater. Dale sighed, Justin was in one of his argumentative moods and did not look like he was ready to budge.

Slightly irritated, Dale stood a few feet away from his father and took a deep breath. 'Dad, look at all the graduates who ain't got a job. Get real. I could be earning a couple of hundred thousand a year by the time I'm twenty. How many rich graduates are there?'

'Hmmph! You little fool. Look at h'all the dangers in boxing.

You'll get your brains scrambled. I'm quite prepared to help pay for your h'education. I've told you that many times h'already. Sounds like you've taken too many punches h'already.'

'Ah dad. Boxing's a science too, y'know. The sweet science. It's not just crash, bang, wallop. There's a lot of intelligence involved in the noble art. The gym is like a university too. The university of life.'

'Noble h'art? Noble h'art? You mus' be mad. You'll get nobbled, not nobled, that's what'll 'appen. Don't you realise 'ow important h'education is?'

'I can always go back to studying after my career's over. I just want to give it my best shot. When I was in Nigeria they treated me like a hero. One of their own, because so few black amateurs go out there. It's always white guys who get on the England team on those trips. I felt so proud. It gave me a great buzz. And you can't deny that you were very proud when I got featured in *Boxing News*, *New Nation* and the *South London Press*.'

Justin fumbled with his cuff links, as he usually did when proved wrong. He had secretly bought twenty-five copies of each and sent nineteen to family and friends in Jamaica. The rest he kept in his desk at work and never failed to show colleagues and new employees. Dale had a sneaking suspicion that his father was proud of his boxing achievements, but he knew Justin was a snob at heart.

That's why he plays golf. He thinks it gives him status. One of my uncles said dad was a brilliant dominoes player as a kid but he stopped playing when he got an education.

'If I was a tennis or golf champion you wouldn't give me such a hard time, would you?'

Silence.

'Mr Stretch has already offered me five grand to turn pro, promised to put me on the big shows at the Albert Hall and Docklands Arena and I think he'll raise it if I push for it. He wants me to sign a contract soon otherwise he's going for someone else.'

'Boxing can wait, son. I just don't want you to waste your life. 'Ow many boxers have got three 'A' levels and a chance to do any academic profession they want? H'especially black ones? Don't waste your opportunities, son. You're luckier than a lot of kids your age - black or white.'

Dale looked down to his feet. He knew his father was right, but there was this burning ambition to be a champion. He loved the physical demands of the sport. And the adulation.

Wow, the adulation.

The back slapping, celebrity status at school. The media interest. Sure, he was good at football and basketball, but they're team games. The thrill of the one-on-one, matching skills, power and sheer will to win against another man. Like Roman gladiators. The lumps and bruises were just a necessary by-product. Death and serious injury was a factor, but like car accidents and plane crashes, they always happened to somebody else. Boxing could not only make him very rich very quickly, he would be famous and idolised if he was really good.

I love that. Boxing is the ultimate challenge. Champion pros get the lot. That's what I want. It takes too long to make the big dollars as a lawyer or architect. I want it now.

'At least have a good think about it, will you son? It means a lot to your mother and me.'

Justin stepped forward and put his hand gently on Dale's shoulder.

'Okay dad, I'll think about it,' Dale mumbled. Justin stepped aside.

Archie was impressed with the way Dale was fitting into his stable at his gym, a converted warehouse underneath a railway arch. The steady rumble of trains passing overhead interspersed with the grunts of fighters working out on the punch bags, thwap! thwap! thwap! thwap! of the skipping ropes hitting the ground and trainers barking out orders to couples sparring. Two four-foot high rings with blue canvases stood side by side on one side of the gym and six leather punch bags swung noisily in another corner.

The black stained floorboards still retained their shine after repeated polishing over forty years and all manner of images adorned the walls. Black and white photos of fighters, fight posters, instruction posters and pennants embellished the walls. Heavy weights were neatly arranged in one corner beside the three full-length wall mirrors for shadow boxing. One area of the walls was devoted to pictures of Archie shaking hands with boxing's luminaries.

Pressing flesh with Don King, Muhammad Ali, Lennox Lewis, Sugar Ray Leonard, Marvin Hagler... There were about thirty photos all with Archie, banal smile dominating the frame, looking like a star-struck schoolboy.

Archie was proud of his achievements. Born in Canning Town of solid working class stock, his stevedore father, Fred, instilled a strong work ethic in young Archie who supplemented his meagre purses as a mediocre light-heavyweight by working as a black cab driver in his twenties. It did not take Archie long to realise that he did not have the talent to be a world champion.

A nose broken so many times it had more turns than a

corkscrew and eyebrows scarred and puffed, testified to Archie's limited ability. So he hung up his gloves for good at twenty-eight, sold his cab and took on two fighters as their manager. Success was immediate for the wideboy Cockney with the charming patter and astute business acumen. The fighters won British titles, earning him the credibility as well as enough money to lease the gym and start establishing himself.

Twenty years, six world champions and countless British and European champions later, Archie was one of the main operators in Europe, respected by the movers and shakers on the other side of the Atlantic. A nine-bedroomed mansion in Chigwell attested to that, complete with indoor swimming pool, horse stables and fifty-two acres of prime Essex land.

That Harrison kid has superb skills.

As Dale finished sparring and started undoing his bandages, Archie called him over to his tiny, untidy room that he occasionally used as an office. Few boxers were ever invited to his swanky offices, in nearby St John's Wood.

'Dale, you've been working really hard since you joined us and I'm impressed.'

'Thanks Archie.'

'You know, you've got great skills, mucker. I like the way you slip the jab and counter with the right over the top. Nice move. As you get stronger, that could be your pay-off punch.'

'Thanks, I've been working hard on that move.'

'Yeah. You've got nice skills. I think you should call yourself Silky Smooth in the ring. Whad'ya think?'

'Silky Smooth... Yeah... Sounds okay to me. Dark.'

Dale was glad that Archie liked him. In the two months he had been training there he felt he had learnt more than in all his years in the amateurs. Top class sparring with Archie's world champions, Bobo Hendricks and Earnie Carson, was great. Occasionally though, Dale got a little too ambitious and when that happened the pros would let go a few full-blooded shots and remind him that he was still wet behind the ears in the pro game.

'You lickle bomba-claat pickney-bwoy. Nah budder fe try shape up like you is a raas-claat big man,' shouted Clifton Buchanan, the Jamaican welterweight champion, after one particularly intense sparring session. 'You is jus' a novice. Seen? Respec' your superiors, yout'.' Dale glared at him. 'What's the matter, Clifton, can't take the pressure from a teenager?' Hendricks and Carson told Buchanan to calm down as Dale glared at him.

Humility was not one of Dale's greatest assets. He loved winding up the boxers so that they would try to take it out on him in sparring sessions. He was so elusive and accomplished at hitting but not getting hit himself, no-one managed to bust him up.

'What de pussy-claat you ah talk 'bout. Me is a champion inna me own right. Nah budda fe try fe gwan bad. Seen? You still 'ave a lot to learn, yout'.'

Dale remained unmoved. *In a couple of years time I'll be able to stand guys like you on your heads. You can't match me for skills. It's just your strength and power I can't match.*

No-one in Archie's gym hated Dale but then again they were not queueing up to invite him round for dinner.

'That kid's got to learn some manners,' said one old pro to another.

'Yeah, I tried to knock the little fucker's head off yesterday but he was too fast for me.'

'Someone will sort him out soon enough.'

Dale enjoyed the pro life. He would jog the half mile to Streatham Common at six in the morning every weekday and run round the Common's perimeter before returning home for breakfast, cooked by Charlene. Steaming mugs of tea with scrambled eggs on toast were his favourite.

Charlene usually had black pudding or fried plantain with hard dough bread before going off to work as a secretary to the managing director of a local second-hand car sales firm. She had worked for a couple of years for her husband when they first arrived in England but could not stand his constant demands which went far beyond the call of duty.

Dale wasn't into Yard food, preferring European and American cuisine. 'How you expec' to get fit and strong if you doh eat Jamaican food, son?' Charlene would often ask.

'It's too greasy and stodgy mum. I can't train on that stuff.'

He reasoned McDonald's and KFC meals he often wolfed down in the evenings were better than the yam and dasheen his mother prepared. He just didn't like it. This rankled with his parents. They wanted their youngest son to be more in touch with his Caribbean culture and so bought him a subscription to the black newspapers *New Nation* and *Caribbean Times*.

It wasn't only the Yard food he didn't enjoy; he had no intention of visiting the Caribbean. The three times the family went on holiday to Jamaica, when Dale was growing up, he found something to moan about and effectively spoilt it for everyone.

The first time he couldn't stand the heat, then it was the mosquitoes and the third time he hated the food.

Dale's greatest holiday was when as an eighteen-year-old he

went to Corfu with three schoolmates. 'It was dark,' he told the envious classmates who did not go. 'All those slappers itching to get waxed. We got off with everyone and anyone. Gallons of local, cheap plonk, lots of vomiting, sing-songs and plenty of burger bars.

'We had a couple of tasty rucks too. I got a real buzz when I floored that leery Scouser with a left hook. Big geezer he was. It gobsmacked their lot. They couldn't believe that a soft Southerner had stiffed their main man.'

Dale did not realise it, but a lot of his father's philosophy had rubbed off on him. 'You guys are easier to get on with and much quieter,' Dale would say to his white friends.

'Anyway, apart from Jesse Jackson how many black people outside of entertainment and sport are doing well? None. After I'm done with boxing, I want to be a media baron like Rupert Murdoch or Richard Branson. Now *they're* the sort of people to be emulated, not just Michael Jordan or Eddie Murphy.'

He thought his father was quite a sell-out but his own sense of values were spot on. Dale could not appreciate the contradiction in his way of thinking.

As he watched TV he answered the phone and turned down the volume of *Blind Date*.

'Dale. Hi, it's Archie.'

'Hello Archie. How're you?'

'Okay me old mucker. I hope you're fit because I've got blindin' news for you.'

Archie paused for effect.

'You're on the Albert Hall bill two weeks' today.'

'Great. Who is it?'

'Dunno yet. I'm talking to a coupla managers, but it'll be an easy one. Don't wanna see you get beat on your pro debut, do we?'

'When will I know, Archie?'

'Not until nearer the date, mucker. But don't worry, you're in good shape and I promise he'll be about as threatening as Papa Smurf.'

'Well, I've got no worries then, have I?'

'Nah. Stick to the plan of bringing you along nice and easy for a coupla years, son, then when you're a bit older, stronger and more experienced we'll start going for titles.

'Listen, this kid will have only two chances of beating you. Slim. And none,' he laughed.

'And slim just left town!' said Dale tired of that well worn joke. 'Sounds good to me, Arch. I'll see you in the gym Monday.'

'See ya, kid. Look after yerself.'

Dale was about to hang up, then remembered something.

'Archie!'

'Yeah.'

'How much am I getting?'

'Seven hundred.'

'Sounds good to me. See you on Monday.'

'No you won't son, I'm off to New York tomorrow on business and I won't be back for a week 'cos I'm gonna watch the Chavez fight in Vegas next Saturday.'

'See you when you get back, then.'

'See ya, mucker. Keep in shape, won'cha? I wanna see you spark the geezer inside a coupla rounds.'

'Yeah, Archie. You can rely on me.'

Archie could hear the blip of the call-waiting facility while he was talking to Dale but had no great impulse to answer it.

As soon as he put the receiver down it seemed to jump back at him angrily. He picked it up slowly as he felt his heart quicken.

'Stretch, nigger says he's not gonna play ball. Sort him out. NOW. You've got twenty-four hours.'

Click.

Archie looked at the receiver, placed it back and went and poured himself a large whisky.

~

Dale was not entirely happy with his purse. He felt that as a top amateur he was worth more. He was sure that Jimmy Blanfield, the white middleweight prospect was earning three times that amount against similarly poor opposition.

Other things troubled him.

He's only watched me in the gym twice in the last three months. How does he know how well I'm doing? Suppose he gives me someone with ambition who beats me? Some debut. My career would be over before it got started. Nah. Archie wouldn't fuck me over. Not yet anyway. That two-year contract guarantees that. Minimum of twelve fights. It was nice of him to get me that deal with Pony. Don't have to pay for any gear now. Pity he couldn't get me a sponsored car. Maybe that'll come soon.

Dale weighed himself the night before the fight and was three pounds overweight. He drank a spoonful of vinegar which Jack swore helped burn off extra fat and went to bed without drinking anything else. Groaning noises from his stomach reminded him of his hunger and dehydration.

~

43

Archie chuckled as he poured himself another glass of whisky.

Dale's going all the way. Should be a world champ in four years. Nice skills and he can bang a bit too. Nice little investment, Archie. Pity he's not white. Would be worth twice as much. Ah well. Niggers dominate the sport now. That's where the dough is. Not like in the old man's day when they got frozen out of championship fights. Niggers and Jews. The colour bar. Great system. Niggers knew their places then.

Wha's the name of that one I beat? Lincoln Kirby. That's it. Good fighter but crap record. Never stopped or knocked out in his whole career. Always got outpointed. Must have won only about ten out of two hundred-odd. But he was smart, old Lincoln. Always put up a good fight but used to allow himself to get beat so that promoters would give him work. I remember someone saying to him 'You're not a bad fighter, why don't you try harder to win?' And Lincoln just grinned and said 'if you saw my house and car you'd know why'. The geezer owned one of those big three-storey Victorian terraced houses in Clapton. No mortgage and nice motor. Zephyr Six, I think. Had his own car mechanics business too. His kids were better off than most white kids in the area. Smart coon. Must have fought three or four times a month for years and never got banged up. Went back to St Lucia and bought a hotel, I heard. Niggers really knew their places in those days. I hope this one don't get out of order.

CHAPTER 4

EATING BABIES FOR BREAKFAST

'Dale, hurry up or you'll be late for the weigh-in.'

'Okay mum, I'm coming,' he shouted from the top of the stairs, rushing out of the toilet. The match was made at the eleven stone ten pounds weight limit and when he had weighed himself that morning he was two pounds over. Even after a good session in the toilet he was still a pound over-weight - and it worried him. He did not want to pay a one hundred pound overweight forfeit.

Dale went downstairs and poured himself another spoonful of vinegar. He was already parched and the sour taste made him wince. Nerves had prevented him from sleeping well. Charlene came down an hour later looking very smart in a burgundy skirt and cream jacket. She was running late for work and only had time for a cup of tea.

'We'll see you tonight at the H'albert 'All, son. We're proud of you.'

Justin came down the stairs and into the kitchen. His navy blue silk tie complemented perfectly his smartly pressed sky blue shirt and black suit trousers.

'Good morning dear, good morning champ,' he said in an upbeat tone.

'Hi dad.'

'All ready for the world title fight?'

'S'pose so. Didn't sleep much, though.'

'It's just nerves son. Don't worry, you'll do just fine. Jus' treat him with respect for the first round. Feel him out. Then wham! Go get him, do it with precision!' Justin smashed his clenched right hand into his left palm for emphasis.

Dale rolled his eyes with boredom. He was not overjoyed that his father was coming. For years Justin's hostility to him boxing had been a bone of contention between them, but as soon as he heard that his son was on a Royal Albert Hall bill, he broadcast the news to all and sundry. He even phoned a cousin who worked at the Jamaica Broadcasting Corporation television station in Kingston to try to get it announced on the island's sports bulletin.

Charlene got up, kissed and hugged Dale and wished him well. She kissed her husband goodbye before getting into her Land Rover and setting off for work.

Justin gulped down his coffee and finished his last slice of toast and marmalade before putting on his jacket. Dale thought he looked more like a dodgy insurance or double glazing salesman than a businessman.

'I won't see you before the fight so good luck son. We'll all be there rooting for you.'

Justin held out his hand and Dale shook it reluctantly. 'You used to hate me boxing dad. Now I'm doing well you want to tell the whole world.'

'Yes Dale, you're right. I was against it. You've decided to go into a very dangerous career, against my better judgement. But it seems you are totally committed to it. The least I can do now is to support you the best way I can. Your mother and I will be praying for you, son.'

Dale was not convinced.

Hypocrite.

Justin walked to the front door grinning, opened it, turned and bellowed: 'Let's get ready to rumble!'

Dale was watching him from the kitchen and rolled his eyes and raised his eyebrows in mock amusement.

You old fool.

His stomach was rumbling. He popped a slice of brown bread into the toaster, poured a small glass of orange juice and sipped it slowly and ate the toast without butter.

After breakfast he picked up his quilted Umbro jacket from the hallway and went for a long walk around the perimeter of Streatham Common. The chilly wintry air helped fully wake him and focus his mind on the fight. When he returned an hour later he looked at the answering machine in the lounge and noticed the light flashing. He pressed the play button.

'Hello Dale. It's Donna. Hope you had a good night's sleep. We're all really excited about tonight. Daddy's bringing all his mates from work. We know you're gonna win. Hope you like the socks. Take care and good luck. Love you lots. Bye.'

There was another message. From his trainer.

'Dale. It's Jack. 'Ope you slept well. Don't worry if you didn't, the other geezer probably had a rough night too. Go for a long walk around the park, then 'ave a rest. Don't eat nuffink 'eavy and I'll pick you up at midday for the weigh-in.'

There were two other brief messages wishing him well. One from Suzanne, an ex-girlfriend who still had a crush on him and from coach Nelson, his old amateur trainer.

Dale put a video tape of Sugar Ray Leonard's greatest fights into the video machine in the lounge and lazed around. He had seen it so many times already that parts of it were worn and slightly fuzzy but it provided some last minute inspiration. He dozed off at the start of the Leonard-Duran II fight and was awakened when the phone rang.

'Dale?'

47

'Yeah.'

'It's Archie. Just wanted to know if you're alright, mucker.'

'I'm fine, Archie.'

'Slept well?'

'Okay, I s'pose.'

'Good. I just thought you might like to know that Chambers isn't likely to have had much kip 'imself.'

'Why's that?'

'Well they decided to come down from Birmingham yesterday because Chambers wanted to sightsee. When his manager asked me where they could stay cheaply, I suggested this bed and breakfast in Earl's Court, owned by someone I know.'

'Oh yeah.'

'But I didn't tell them it was right beside a gay nightclub. The all-night music and those poofs creating outside will have driven them gaga.' His booming laugh made Dale pull the receiver from his ear.

'Those noshers must have really fucked them up!' Archie bellowed again and Dale slammed the phone down in relief.

Charlene came home for lunch. She kissed Dale who was lying on the leather Chesterfield watching a Muhammad Ali video for the thousandth time before going into the kitchen to prepare herself a snack.

The doorbell rang. Charlene answered it.

'Dale, Jack is here. Hurry up, son.'

'Alright mum, tell him I'll be down in a minute.'

'Come in Jack. He's just getting ready.'

'Thanks Mrs Harrison.'

She showed Jack into the lounge before offering some refreshment.

'No thanks, we're running late,' he said.

Jack told her how excited he was at Dale's progress in the gym and what high expectations they all had for him.

'I know,' she said. 'E is h'always talking 'bout 'ow 'e is going to be a worl' champion. But to tell you the trut' Jack, my 'usband an' I do not h'approve of 'im being a boxer. We wanted 'im to be a h'architect or 'ospital surgeon.'

'There's no reason why he can't do that after boxing, Mrs Harrison. He's a bright kid.'

Jack was amazed that Dale had three 'A' levels but preferred to box. 'Never met a smart darkie boxer before,' he sometimes said to his wife Stella. "E must be one in a million,' she would reply chuckling.

'Smart fighter, though Stella. Nice moves. And 'e knows it. Likes rubbing the old pros up the wrong way. Someone's gonna chin him one of these days.'

Jack put a Status Quo tape on in the car, on the way to the weigh-in and was genuinely surprised that Dale didn't like it.

'That's young people's music, ain't it? Nicked it off me daughter.'

'Well she ain't my music guru, mate. Here. Drop this.' He pulled out a Rob Base and DJ E-Z Rock tape and started bouncing to the 'It Takes Two' track.

It takes two to make everything alright.
It takes two to make it outta sight....

Then Dale switched over to a jungle tape mixed with some hip hop stuff by Snoop Doggy Dogg.

Jack's grimace was an eloquent explanation of what he thought of it.

Dale effected a mock American accent. 'Hip hop, bro. Get wid the programme, man. It's kickin'.'

Jack was not amused and stayed silent for the rest of the

journey.

They arrived just in time at the weigh-in in a huge function room in the bowels of the Cumberland Hotel in Marble Arch. Dale hurriedly stripped off his Fila tracksuit and stepped on the scales in boxer shorts.

'Dale Harrison. Eleven stone, eleven pounds,' announced an official peering at the scales.

A slightly built, grey-haired man in his fifties stepped forward. It was his opponent's manager. 'You'll have to take that extra pound off, lad,' he said in a thick, nasal Brummie accent looking at his watch. 'You've got half an hour to lose it.'

Dale sighed, looked at Archie standing nearby who nodded compliance. Archie knew this manager would not compromise. Dale put his tracksuit back on and told Archie and Jack he was going for a run in Hyde Park. Twenty minutes later he returned, sweating heavily.

Jack rubbed him down with a towel. An official told him to strip off and get back on the scales and Dale did, nervously.

'Dale Harrison. Eleven stone nine and a half pounds.'

He breathed a sigh of relief and thought back to the previous night when he ate two bowls of tuna and pasta.

Next time I'll just have some fruit, like Jack told me to. He knows I don't like fruit much though. Says eating it gives him the pip. Hah.

Archie and Jack looked relieved too. 'Don't cut it so fine next time, Dale,' Archie said sternly.

In the confusion of arriving late, Dale saw his opponent for the first time. Archie nodded towards Stewart Chambers who was talking to his diminutive manager. Dale's mind was immediately set at ease. Chambers was a tall, angular man with short, reddish hair that receded at the front, his face sprinkled with freckles around a lean, pointed nose that had evidently been broken several times judging by the jagged route it took.

'He doesn't look much Dale but he's durable,' Archie whispered conspiratorially. 'Been in with some good 'uns and lasted the distance most of the time. Got an awkward long jab, ideal for you to counter with the right over the top.'

'What's his record like, Jack?' Dale asked.

'He's only won three out of twelve, but never been stopped.'

'Must be a light puncher, eh?' Dale asked.

'Couldn't break out of a wet paper bag, mucker,' Archie smirked. 'We don't wan'cha to lose on yer debut, do we?'

'S'pose, Archie. Doesn't look like Godzilla, does he?'

'Don't worry about that lad. You're gonna win. That's the most important thing.' Archie walked off to speak to some of the other boxers he had on the bill.

Dale opened a can of Isotonic drink he had in his kit bag and gulped thirstily. He finished one and cracked open another as he picked up a phone in the hotel foyer.

'I had to have a run to make the limit,' Dale said to Donna.

'That's bad. I told you not to have all that pasta.'

'Okay, Donna. Okay.'

'What's your opponent like?'

'Looks as hard as nails. About seven foot six and got muscles coming out of his ears. I saw him eating a baby for breakfast.'

She drew a deep breath. 'Is he really that frightening Dale?'

'Yeah. But I'll beat him.'

'I know you will, sugar. Are you coming round for lunch now? Mum's making shepherd's pie.'

'Jack wants me to stay with him. Then he wants me to go

home to rest.'

The silence spoke volumes.

'Donna, Jack doesn't want me to have any distractions.'

'Can't you just pop round for a few minutes? Please.'

'No, I'll see you later. Got to go now, Jack's waiting. See you after the fight, okay.'

'Good luck, Dale. I love you.'

'Yeah. Alright. See ya later.'

Dale and Jack went to a small Italian restaurant in Queensway. Dale had lasagne and Jack ordered fish and chips. 'Don't like any of that fancy stuff,' he always said, meaning anything non-British. 'Don't mind a Ruby now and then though. Can't beat a good curry. It's funny how curry houses have become almost British now, innit? One in every high street in Britain.'

Dale thought it was strange that such a hardcore nationalist like Jack enjoyed eating in Indian restaurants, but he was full of contradictions. A portly ex-welder in his early forties, he had only boxed to amateur club level and was barely literate, but could talk with passion and conviction on subjects he barely knew anything about.

Being a black boxer did not mean he was a stereotype. Donna's parents adored him, not least because he was a local celebrity with enormous prospects. Donna doted on him.

She always bought him a new pair of white Nike socks for every fight and loved to count how many sit-ups and push-ups he could do after they made love.

The manic exercising after sex was Dale's way of refuting the archaic notion that sex before a fight hampered a boxer's performance. Donna's parents were always working or socializing at weekends which gave the young lovers plenty of opportunity to satisfy their sexual impulses.

Short and petite, Donna was proud of her flowing, dark hair that stretched halfway down her back. Long eyelashes and a little button nose gave her doll-like qualities. Despite her stumpy legs, she liked to wear stilettoes and mini-skirts to make her look taller. She looked much younger than her twenty-one years but Dale, being two years younger, liked the idea of going out with an 'older woman'. At that age two years made a lot of difference.

He thought she was a little too serious about the relation-ship, but he didn't mind. Donna was sweet and sexy and she had a bit more attitude than the other, younger girls he had been out with.

As he walked into the Royal Albert Hall, Dale felt a great sense of euphoria and self worth.

Wow. Pro debut at the Albert Hall.

CHAPTER 5

LET'S GET HITCHED

Dale and Jack were shown to a dressing room with a hand-written sign pinned to the door that had a list of six names. Harrison was at the bottom of the list. The old, expansive dressing room had a strong musky smell. There were other boxers already there Dale recognised from the gym and around the boxing circuit. He said hello to a few, put his kit bag on a wooden bench and sat down. Somebody was playing some soothing R. Kelly on a portable stereo.

Doctor Vyas, a slim Indian man in thick, tortoiseshell glass-es wearing a smart, beige double-breasted suit, briefly inspected Dale's hands, eyes, hearing and heart before pass-ing him fit to box.

Dale placed a towel on a wooden bench and lay down to rest, hearing the peripheral noises much more intently than he really wanted to; the dull drone of the traffic, boxers mov-ing around, crowds arriving, announcements on the house tannoy.

An hour later the whip came in to announce the running order as Dale was getting taped up by Jack. 'You're on second, Dale,' the whip, Ernie said. He was a slightly built, middle-aged man in a flat cap and tweed jacket. 'The first one's four three-minute rounds so be ready.'

Jack was tense. He grunted to anyone who spoke to him without looking up from applying strips of sticking tape to Dale's bandages. An official from the British Boxing Board of Control arrived to inspect the bandages before giving Jack a pair of red eight ounce gloves.

Dale was so nervous he kept on trying to pee. Four times in a quarter of an hour. Jack told him to relax and start warming up.

As the first fighter on the bill walked out with his trainer, Jack got out his hand pads and made Dale punch out quick combinations. After a couple of minutes, Dale had worked up a sweat.

Jack told him to practice his jab then told him to walk around and stay loose. Dale's bladder felt tight again but he knew nothing would come out.

Jack asked him to calm down and started tweaking his neck and shoulder muscles to help relieve the tension. The whip appeared.

'You're on kid.'

Jack held the fighter's face between both palms and stared into his eyes. 'Don't worry, Dale, you're gonna piss this one. Just keep your jab going - boom, boom, boom - and be careful of his fucking right cross.'

Dale nodded. His heart was thumping as hard as a Soul II Soul bassline. Self doubt enveloped his thoughts.

What if I lose? What will Donna think? Archie won't wanna know. Dad will be so ashamed. Shut up you fool. Of course you're gonna win. Chambers is nothing.

As they emerged from the dressing room, he could hear the crowd. It gave him a buzz. Nerves and excitement played ping pong with his emotions, as he felt a cold trickle of sweat running down his back underneath his blue satin dressing gown that had 'Silky Smooth' emblazoned in white on the back.

I've trained hard and I've got the punch and amateur experience to beat Chambers. He can't possibly win. No way.

As Chelsea was his favourite football team and the Blues Brothers one of his favourite films, Archie had come up with the idea of wearing a blue kit.

What happened next took Dale completely by surprise.

Archie was waiting for Dale as he stepped out of his dressing room and put a pair of Rayban shades and a black trilby on a bemused Dale. The crowd murmured in amusement as he emerged into the arena. Jack and the bucket man mumbled their disapproval. 'Archie finks this is fuckin' showbusiness,' grunted Jack.

Dale was thankful for the shades as he stepped into the ring as the overhead lights seemed to rage down on him. Jack took the dressing gown off, then the shades and trilby.

The referee, Bert Adams, checked that Dale had an abdominal protector on, no earrings and his gloves were properly laced. Dale looked across at Chambers. He looked even paler under the harsh lights than at the weigh-in, but paradoxically, he looked taller, slightly more muscular and his stern face and fixed stare made him slightly intimidating.

He's got bigger since this morning.

Adams called them to the centre and said something about a good, clean fight, obeying his commands and protecting themselves at all times. They were sent back to their corners.

Ding! Ding! 'Round One!'

Dale stepped forward and as he met Chambers in the middle threw a long left jab. Chambers slipped underneath it and landed a left hook to the body. Dale was surprised rather than hurt that Chambers evaded his punch. Dale shot out a double left jab and this time the second shot landed and made Chambers step back.

For the rest of the round Dale threw his jab like Jack had

56

nagged him to do and by the end of the session he was in firm control. Chambers' pasty face was now a map of red blotches.

Jack was pleased with Dale's start. In the one minute interval he told Dale to keep the jab going but this time whip over the right hand with more conviction. Half way through the second, the right cross landed on the top of Chambers' head and he keeled over. Referee Adams did not even bother to take up the count.

As Chambers rose on unsteady legs, Adams waved it over. A joyous Dale raised his arms triumphantly. Jack kissed him on his forehead when he returned to his corner then told him to go and check on Chambers who by now was sitting on a stool being inspected by a doctor.

'Yeah, I'm alright thanks. Good fight Harrison. I've never been hit that hard before. You're going a long way.'

Dale felt like a world champion already!

'Oh Dale I'm so proud of you,' said Donna hugging him outside the dressing room afterwards. 'You're gonna be a big, big star.'

'Thanks Donna. It was great. I loved it, but boy, was I nervous. Come on. What's that surprise you wanted to tell me?'

Are you sure you're ready for this Dale?' she said cheerily.

'Of course. C'mon. What is it?'

'Mum and dad think we should get engaged.'

'What? We're too young.'

'Yeah. But we've been together two years now and they said they can see we're really in love and we should be making plans to get married and have lots of little champions.'

'Well, I dunno. I have to give it some thought. There's a lot happening in both our lives at present.'

He paused as her head bowed in disappointment.

'How come your parents didn't mention it to me?'

Donna's smile disappeared. She looked away, tears welling up in her eyes.

'Let's talk about it some other time, Donna, eh?'

'When, Dale?'

'Not for a while. Let's wait until I've at least made some money from boxing. Anyway, why is your family suddenly so anxious to get me hitched?'

Tears rolled down her face and dropped into her blouse. 'I don't want to lose you, Dale. You're special. I thought you loved me.'

'I do Donna. But... But...it's just not the right time to discuss things like that. We're too young.'

They walked into a bar where about fifty of Dale's family and supporters were waiting. Trevor Driscoll, a friend from schooldays who had sold loads of tickets, hugged Dale tightly. Trevor was a big, red-haired man, London-born nephew of a former All-Ireland light-heavyweight champion. He tried boxing as a kid but soon realised he preferred Guiness to gym work. Supporting Dale was the next best thing to being a champion.

'I'm so proud,' Trevor said. 'I put hundred nicker at fifty-to-one on you at the bookies that you'll be world champion Dale. I know you can do it geezer. The best investment I ever made. I'll get five grand in a couple of years.'

'Thanks Trev,' he said as the crowd broke into spontaneous applause, cheering and whistling as if he had just knocked out Mike Tyson. Dale felt embarrassed and wanted to turn back but before he could, he was engulfed by back slappers and well wishers.

'You're gonna be a champ,' everyone was saying, ignoring

the fact that Chambers would not have troubled Dale's eighty-year-old grandmother.

Dale smiled.

God knows how crap the three guys he beat must have been. Coach Nelson says 'a win is a win is a win'. Phew.

A few minutes later Archie arrived with Jack, both smiling broadly.

'Great start Dale,' said Archie, hugging him. 'The crowd will warm to you. They loved your Blues Brothers image too with the *Minnie the Moocher* record. Your mate Trevor reckons he can sell twice as many tickets next time at his cab firm.'

'It was a bit over the top, Archie,' Dale said.

'Well, that's what you need nowadays, mucker. An image. It's not enough just to be a good fighter. You can reach a wider audience just by catching the public's imagination. Ali used all those gimmicks and it worked.'

'Well I'm not totally comfortable with it, Archie, but if that's what you think can work I'll toe the line.'

'Nice work, Dale,' said Jack. 'You used the jab well. Got to keep your left 'and up though. You're not Tommy Hearns, y'know.'

'I will be one day Jack. Trust me.'

'You know what your great problem is, don't you, son,' said Archie.

Dale pulled a quizzical face.

'Your lack of confidence.'

All three laughed together.

'Come outside, I've got something for you, Dale,' said Archie.

In a little alcove off the main corridor Archie handed Dale a white Manilla envelope stuffed with twenty pound notes.

'There's seven hundred there, son. You've earned it. I've paid Jack separately but normally he gets ten per cent of your purse. When you start earning better you'll 'ave to pay him.

'I usually charge three pounds a session for the gym but I'll waive that for the time being. And I'll leave you to sort out your income tax. I can put you in touch with an accountant if you 'aven't already got one. I won't charge you for all the bandages you've 'ad and the boxing boots were a present. But you'll 'ave to buy your own from now on son.'

'Thanks Archie.'

Dale was reasonably happy with his purse. He knew that Jimmy Banfield earned over two thousand pounds for his professional debut, but then again Banfield had sold over five grand's worth of tickets, making Dale's modest sales look pretty insignificant.

'You brought a reasonable crowd down with you tonight, Dale. You know you can earn yerself extra money if you bring punters in. Fink abaht it.'

'Yeah. Alright, Archie. I'll think about it.'

Archie held his hand out. When Dale clasped it his manager-promoter held on to it.

'I've got big plans for you son.'

As Dale walked away Archie smiled broadly.

Dale got out of his dad's car to walk Donna to her door, kissed her and left.

~

Donna lay awake in her bed, thinking deeply.

I hope fame and fortune doesn't go to his head. He's so nice, wish we could marry tomorrow. And live in a big house in Sussex and have three beautiful children. Sleeping with him is fun, but I don't like it when he does that anal penetration stuff. It really hurts at first. He seems to like it better than my pussy. Bit weird, Dale.... Anyway, we'd have a Mercedes Sports each. I wouldn't work, of course. No way. Just look after the house and kids. All the Versace and Christian Dior money could buy... Harrods and Harvey Nicks will love me. Hope he believed that stuff about my parents wanting us to get engaged.

CHAPTER 6

OPEN WIDE ESTHER

'Bwoy, Lonnie, I can't wait to leggo dis lame building work,' said Tiger. 'All my breddren t'ink sey I'm dissing dem 'cos I don't check dem no more. I'm either working or training. Life's a bitch right now.'

'You've gotta stick it out kid,' Lonnie said. 'It's only for a while till you're earning some good purses.'

Tiger had just showered and dressed after a gym workout and they were getting into Lonnie's old Peugeot.

'How much longer, though, bro? I'm nineteen. Unbeaten in nine fights. I should have the most criss garms and serious wheels, man. I ain't even got a moped! I must have had these Reeboks,' he pointed at his feet, 'at least four months. Dat ain't no good for a yout's profile. Man has to look criss to round up the punany. Know-ah-mean?'

'Let's see,' Lonnie said mockingly, 'you've got to have designer street clothes to pull the blindin' birds, correct? And a nice car to complement it all? Do I know what you mean?'

'Yeah. Right. When a gyal sees a yout' boxing on TV, two-twos she expects him fe have all de lifestyle otherwise she's gonna diss you, big-time. It ain't easy maintainin' your profile on forty pounds a day labouring wages and your best pay for a fight is seven-fifty when you're supposed to be a worl' champion prospect.'

'Good things come to those that wait Tiger. You know that.'

'Fuck dat patience shit, Lonnie. I ain't got de lifestyle I want, man. Can't even afford a 2CV much less for a Ferrari dat me wanna get when I'm champ.'

Lonnie laughed at the teenager's fanciful notions. He was a mousy-blond, heavily-built man who looked younger than his forty-three years. A part-time minicab driver he had been juggling his finances for years trying to keep his ex-wife and two small children in a lifestyle that she wanted to become accustomed to.

When the courts came and whacked him for double the sixty pounds a week he was already paying her, the thought of buying hundred pound Nike trainers seemed like the height of extravagance. His only luxuries were a couple of pints in his local a few nights a week and the thin Old Holborn cigarettes he rolled incessantly.

Tiger thought Lonnie's dress sense belonged to the Iron Age. He still wore brown Farrah slacks, polyester shirts opened to the waist and a tatty Crombie coat in the winter. 'You're sort of Kray Twins meets James Brown, Lonnie,' Tiger laughed, 'wid a touch of Del Trotter!'

The only time Tiger saw him in a suit was at the Boxing Writers' Club annual dinner at the Savoy Hotel. It was a double-breasted, navy-blue, serge suit with lapels so big they looked capable of taking him off his feet in a strong wind. By the proud look on Lonnie's face, Tiger could tell he thought he was the bees knees. 'More like a dog's dinner,' Tiger mumbled to a mate. 'Oxfam must ah seen him coming.'

Boxer and trainer were so opposite in style and taste, it was a wonder they got on at all; when it came to music Lonnie thought Public Enemy was a radical political organisation and Barrington Levy a Jewish rap artist. Tiger thought Genesis were a gospel band.

The only two things they really had in common was a good

heart and an immense love of boxing. Despite his lack of funds, Lonnie was a soft touch for fair-weather friends, often tapping him small amounts he could barely afford - and never got back. It infuriated Tiger. 'Dem man dere take you for a pussy, Lonnie. You've got to wise up, my friend, otherwise you're always gonna be broke. Believe!'

In that respect, Lonnie reminded Tiger of his father.

Dad wasn't exactly a soft touch but him and mum was always helping out people who hit on hard times. Dey couldna hardly got any t'anks for it, much less their dollars back. No-one's gonna teef my hard-earned dollars when I make it. Jah know.

Derek 'Colly' Coleman, Tiger's manager, was European lightweight champion in the Sixties. But you wouldn't believe it judging by the size of his waistline now. After years of absti-nence some boxers bloat out when they retire. Colly was one of them. He went from a sylph-like nine stone fighting weight to over fourteen stone within a few years of retiring. Despite his weight, he teased Tiger about how fit he was and was able to keep up with the young fighter on long runs.

A handsome, dark-haired father of two teenage daughters, he had a charisma as a fighter that used to pack out the small venues around London and when he retired he used his sub-stantial earnings to start a property development empire with his builder father.

Colly didn't have the patience to train and nurture fighters, but loved the cut and thrust of the business side, so he became a manager and promoter. His immense business acumen made him a natural rival to Archie Stretch in the pro-motion game. Colly showcased his fighters on BBC and Archie had a deal with ITV. When satellite TV came along, both promoters benefited; Archie on Sky Sports and Colly on Eurosport.

Colly appreciated Tiger's talents from the moment he saw him as a sensational sixteen-year-old amateur. 'This kid's going all the way,' Colly whispered to Lonnie who nodded agreement.

'Mrs Crawford, I can assure you Tiger's got all the makings of a champion,' Colly said when he went to discuss signing him as a pro.

'Yes, I know dat, Mista Coleman,' Iris said. 'But 'im is jus' a bwoy. Seventeen years ol'. Me don' like to t'ink of de pain and sufferin' 'im can get as a professional. It was bad enough when 'im was fightin' amateur. But dem man dere could jus' mash up 'im face.'

'I can assure you Mrs Crawford that Tiger will be well matched and earn good money in the process. I'm prepared to pay him a two thousand pound signing on fee, give him a job with my building company and allow him plenty of time off to train.'

Iris relented on Coleman's third visit. She sensed he was a good man 'unlike dat 'orrible Mista Stretch who jus' seemed interested in makin' money out of my baby.'

Tiger's first three opponents only lasted a round each. Nor did his next three last much longer; two, four and three rounds respectively.

'Tiger, you're making things very hard for me to match you,' Colly said after his sixth victory on a bill at the York Hall, in east London's Bethnal Green. 'I'm already paying them over the odds just for them to step in there with you. Looks like I'll have to start importing some Yanks.'

'By any means necessary, Colly. Bwoy, me want a title bad.'

Tiger was happy at how well his first pro year had gone but was frustrated that he hadn't fought more often. Suitable opponents often demanded way over the norm to fight him. He appreciated Colly giving him regular labouring work and understood that his promotions did not generate as much as Archie's, but like all ambitious teenagers he was impatient. Never too impatient to contemplate resorting to his old criminal ways though.

Tiger needed fights to stop him being distracted. He had discovered girls in a big way and chased anything in a skirt, batty riders or pum-pum pants. He moved out of his mother's place to rent a one-bedroomed flat in Lewisham, just behind the High Street.

It was tiny, cold and damp. There was no heating and the threadbare carpet and tatty furniture did not suit the image he wanted to give female visitors.

So he painted the walls white, fitted the whole flat with tasteless MFI furniture and bought some cheap brown carpet. Pride of place went to his treasured boxing trophies on the mantelpiece over the boarded up fireplace.

What it lacked in taste he made up for it in cheerfulness. Tiger had an insatiable hunger for casual sex. Girls passed through there faster than a yuppie's Porsche. David Marrow, a bespectacled civil servant in his fifties living on the ground floor looked like 'a bona fide bachelor living a sad life,' Tiger used to tell his mates.

David's thick glasses, thin grey hair and acrylic cardigans made him look much older. His frumpy image and apologetic way of speaking gave Tiger the creeps.

As Tiger rushed down the stairs on his way to the gym, David opened his own door.

'Eh. Excuse me Tiger.'

'Yeah. What's up?'

'I was watching a bit of TV last night. Fight Night actually. And I saw you boxing. I didn't know you were a professional.'

'Yeah. Dey showed a recording of my last fight.'

'You were jolly good. Really bashed up that poor chap.'

'See me, I don't get paid overtime for going de distance. Believe!'

'Eh, I was wondering, Tiger.'

David looked at his feet as if too embarrassed to continue.

'What is it David?'

'To tell you the truth I've always been a boxing fan. You know, Muhammad Ali was great. And I just wondered if it was possible to purchase a ticket to watch your next fight.'

Tiger was surprised. They had rarely exchanged more than pleasantries since he moved in three months earlier.

'Okay. I'll get you a ticket. I'm on at de York Hall on the six-teenth of next mont'. How much do you wanna spend?'

'I want two. How much are they?'

'Tenner up to t'irty-five ringside, but you might as well have two tenners cah the venue's small.'

'I'll have two tenners then.'

'Cool, I'll drop dem in tomorrow.'

Tiger notched another easy win a month later, knocking out a hapless journeyman in the fourth round. He showered and collected his money from Colly. He was walking down the venue's steps and heading towards the mini-cab station to go home when he bumped into David accompanied by an attractive woman.

'You were fabulous Tiger,' he said. 'World champion in the making. Brilliant. I was very proud to watch you.'

'T'anks David. I'm glad you came along.' Tiger's eyes flicked to the woman smiling beside him. Her firm breasts under a lycra white top and cotton tassled jacket were mesmerising. Her crinkly mousy-blonde hair sat neatly on her shoulders, contrasting vividly with large, hazel eyes in the night's dimness. David noticed the eye contact and said:

'Tiger, this is my daughter, Esther.'

They shook hands.

'Hello Tiger,' she smiled.

'You didn't tell me you had a beautiful daughter David.'

'Like Michael Caine says, not a lot of people know that. They think I'm a confirmed bachelor.'

'Daddy guards his privacy like an errant Tory MP,' Esther said. 'It seems like he's ashamed of telling people about me.'

Tiger was intending to catch a cab straight home but Esther changed his plans. 'David, why don't we go for a drink across de road dere.'

The two looked at each other inquisitively before turning to him and saying in unison: 'Alright.'

In the pub opposite they spent the next half hour until closing time laughing and swapping anecdotes. David talked about life in the computer department of the civil service and Esther chatted about the people she encountered as a dentist. Tiger tolerated David's dry stories but enjoyed her bubbly personality.

'One client,' she said, 'had such bad breath we could smell him coming before he even got off the bus!'

'Bwoy, I hate going to the dentist,' Tiger said. 'I'd rather fight Mike Tyson.'

'Me too,' said David.

'Me three,' Esther echoed. They all laughed.

'Some people are really scared of dentists,' she added. 'I used to see this huge bricklayer who looked so nervous we thought he was going to faint. He only came in for a couple of fillings and got his mother, a dear little frail woman, to come in the surgery. We could tell he wanted her to hold his hand but he was too embarrassed. Apparently, when he was a little boy his mother told him it wouldn't hurt, he was shocked out of his wits when it did. His mother's had to go with him ever since.'

Tiger warmed to Esther. She was a lot more mature than the young girls he'd been dealing with. He liked her plummy voice, natural wit. And those titties! He couldn't help appreciating the curvy outline of her backside and thighs underneath her black leggings.

'Ralph will be sorry he missed this,' she said.

'Who's Ralph?' he asked already sensing the answer.

'Oh, my boyfriend. He wanted to come but he's an estate agent and you know how busy things are right now. Even before a property goes on the market he's got half a dozen buyers willing to pay the asking price. Then he gets into a gazumping situation. It's totally mad. Work, work, work. That's all he does, boring bugger.' She shrugged her shoulders as if to say 'but what can you do?'

They all got into a cab which dropped Esther off on the Essex Road in Islington before taking David and Tiger home to Lewisham.

Tiger lay awake that night thinking of Esther. Wonderful Esther. He tugged himself off thinking of her.

I hope she really meant it about coming to see me fight again. Bwoy, I'd like to wax dat bitch. Bet she could show me some moves. Pity about her idiot bwoyfriend. Bet he can't do de works. And when he does he lasts two minutes. Including fore-play. You never know... David's a bit of an undercover mover, eeh? Everyone thinks he's a lickle hermit. Who would t'ink that ugly fucker could produce such a beautiful pickney.

The next morning, as Tiger walked down the stairs, David popped his head round his door.

'Hi Tiger. How you feeling, today?'

'Yeh man, cool.'

'Well Esther just rang and she asked me to give you her number. She says she wants to keep in touch so that you don't forget to tell her when you're boxing again.'

'Dat's nice.'

Tiger waited a few days before calling Esther at work.

'Hi Tiger. How are you?'

'I'm cool. Wha'you sayin'?'

'I beg your pardon?'

'How are you, Esther?'

'Fine. Fine, I think. I just had a patient with the most horrendous BO. It made me feel sick. One of the pitfalls of the job, I suppose. Maybe I should change careers and become a boxing manager. They seem to have a lot of fun.'

'Yeah. Deh make nuff, nuff money. And deh don't have to take any punches.'

'Sounds good to me.'

Pause.

'Your farder said you wanted me to have your number.'

'Yes. I want to keep in touch with the future world champion,' she teased.

Tiger chuckled.

'Well him only live downstairs an' I was gonna let 'im know when I'm out next.'

'I don't want to rely on daddy. He's so scatty.'

There was another pause as if she was choosing her words carefully.

'Anyway, Tiger, I thought maybe one evening when you're not doing anything we could go for a drink. Fancy that?'

'Bwoy, I don't drink, but I'm willing to break a rule.'

'Good. Let me check my diary.'

Tiger laughed. They arranged to meet in The Z Bar, a wine bar on Acre Lane, the next Monday.

As he was about to hang up, Tiger heard her call.

'Oh, Tiger.'

'Yeah.'

'Don't tell daddy, will you? I don't want him getting the wrong impression.'

'Wha' dew mean?'

'Oh daddy's such a prude. He'll jump to the wrong conclusions. He really likes Ralph and wouldn't approve of me having a drink with another man.'

Tiger smiled.

'Okay Esther.'

The four days to their meeting seemed to drag for Tiger. The excitement and anticipation was excruciating. Esther sounded so mature and worldly wise. And she had a fit body.

Lonnie held him up after training that Monday night, wanting to discuss his next fight, but Tiger couldn't concentrate.

He had borrowed Junior's ten-year-old XR2 and pulled out of the gym car park like a Formula One racer, arriving at seven-thirty. The fact that he did not possess a driver's licence and there was no tax, insurance nor MOT was of little importance. He parked hurriedly at a bad angle to the kerb and ran into the wine bar, puffing more from nerves than exertions.

Esther wasn't there.

He ordered a fruit cocktail and sat near the entrance to ensure he did not miss her. As the place was not much bigger than a boxing ring, there was little chance of that. Half an hour later Esther breezed in.

'Sorry I'm late, Tiger,' she said, pecking him on the cheek. 'But I came on the Northern Line down to Stockwell and you know how unreliable it is.'

'Dat's alright Esther. Bwoy, I was worried dat you weren't gonna show.' As she settled down his eyes ran over her long-sleeved viscose top that zipped from the waist to the neck but was only done up to the titties, revealing plenty of heaving mammary.

'Wha' cha drinking Esther?'

'Oh, I'll get you a drink. It's the least I can do for keeping you waiting so long.'

He didn't protest as he was used to picking up the tab on dates. He couldn't help noticing her strong legs and round backside under the tight skirt as she leant over the bar to look at the expansive rum collection. He smiled as he felt a twinge inside his jeans.

She came back with another fruit punch for him and a white rum and coke for herself. 'I love white rum,' she said after a sip, dramatically closing her eyes and trembling to tes- tify to its potency. 'Got the taste for it when I was in Jamaica.'

'Must ah been a wicked experience.'

'Oh yes. With Ralph last year. We were mostly in Kingston. Stayed at the Wyndham. Everything was great, except dealing with the higglers.'

'Higglers? How you know about higglers, Esther?'

'So many approached us, trying to sell this that and the

other, you couldn't but help realise who they were.'

Tiger was a bit embarrassed to admit that even though he had lived in Jamaica as a child her knowledge of the island was far superior.

'But as soon as I make some corn, Jah know, me ah fly out fe see my farder, in Bull Bay, just outside ah Kingston.'

They swapped stories about their lives for the rest of the evening. Tiger kept to his fruit juices as she knocked back one rum and coke after the other. As she got tipsier she revealed more and more about herself. She lived alone in a flat she bought off Ralph, which is how they met. He worked too hard and she rarely saw him and she was thinking of dumping him. She had always liked boxing, because 'Sugar Ray Leonard was so cute and Muhammad Ali was such a noble man. Even with Parkinson's disease he's a remarkable fighter. A great example to others'

Esther learnt more about how black people think and their attitude to life in Britain that evening than in her previous twenty-six years. She had always wondered why the National Front and BNP went on about young black men being rapists and muggers. 'I'm not saying there's any great truth in that, Tiger, but there does seem to be a lot of unemployed young black men around, doesn't there?'

'Dat's only because of discrimination. We get prejudice at every level. Believe. Teachers at school. Police inna de street. Employers at work. De whole ah dem against we. You get me?'

'I suppose so. But a lot of those young chaps seem to drive very nice cars, don't they?'

'Yeah. But check out where dem live. Most of dem in coun-cil flats on dreggy-dreggy estates dat most people would never set foot pon. Dere wheels are just a token status symbol. I know some of dem jus' duckin' an' divin' fe make a little sheckle, but dey ain't gonna be barristers and doctors. Believe. Most people t'ink dat a black man with a job should only serve Big Macs and Happy Meals.'

She laughed loudly and stopped when she saw him looking at her sternly. 'Drug dealing and gangsta business is de only way some brothas and sistas can make dere change. Social security don't pay shit. You get me? With a bad address, no qualifications and black skin, some of my breddren have no choice. I ain't condoning it, jus' trying to put t'ings into perspective. White folks don't know ah wha' gwan.'

Esther was fascinated.

This is not your average dumb black guy. He's a thinker with a conscience. Nice body too. Must be better than Ralph. Hah. Even Alf Garnett's got more stamina than Ralph.

Two hours later she was pretty drunk and asked him to call her a cab. Tiger detected a tinge of faked surprise when he offered to give her a lift home.

'Oh no, I couldn't. It's completely out of your way.'

'Dat's alright.'

She claimed to like the ragga music booming out of the car's stereo.

'But I'm not always sure what they're saying. I prefer rock and classical really.'

They pulled up outside her flat and Tiger held out his hand to say goodbye.

'Coming in for a coffee, Tiger? I don't want you falling asleep.'

It was nearly midnight and Tiger was very sexhausted but the fragrance of Esther's expensive perfume was still stronger than her rum breath.

74

He sat on the black leather sofa in her flat and admired the equine prints dotted around with images of household pets and flicked the TV remote through the channels. Esther kicked off her shoes and put a tape of Bob Marley's Survival album on the hi-fi. Tiger laughed at the stereotyping.

Why do white people only play Marley when dey drop some reggae?

She went in the kitchen and came back a few minutes later with two mugs of coffee and rested them on the coffee table in front of him. She dimmed the lights, undid the top button of her skirt and sat beside him. She picked up the TV remote and switched it off.

'Thanks for a wonderful evening, Tiger. You're a lot of fun.'

She leant over and kissed him softly on the lips. Tiger placed his mug on the coffee table and pulled her towards him. Their lips locked like two pieces of velcro. The kissing and a lot of fumbling continued until she pulled away, stood up and took hold of his hands and started pulling him down the corridor and into her bedroom. Tiger did not resist. His dick was throbbing with excitement.

She pulled him on top of her onto the bed, tugging at his clothes whilst kissing him all over his face, running the tip of her tongue over his thin moustache and trim beard that ran vertically down from the corner of his mouth. He stood up and pulled off his jeans and sweatshirt as she unzipped her top and peeled off her skirt.

'Put this on please, Tiger,' she said, producing a condom. 'No glove, no love, sweetheart.' He tried to but it only came halfway down his dick. She pulled it off and gave him another one. That one did not go much further. They laughed and Esther gave him a third one. It just about fitted.

75

'So it's true what they say about you black guys.'

'Not really. Deese t'ings wouldn't fit a squirrel.'

Esther gave a deep moan of satisfaction as he entered her. Tiger was beside himself with excitement. Girls had come on to him before but this was his first woman. And she felt hot.

Wait till I tell Junior. I'm gonna give him de coup.

He smiled and looked into Esther's hazel eyes. She smiled back then started moving her hips in rhythm with his deep thrusts.

'Fuck me, Tiger. Fuck me good,' she moaned and started moving faster. Being a dentist he half expected her to say: 'Open wide.'

He bent down to kiss her nipples and she moaned again. Her coarse language excited him even more. A few minutes later he was a spent force. Overcome by her seduction routine, he had not been able to sustain the action any longer.

'Oh Tiger. You won't last in a twelve round fight at that rate, will you?' He grinned sheepishly. 'Never mind. We'll just have to do it again to make amends.'

She peeled the condom off, wrapped it in tissue and threw it into the bedside bin before pulling out another one. His dick flickered into life again as she caressed and kissed it. The dimness of the bedroom made his dick look huge in silhouette.

He lasted a lot longer and knew she was satisfied this time judging by the fingernail marks left on his back as she climaxed. Completely exhausted, he was amazed when she reached out for another condom.

'Bwoy, Esther, I don't t'ink I can rise to the occasion again. Believe.'

'We'll see,' she said defiantly, stroking it lovingly. Two hours later and after their fifth session, Tiger pushed Esther away.

Dis one's a nympho.

'Where's your bat'room? I've got to go now.'

She led him into an adjacent room, switched on the shower and gave him a towel from the airing cupboard as he got in.

'Do you want some company, Tiger?'

'Bwoy, me can't tek anymore.'

'I promise I won't.'

She got in under the water and sure enough, began kissing him on the chest. He laughed and pushed her gently out, overcome by tiredness and a sore dick.

She went into the bedroom and returned wearing a lilac bathrobe.

As he dried himself she took his towel and started patting him dry, deliberately leaving his genitals till last, kissing them gently before wiping them slowly and looking up at him lustfully. Tiger could only laugh.

He got out whilst the going was good, walked into the bedroom and started dressing. She sat on the end of the bed watching him attentively.

'You've got a really nice body. Not like Ralph. Hah, he's all flab. You're dark, aren't you?'

'Dat's right. You know the saying - de darker de berry de sweeter de juice. Dat's me!'

Esther giggled.

He used her Oil of Ulay lotion as his kit bag was still in the car. She was mildly amused that a champion boxer was using her feminine creams.

'Black skin is not designed for dis cold, nasty climate,' he said by way of explanation.

He could tell from their conversation in the wine bar that

there were many things about his culture she was curious about. She asked things like why do black house parties never kick off until midnight and why those born in Britain still considered the Caribbean or Africa their true homeland. Black people are never punctual, she said. They always seem to go to church and sing gospel at the top of their voices. There are so many single mothers with no fathers about. Young black men always have a swarm of girlfriends...

Tiger hummed along to the revival tune on Choice FM as he drove home. Very appropriate, he thought.

Tonight is the night that you make me a woman.

You said you'll be gentle with me and I hope you will.

I'm nervous, I'm trembling...

He felt he had really become a man tonight.

Bwoy, dat was sweet, eeh. Esther likes her t'ings. I can't wait for next Monday.

The highlight of both their weeks was the Monday night tryst. Tiger learnt more about sex in that time than in the few years since he lost his virginity in his mid-teens. Sex with her was wild and uninhibited. It was like living out a fantasy. Exhausting but always exciting.

They did it in every room in her flat then started venturing outside. In Junior's car. Behind a cinema. Down alleyways. A telephone box. The more daring the place, the more exciting it was.

Their most daring place was at an Albert Hall boxing show. It was poorly attended and they found a secluded spot in the uppermost balcony of the vast building. There was a curtained off area never attended by staff until closing time. Tiger had found it by accident when as a poor amateur he slipped past security, got chased by a commissionaire and ended up there.

Tiger got a thrill out of giving Esther a back shot as he peered between the curtains, looking down on the unsuspecting spectators and boxers below.

'Lonnie gives me nuff grief about coming to de fights to learn some new moves,' he said to Esther. 'Well him not wrong!'

'It gives a new meaning to job satisfaction,' she laughed, in time with his thrusts.

When Tiger phoned her at work to confirm their date that night, Esther sounded glum.

'Tiger, we can't meet anymore.'

He kissed his teeth. 'Why?'

'Ralph gave me an engagement ring yesterday. It was our second anniversary and he asked me to marry him. Now I feel guilty about us.'

Tiger tried to persuade her to meet him that night, if only to say goodbye, but she wouldn't have it. The property market was still bouyant and Ralph, now very wealthy, wanted to devote more time to the relationship.

'Dat is a pity, Esther. I'll miss you. Monday nights will never be the same. Are you sure you don't want dis fe continue?'

'Yes,' she replied hesitantly. 'I think it's for the best. Bye Tiger. I'll miss you.' She hung up.

He felt hollow as he looked at the receiver and contemplated smashing it. The last few months had been the most exciting so far in his short life. It wasn't just the sex; being older and a professional, she was intellectually stimulating and enlightening. He even hoped they could become an item, even though he had never been seriously attracted to white women before. He had become so focused with his boxing and labouring job that he rarely slept with anyone but Esther. The void she left made him feel empty. He decided from that experience never to rely emotionally on just one woman again.

It don't worth it. She liked her undercover jooky-jam but she decided to stick wid him. I ain't going through dat emotional shit again. Women 'ave to respec' me from now, cause me ah run t'ings, t'ings nah run me.

CHAPTER 7

UNGRATEFUL TOE-RAG

'I'm glad you're not going to box any more, son,' Charlene said, clasping Dale's face between her hands and kissing him. Justin, puffing furiously away on his pipe, looked at his son curiously.

'But I thought you said you wanted to be world champion.' Justin put down his copy of *The Gleaner* to talk.

'Dad, I thought you'd be pleased that I was packing it up. You didn't like me boxing in the first place.'

'True, son, true. But I did think you was going to see it through before you returned to studying. Twelve fights unbeaten, you was in line to be British champion. Could have won one of dem magnificent Lonsdale belts, eeh!'

'Nah. Boxing's not for me any more. There's too much corruption and slippery people. The boxers take all the pain but everyone else gets paid. I love the glory, being the centre of attention. It's the most beautiful feeling when the ref raises your hand in triumph and the press ask you for interviews and people stop you in the street for your autograph... but it's a mug's game.'

'So what you going to do then, son?' Justin asked.

'I wanna get a degree in economics and then get a job in the city or with a multi-national.'

'How will you pay for your studies? We can't be subsidising you forever, y'know.'

'Don't worry. I'm sorted. I made sure I earned enough from those fights to put some away and through the people I've met in sport I'll be able to work in leisure centres and gyms as a boxing coach or fitness instructor in the holidays.

'What does Mr Stretch think?' Charlene asked.

'Well, he's not exactly thrilled. Says he's invested a lot of time and money in me. Wants to talk to you two, but my mind's already made up.'

'Okay son,' Justin sighed. 'If that's what you want to do, we'll stick by you. But if you want to go back to boxing I won't mind.'

Justin had become so used to Dale's increasing celebrity status, he even hung two miniature leather gloves in the Jamaican national colours from the rear-view mirror of his car.

He loved boasting about how rich and famous his son was going to be when he won the world title and was pleased that he had been featured on national TV and his latest wins were mentioned in the national papers, albeit two-paragraph fillers. Having an aspiring champion for a son added lustre to his bragging rights at the golf club.

'Donna, I've retired,' Dale said, preferring to look at the bowl of chicken chow mein on the table rather than into her eyes.

'What?'

'I've stopped boxing. I've quit to go to university.'

They were in their favourite Chinese restaurant, Mrs Wongs, in Streatham Vale.

'But... but... why?'

'I'm not in love with it anymore. There's too much corruption and underhand dealings. Yesterday a manager offered me five grand to fight his boy who they're trying to build up for a world title. I was surprised because I would start favourite.

'We both know that. But then he offers eight if I was prepared to lose on points. Ten if I take a drop and fake a knockout... The worse thing about it was that Archie was considering taking it. I hate it.'

Tears welled up in her eyes.

'But Dale. You're doing so well. Thought you wanted to be world champ. You haven't even got the Southern Area title.'

'I can't stand all the wankers and thieves in the game, Donna. Look at Stretch. He must be worth millions but what am I getting a fight? Two thousand. That's all. No TV money, neither. It's out of order. My opponents, until recently, have been crap. I'm glad for the support of my fans though. Trevor's been brilliant. He's sold thousands of pounds of tickets for me through his contacts at his cab firm. He stands to make at least twenty grand from all the bets he's put on me to be world champ if I win the title.

'But the guys I've fought in my early fights were all roadsweepers and ex-cons just out of the nick and desperate to earn something. Crap fighters with fuck-all ambition. Stretch said that if he found they had a pulse he wouldn't take the match. Stiffs. I had tougher fights in the amateurs.'

'It doesn't matter Dale. That's the name of the game. Everybody knows that. Anyway, Stretch started giving you some better fighters in your last two bouts. And you stopped them.'

'You don't know the half of it, Donna. That American kid I had two fights ago had been inside for two years. He told me when we had a drink after that he'd only come out of the pen three weeks before and took the fight because he was so desperate.

'He arrived at Heathrow the morning of the fight and was so jet lagged that he was too exhausted to come out for the sixth. That was bullshit about him damaging an old shoulder injury. He was just too knackered.'

'Okay. What about your last fight. That kid from Wolverhampton.'

'Leave it out. Another desperado. He'd lost about thirty out of forty-two. He came down by train and got lost at Euston. Missed the weigh-in and spent all afternoon sitting in a McDonald's because him and his trainer were broke.'

'So what. You won. And anyway, Stretch was lining you up for a big fight, maybe a British title eliminator.'

'I'm not interested Donna. Don't you understand? Boxing's a shit sport for shitty people who don't give a fuck about each other. It's a mug's game, as Eubank said. Jungle mentality.'

They finished their meal in silence. Donna slipped him a twenty-pound note because Dale had conveniently forgotten to bring his wallet, again. He walked her the short distance home.

'So what's going to happen to us, Dale?'

'Nothing needs to happen. I've been accepted at the London School of Economics so I won't have to leave home to study.'

'I hope you don't meet some brilliant, beautiful student there and dump me,' she said wistfully, grabbing his arm tightly.

'Nah. I couldn't do that Donna. Not after all the support you've given me.'

'Do you really mean that, Dale?'

'Of course,' he said. He bent down and kissed her on the forehead.

'Are your parents in?' he asked smiling.

'No. Mum's gone to bingo and dad's working.'

'Good. Let's go home then.' He pulled her along.

As he was putting the condom on, the naked Donna sat up in her bed.

'Dale?' she asked emotionally.

'What?' he replied testily.

'You do love me, don't you?'

'Of course I do.'

He tried to push her down but she resisted.

'Something's bugging me. You're going to the London School of Economics.'

He knew what was coming but still said: 'So?'

'That's where Suzanne goes.'

'What's Suzanne got to do with it?'

'She's your ex and I know she still likes you.'

'Why d'you think that?'

'I know. Believe you me, I know.'

There was a long silence.

'Dale?'

'Yes,' he replied not disguising his impatience.

'You're not going to dump me for her, are you?'

'Shut up Donna. You're talking crap.' He pushed her onto her back, but she sat upright again.

'No, I don't want to. I'm not in the mood.'

'Well, I am,' he said defiantly pushing her down again.

She did not resist this time and just lay there limply as he selfishly pumped away with little regard for her feelings, letting out a long, low grunt when finished. He got up, dressed and left without saying a word as she sobbed underneath the quilt.

'Call me, Dale,' she pleaded as he walked out of the bedroom.

'Yeah, right.'

Despite numerous phone calls, Donna could never catch him in. She finally got the message when she called at his house and Charlene told her, unconvincingly, that Dale had gone to Jamaica for a long holiday the previous week. She knew it was a lie; one of her friends had seen him in a nightclub the previous night with an attractive red-head fitting Suzanne's description.

Dale was glad Donna was finally out of his life.

She was getting too heavy. All that talk about getting engaged and married. I'm too young and free spirited for that bullshit life. Suzanne's cool. Much more relaxed. Doesn't hang onto my every word. Plus her dad's a stockbroker. He'll be able to get me into the City. I don't expect to miss boxing, either. Fucking Stretch was so racist. It's not like I was some sort of ignorant rude boy with a chip on my shoulder. Like Tiger.

Dale remembered the time he found out that Jimmy Banfield, the blond fighter Stretch pinned his hopes on becoming a world champion, had got a signing on fee of twenty thousand, an Adidas sportswear contract and a sponsored car. Banfield did not live up to expectations in the pros, despite getting even worse stiffs than Dale was being spoon-fed with.

Dale was a far better prospect judging by his amateur record but only received a three thousand signing on fee and no other inducements.

When Dale questioned Archie about it he just shrugged it off. 'A couple of big name American managers offered him the same deal and I had to match it.'

Then there was the episode with Mark Higgins, known in boxing as a 'bleeder' because he cut so easily. The moment Dale saw all the scar tissue around Higgins' eyes at the weigh-in, he knew he was in for another easy night. Sure enough, from Dale's first significant punch, a right cross, he opened a two-inch gash above his left eye in the second round. The referee called it over seconds later.

'That kid shouldn't have been in there with me, Archie.'

'Well, he passed his medical, son,' Archie flashed that cheesey, infuriating smile again and winked. 'Lighten up, son, you're still unbeaten.' Dale didn't feel good about what was going on.

~

'Look, he's not going to chuck it, right. The little coon wants that title and he won't be intimidated,' Archie pleaded to the three leaders of the Murray gang. 'He wants to be world champion more than anything.'

'Well, that's too bad, Archie. We'll have to sort him out.'

They left as Dale rang the doorbell.

On the way to Archie's office to annouce his retirement, Dale was filled with a strong sense of foreboding. Archie already knew what Dale was going to say but there was the little matter of contractual obligations to sort out.

Archie sat imperiously behind his desk, looking intimidating in his huge chair. He did not offer his hand to Dale when he entered the vast office, merely motioning him to sit down.

'I won't beat around the bush, Dale. I'm not happy about this situation. You've still got eighteen months of our three-year contract to go.'

'Yes Archie.'

'Well how am I gonna make my money back on ya? I've done my money promoting you, son.' Both knew that was a lie but Dale didn't know how to prove it.

'I'm sorry Archie but I just don't feel like my heart's in it anymore. Never know, I might change my mind and come back. I'm only twenty.'

'Well if you do come back mucker, make sure it's with me. Goddit? I invested plenty with you Dale and I don't like losing out. I'm a businessman and hate not t'see some sorta return on my investments.'

'Yes Archie. I get the point.'

Archie twitched a hint of a smile then reached into a drawer and pulled out some papers.

'Here, sign this.'

'What is it?'

'Let's call it a loyalty contract. If you do decide to come back within the eighteen months, this is your pledge to be managed and promoted by me.'

'I can't sign that.'

'Why's that?' Archie's voice deepened.

'Because I might want to keep my options open.' Dale looked down at his feet, not daring to look Archie in the face.

'You ungrateful little toe-rag. What the fuck are you talking about?' he roared, banging a fist on the table. 'You'd better sign here, right now or you'll never, ever fight for anyone, anywhere. Understand? You owe me money which I was prepared to waive. I never took my manager's twenty-five per cent. Jack never took his trainer's ten per cent and I never took a penny in training fees and for bandages and other bits 'n' pieces.'

Archie paused to let his outburst sink in.

'Are you gonna do us both a favour now?' He held out a pen

and pushed the papers forward. Dale reluctantly signed. He thought of taking them away to get a lawyer's opinion but decided there was no point. Nobody ever beat Stretch on contracts. Anyway, he could not be sure whether the threat was to prevent him through litigation or in a more direct, sinister manner.

'Now that's better.' Archie smiled. 'I'm glad we came to an amicable understanding, Dale.' He leant forward and offered Dale his hand. Dale shook it weakly and left.

Archie sipped from his glass of whisky as he spoke on the phone to Jordan. 'The little coon was so ungrateful 'e said if 'e ever came back 'e might not sign wiff me, Jack.'

'Fuckin' slag,' responded Jack. ''E never bothered t'come an' see me t' tell me. Jus' phoned me las' night and said summink abaht going back t'school.'

'Well if 'e ever comes back he'll 'ave to rejoin us. I got 'im t'sign a loyalty contract, the little shit.'

'Nice one, Archie. Ooh says the slave trade's over.'

They laughed in unison.

~

At first Dale enjoyed university life. The London School of Economics was an institution revered around the world that counted heads of state and world figures as former pupils.

His mate Trevor would drop in for a coffee if his cab route took him anywhere near the university. There was not a hint of bitterness from Trevor towards Dale for retiring. 'As long as you're happy, Dale, that's good enough for me, geezer,' he said. Dale appreciated that and reciprocated by dropping in at the Hope and Anchor pub in Tooting Broadway occasionally for a drink with him.

Dale was something of a celebrity at the LSE and although his relationship with Suzanne lasted throughout his three years there, he took every opportunity to enjoy himself with impressionable girls excited by his status. Significantly, he never stopped training in boxing gyms and still sparred with top amateurs.

A naturally gifted student, he did not work too hard to get a 2:1 pass for his degree. In fact, he spent more time in the poker card schools that were always running in the students' common rooms than in lectures and loved beating the rich foreign students out of huge chunks of their generous allowances.

His ploy was to play badly at first and lure them into a false sense of security, win it all back and then clean them out. Dale more or less financed himself throughout his time at the LSE with his card school winnings. He was so good that many thought he was cheating but no-one could figure out exactly how. Being an ex-boxer they were too frightened to confront him anyway.

CHAPTER 8

X-RATED VIOLENCE

'You'll be ready for the British title soon, Tiger,' Lonnie said as they finished off a gym session. 'I'm putting your name forward for a British title eliminator. Just keep winning, kid and you shouldn't have any problems.' He rolled a cigarette.

'You got it. I'm ready.'

Tiger was building up a reputation as one of the most exciting fighters in Britain. Unbeaten in eighteen fights, only one opponent had lasted the distance.

'I'm gonna be de next Marvin Hagler,' Tiger often said. 'He had it all. Speed, power, style and confidence. Nice of Adidas to give me a deal. Not as good as Hagler had, but see me? Ooh. My time will come. You get me?'

'Just one problem, Tiger.'

'What's dat?'

'We've discussed this before, I know, but I feel it must be aired again. I've seen so many talented fighters ruin their careers by outside distractions, be it drugs, drink, gambling, women or a combination of those.'

'Yeah, so what's dat gotta do wid me?'

'I know you like girls Tiger, but you seem to be spending an inordinate amount of time with them outside the gym.'

'Relax Lonnie. Man's gotta have some relaxation. If a breddren's gotta profile with the punany den he can't spread 'imself too t'in. You get me?'

'There's nothing wrong with having a healthy interest in girls, Tiger, but you seem to be taking it to excess. Don't forget there's sexual transmitted disease and a little killer called AIDS flying around. Now that is serious shit.'

Tiger laughed. 'You know my motto is no glove, no love. Don't worry 'bout me, star, I ain't met a beenie yet that can jeopardise my career. I'm just flexing wid dem.'

'Flexing? Careful you don't snap.'

Tiger laughed.

'You know I've gotta main squeeze now. Taneesha. Fit or what! She's so criss you wouldn't believe. I give t'anks to Jah every time I see her. Like Richard Pryor says "she's so fine I could kiss her father's dick". But she's a student and can't see me in de week so I have fe get some little side squeezes to keep me sweet. Know-ah-mean?'

'Just make sure you don't get caught out, Mr Loverman, otherwise you might not have any balls left to squeeze.'

'Champion schemer, dat's me. Taneesha t'inks I go to bed at nine-thirty when I phone her, but little does she know dat's when I'm getting ready fe rave.' He began showing Lonnie his latest dance moves.

'You'll have to cut that down now you're moving up in class. They're not always going to go when you hit them like before.'

'I'm ready for any pussy-claat bwoy. Believe. Nobody can withstand the Tiger T'ump. When I t'ump dem down, dey stay down.'

'Seventeen knockouts in eighteen fights proves you've got the power, but only at this level. Plus your defence still ain't great. You've got to work harder on that.'

'Yeah, yeah. I know dat. But I take a good shot. Y'know dat. Rock solid chin, star. God blessed me wid dat. You can't put muscle on a chin. The fans want X-rated violence and dat's what I give 'em.'

'I sold nineteen t'ousand wort' of tickets for de last fight. Not bad for a Brixton yout', eh? Pity I'm not an Archie Stretch fighter den I'd be on Albert Hall shows.'

'But you wouldn't have a pot to piss in though.'

'Dat's true. I wonder why dat fool-fool bwoy Harrison really did pack up. Probably can't afford de bus fare to the gym. Anyway, him have him daddy's money, lickle spoilt brat.'

The animosity between them had not diminished over the years. Whilst studying Dale grew increasingly frustrated reading about Tiger's exploits in the press and seeing him on TV.

If I came back tomorrow I KNOW I could beat him. Tiger ain't saying shit. My skills would negate his raw power.

Dale resented Tiger becoming a celeb, being featured in the sports sections as well as in the fashion, gossip and news pages.

I'm more skilful, better looking and more articulate than that low-life son-of-a-bitch. I'd be better for boxing than he is.

By the time Dale received his economics degree, he knew exactly where he was heading.

And it wasn't the City.

CHAPTER 9

I'M NOBODY'S PLAYTHING

Tiger was working at the Earl's Court Motor Show promoting the new Honda Tiger model with the slogan: UNLEASH YOUR TIGER AND LET IT ROAR LIKE A CHAMPION.

The advertising posters showed him on all fours, in a feline pose on the bonnet of the two-litre, turbo-charged sports car and had been the company's best promotion for years. Tiger was a cult figure and sales of the nineteen thousand pound car had escalated in the two months since it started. A couple of rude boys on the Brixton front line had even bought - sometimes stolen - models as a mark of respect to their hero.

'So *you're* Tiger Crawford,' Yolanda said looking him up and down in his incongruous tiger-skin boxing boots, shorts and vest.

Immediately struck by this vision of loveliness, he could not wait to bid goodbye to a teenager whose father had just taken a photo of the two of them. The sweet fragrance of Yolanda's seductive perfume wafted his way. *Rahtid, she smell GOOD, eeh.*

Her smooth, dark-brown skin contrasted perfectly with her cream silk blouse, reminding him of a white truffle. A peek of gently moving breasts made his dick twinge into life.

'You look more like a kitten actually,' she added to a grinning Tiger after the fans moved away. 'It should be the Honda Tabby, shouldn't it?'

'Well I ain't no pussycat, sista,' he replied leering at her cleavage.

'But I could do with some pussy, know-ah-mean?'

Would you like to suck my dick?

Oh no, not another crude bastard.

Incensed, she crossed her arms. 'I shouldn't have expected anything better from the likes of you.' And before he had a chance to answer, she was marching away.

'Woah, who started de insults in the firs' place?' he said defensively, now feeling guilty. He pulled on his tiger-skin dressing gown and dodged between onlookers in pursuit of this feisty girl striding angrily away. He couldn't help but look down to admire her tiny waist that curved out into tight, inviting buttocks underneath a spray-on skirt.

'Yo. I'm sorry sista. From de 'eart an' soul. I'm sorry. BELIEVE. I was outta order. F'real.'

She stopped but refused to face him so he grabbed her arm and tried to turn her around. By now, dozens of fascinated eyes were focused on this famous boxer arguing with this gorgeous female.

Yolanda pulled her arm out of his grasp and turned round sharply, her large brown eyes glowering. 'I'm not one of those roughneck women you're used to. Nobody talks to me like that. I don't care who you are!'

'Easy. Easy, repec' due. To de max. I'm sorry. Right? Me know dat man like me 'as a reputation for mashing up everyt'ing inna de ring, but I'm not completely outta control. I do know how to treat a woman correct. Believe.'

'Yeah, well you've got a funny way of showing it.'

He looked into her eyes intently and decided to take a chance.

'Easy. A criss sista like you deserves de fullest respec' from a bona fide breddren like me. So, when me can tek you for de

95

most wicked dinner you ever had?'

'Are you mad? After the way you just spoke to me...'

Tiger bowed his head.

'Bwoy, you don't ramp, d'ya?'

'Anyway, how do you know I'm not already seeing some-body?'

'Hey jus' cool. Seen? I jus' asked you to go to dinner, nut'un else. At least gimme a chance, noh?' He looked pleadingly at her. After what seemed an eternity, her features softened and a smile formed around the corners of her mouth.

'What's your name pretty lady?'

'Yolanda, *Claude*,' she smirked at saying his real name.

'Yolanda. Dat is the most beautiful name I've heard in the longest time.'

She put her hand to her mouth, feigning a yawn.

'Get some fresh lyrics, geezer,' she said.

'What about dinner. *Tonight*?'

'I don't go out with strange men.'

'Cha! Dere's nothing strange 'bout me.'

'Yeah, well how come you can stand in the middle of thou-sands of people in a tiger-skin and not be embarrassed?'

His face dropped.

They stared at each other for a few seconds before Yolanda began laughing uncontrollably. The tension amongst the crowd watching eased and they started smiling too.

'You're funny,' she gasped, trying hard to suppress the laughter.

'Listen, I'm not free for a couple of weeks.'

His face dropped again.

She's not interested.

'But I do like soul food.'

She IS interested.

They both smiled.

'Give me your number and I might call you when I'm free, Tiger.'

The onlooking crowd, satisfied with the outcome, broke into spontaneous applause.

'Am I forgiven den?' Tiger looked at her pleadingly. She smiled and without saying a word, held out her hand. He took it and kissed it very gently, oblivious to the audience or the flashing cameras.

The next day, their picture appeared on the gossip page of *The Globe* under the headline:

Picture exclusive: TIGER'S NEW PLAYMATE

Champion boxer Tiger Crawford had more than promoting sports cars on his mind at the Motor Show yesterday. He was seen chasing this mysterious beauty through the crowd. Eye witnesses reckon they had a blazing row before making up, embracing each other and kissing passionately in front of stunned onlookers...

'It's total crap,' fumed Yolanda. 'I'm nobody's plaything. Crawford's got another think coming if he thinks he's bagged another star-struck groupie. Anyway, he only shook my hand. *The Globe* always lies.'

Within a few weeks though, things were very different. Tiger's allure had worked again. He was not the monosyllabic musclehead she half expected and turned out to be witty, attentive and very charming. She loved the way he spoke, bouncing from south London Cockney to hardcore Yardie to New York rap, sometimes all in one sentence.

Girls were always surprised by his personality and good humour, unlike the demonic fighter's image he cultivated.

Sure, he was a bit of a geezer, and obviously a ladykiller, proud of his physique and macho image, but he was also a generous and humorous man who ensured that his friends enjoyed themselves as much as he did whenever they were out.

Champagne always flowed wherever Tiger partied, but he rarely drank to excess. Getting drunk was not his idea of fun. Yolanda was impressed with the way he handled adoring fans. No amount of autograph signing and photograph taking was too much for him, wherever he was.

His attitude was that it was the paying public that made him very rich and famous and serving the public was only part of his job. Pressing flesh and posing for photos were all part of the package. He particularly liked attending children's charity events and loved the kids swamping him and having mock fights with them.

The media rarely attended these events, he just loved to help bring some happiness and inspiration into their lives. He enjoyed dressing up as Santa at Christmas time and going to as many Barnados homes for orphaned children as possible.

~

Dale spotted Yolanda at a charity fashion show at the Cafe Royal. She was the first black girl he had ever fancied, as much because of her celebrity status as for her stunning appearance. He made a beeline for her when all the models were streaming out of the dressing rooms.

'Hi, I'm Dale. Fancy going for a drink in my Beemer?'

'Fancy yourself, dont'cha?' she replied disdainfully.

'No. I just know class when I see it. What's your name?'

'Dora. And I wouldn't be seen in anything less than a Porsche, darling.'

'Sorry, that's my other car.'

'Huh. Can't you come out with some better lyrics than that?'

Before he had a chance to answer, Yolanda's friend Unal was pulling her towards two men who had obviously arranged to go somewhere.

Yolanda smiled and shrugged her shoulders as if to apologise. She liked the look of this very forward geezer but he would have to try harder. Much harder. Dale was annoyed but did not show it.

To cheer himself up, he went round to Shane's who lived in a flat a few doors from Peckings record shop in Askew Road, Shepherd's Bush. Sometimes they could hear the pounding basslines coming through the floorboards in the mornings like minor earth tremors.

Dale thought it was ironic that he hated reggae, especially Studio One classics that Peckings specialized in, yet Tiger loved it. Tiger was often in the shop so Dale was mindful when he visited Shane during shop hours to avoid bumping into his rival.

Shane's flat was spacious and tidy with lots of artefacts from all the places he had travelled as a session musician. His father was a Nigerian textile dealer and his mother a Scottish lecturer and his flat reflected the fusion of cultures; bagpipes in one corner and African drums in another. His parents met and fell in love while at university and were still together living in homes in Lagos and Belsize Park.

When session work dried up, Shane used his tall, lithe physique and chiselled features for catalogue modelling work to supplement his income. Dale enjoyed Shane's company because he was so different. A deep thinker who was into tai chi, philosophy and astronomy. He spoke French and Spanish fluently. Dale found him stimulating, spending hours in the flat, often staying overnight.

The only aspect of his character he disliked was Shane's penchant for snorting coke. Daily and to the extreme. Although he did not admit it, Dale suspected Shane was a drug dealer. There were too many people phoning and passing through the flat at odd hours. When he confronted him about it Shane just laughed it off. 'Remember what Al Pacino said in *Scarface*: "Never get high on your own supply",' was always his cryptic response. Nevertheless, Dale was a little disturbed.

They lost touch for a while after leaving school and met again at a Lennox Lewis celebration party in the West End and although Dale was not the sort that struck up friendships with men easily, there was always something magnetic and appealing about Shane.

Being in showbusiness himself, Shane was neither impressed nor intimidated by Dale's celebrity. After all, they came from the same background. Dale could relate to Shane partly because he never felt close to his father and brothers and Shane filled a powerful emotional void in his life.

~

A tiger in the ring but a pussycat out of it. He's nice and dark too. None of that light-skinned-so-I'm-better-than-you-shit.

Yolanda liked what she saw. What's more, he hadn't even tried to sleep with her on the first date, like most men tried to.

This black man has brains, money and fame, and does not seem to think entirely with his dick. God, let's hope he's genuine.

She crossed her fingers and looked upwards.

There were no obvious signs that he had a harem of women in tow as the press was always claiming, but then again, she wasn't with him all the time.

Tiger always made sure to turn off his mobile phone when they were together. *Me nah want no gyal come phone at de wrong time. Dem gyal deh too rahtid jealous. Me nah like no fuss an' fight wid no gyal. Just keep the vibe sweet with de whole ah dem.*

On their first date, they went to The Mango Rooms in Camden Town, for a Caribbean meal and he had been the perfect gentleman.

They chose The Mango Rooms' authentic Caribbean setting with its colourful murals of tropical beaches and latticework and drank rum cocktails.

They sang along to the lyrics of the thumping reggae basslines in the background as they ate yam, banana, ackee and saltfish.

Tiger was mesmerised by Yolanda's beauty. He liked the fact she was dark-skinned. He thought it complemented the whiteness of her eyes and teeth. The soft candlelight twinkled in her sparkling eyes. Her smile was made for a Hollywood romantic blockbuster. Kissable or what!

A perfect face, he thought, encased by thick, relaxed hair in a bob style. Her long mane sat atop wide, athletic shoulders and he could not help but notice her firm breasts underneath a black Chanel jacket. He was in blue 501s, as usual, with a black polo top and pin-striped Versace jacket.

He felt good. Getting female company was no problem, it was just their calibre that was lacking.

Too many tarts and not enough gateaux.

For a while now he had been searching for someone special. Yolanda certainly fitted the bill looks wise and he was keeping his fingers crossed that her intellect and personality matched expectations. She was certainly feisty, as their first meeting showed. And although she was aware of his fame, she did not seem the star-struck bimbo type.

I like dat. At last, I've found my main squeeze.

Yolanda had been out with lots of taller, more attractive men, but there was something about Tiger she was instantly attracted to. He was good looking but not handsome in a classic way. His smooth, dark skin belied his tough profession.

Only a couple of small scars over his left eye gave notice to his brutal trade. His head, shaven around the back and sides with a cluster of baby locks on top, looked like little shoelaces. She liked the thin moustache that tapered down the corners of his lips into a neatly trimmed goatee. It showed good grooming.

He's more a little boy than a brute of a man. That rough image is not the real him, I'm sure.

Yolanda's initial impression after their first meeting was confirmed at The Mango Rooms.

He's more intelligent than I thought. Bit of a charmer. But all those girls! He must have had more women than Magic Johnson - and look what happened to him.

The conversation flowed without pause with no embarrassing moments. Yolanda was surprised by how attentive he was. Yes, she preferred 'Yard' food to English cuisine but could not eat it too much because she wanted to stay trim.

He loved soul food too, but like her, had to watch his weight. Even between fights he had to be careful, lest he ballooned. He had been known to blow up to over thirty pounds above his fighting weight of twelve stones in his more indisciplined days.

'Bwoy, I tend to pig out after a fight. You get me? I'm not really a drinker and I love my mum's home cooking. Vicious. Jah know. But all dat stodge and fried food makes Bernard Manning look t'in.'

He liked reading biographies, playing Scrabble with his brother Cassius and, surprise, surprise, watching sport on TV.

'Don't all men watch sport?' she said. 'That's your favourite past-time. Isn't it? I don't know any men who don't. Football, football, boxing, horse racing, football, athletics, football, rugby, football, snooker, football, cricket, more football plus a little bit of football. If you're not playing it, you're watching it live. Or on TV. You flick over the channels watching about three sports at once. I've even seen my uncle watching two football matches by flicking back and forth. What is it with men and sport? When you're not watching it, playing it, reading about it you're talking about it. You bet on it. You name your kids after whole teams. You get tattoos of your favourite players. And you even fight about it. Look at football hooligans. I'm quite jealous. I mean, I like sport, but Jesus Christ, does it have to dominate your lives?'

Tiger buried his head in his hands in mock surrender. He couldn't argue with that.

After studying for her degree in media studies at Goldsmiths in south London, she started working in public relations and was now working for a PR company in Covent Garden specialising in sports personalities and sportswear. She enjoyed working for Sporting Excellence, SPEX for short, and hoped to branch out one day with her own company. No, she wasn't a boxing fan. 'Too barbaric.'

But she liked football 'those lovely, strong thighs', athletics 'isn't Colin Jackson gorgeous?' and gymnastics 'their bodies are so supple and strong'.

She used to smoke cigarettes and occasionally enjoyed a spliff - but never touched hard drugs. She liked the odd glass of wine and loved champagne but could go 'absolutely ages without touching a drop of alcohol.' Her father was dead and her mother worked as a foster mother in Hulme, Manchester.

They discussed their tastes in music and literature but steered clear of religion and politics - taboo subjects for a first date. Virtually everything light and superficial was talked about until every subject seemed to be exhausted.

There was a long pause and the inevitable topic just had to come out.

'So, do you have a woman in your life? Or should that be plural?' He had been wondering how long it would take her.

'Bwoy, dere's no-one serious in my life, 'cos true sey I love boxing more than anyt'ing else,' he said quietly. 'I'm just enjoying my bachelor status to de max. F'real.'

He insisted he wasn't romantically involved with anyone, although he did admit he was not short of women friends.

'Huh,' she said. 'That's an understatement. Next you'll be telling me you're a Trappist monk.'

He laughed nervously. His hectic love life was always being splashed in the tabloid press. He quickly turned the conversation around to her and asked whether she was dating.

Yolanda told him she had been seeing Eugene on and off for two years. Eugene, an American banker, was based in New York and because they rarely saw each other it was not really a functional relationship.

'Anyway, Eugene may be wealthy but he's a little boring and too predictable. I got fed up with the egotistical male models and flash actors I was meeting. I tell you, they're so full of shit it's untrue. You know what one model said? That he was much better looking than me and he was doing himself an injustice being seen with someone not up to his standard. The cheek of it.

'The final straw came when this actor I had been seeing for a couple of months dumped me. He was a real hunk and all the girls fancied him. But guess who he left me for? Another man! For a long time he thought he was bisexual but decided that he was exclusively gay. Pity, he was gorgeous.

'I wondered why he couldn't perform when we finally tried to... you know. That's when I decided to go for a quiet, professional man in a steady job. I met Eugene on a business trip soon after. Good looking, well dressed, rich and stable. But he is *too* straight for me.'

She started giggling and put her hand over her mouth. 'You know that buppie type character in *She's Gotta Have It*? Greer, who takes ages to fold his clothes up neatly before he's ready to make love to Nola? *That's* Eugene.' They laughed so loudly that diners on adjoining tables fell silent and looked up at them curiously.

Still laughing, Yolanda added: 'He must have been Mr Bean's brother.'

She liked bubbly, fun-loving men. Guys with *attitude*. Tiger had that edge. And not just because he earned a living from such a dangerous profession. It was evident that he was a rough diamond.

'Not particularly well educated, but far from stupid, with a good heart. At the end of the evening, he dropped her home in his gleaming black Suzuki Vitara with wheels so wide they made her think of a tortoise.

'Dat is my runaround,' he said proudly. 'De Mercedes 500SL comes out for weekend runs and I only drive de Honda Tiger when Honda use me for publicity.'

He took up her offer for coffee, but merely pecked her on the lips before leaving immediately after he finished his first cup. In the hallway he held her hands in his.

'Yolanda, t'ank you for a wonderful, concrete, bona fide, experience.'

'The pleasure was all...yours,' she laughed. Tiger grinned. They pecked again and he left.

He waved up to her when he reached the courtyard and as he walked around the corner towards the car park, did a Muhammad Ali-type shuffle, spun around on one leg, threw a ten-punch combination, then threw his arms up in the air as if he'd just won a world title.

'Yes! Yes! Yes!' *Dis is it. Dis one's f'real.*

As he got into his car he noticed the wobbling of net curtains opposite. An old woman watching from the side of her curtains recoiled in alarm in case this mad black man came up to murder her. Tiger laughed and blew her a kiss. Horrified, she scampered off to make sure the three locks and two bolts on her front door were all secure.

Yolanda still had a smile on her face as she took off her make-up in front of the bathroom mirror.

He's nice - and he knows it. Good manners... Horny body. But all those girls. He must have an army of them on tow. Be careful Yolanda. This guy MUST be a schemer.... You ain't going to bed me that easily Mr Loverman.

They saw each other regularly after that, talking every day on the phone and canoodling in all the fashionable London nightspots, much to the delight of the marauding paparazzi.

The inevitable headlines of BEAUTY AND THE BEAST emblazoned every national tabloid page as the paparazzi tried to out scoop each other for the most intrusive pictures.

Tiger was enchanted not just by Yolanda's good looks but her captivating conversation and infectious laugh.

There was a gentleness about her that made him feel protective, yet there was still a tough streak, a no-nonsense demeanour in the way she spoke about her relationships with people and the way she handled her affairs.

In a Covent Garden restaurant soon after they met, she chastised a waiter for taking too long in bringing their drinks and insisted that the smoked salmon and garlic mushrooms were not 'quite seasoned and cooked the way I would expect from a restaurant of this quality.'

'Bwoy, Yolanda, I wouldn't like you to train me,' Tiger said. 'You're too tough, man. You nah ramp. You'd bus' me up in two days.'

They both laughed. Laughter was something that came easily and often.

He's lovely.

She's purrfic.

CHAPTER 10

I COOK A MEAN BREAKFAST

Yolanda was surprised that Tiger did not push for sex and started wondering whether he was gay. Then again, she didn't mind. Being celibate for a while was no great hardship.

One night, a month after they met, they had dinner at San Lorenzo's and canoodled in a Soho basement club that specialised in r'n'b. Tiger phoned her at work that day and insisted she brought her toothbrush when they went out that night. 'What for?' asked Yolanda.

'Well, you'll need to brush your teet' after breakfast.'

'I never eat breakfast.'

'I cook a mean breakfast,' he said hopefully.

'Darling, it's oysters, fresh squid and quail's eggs on toast if I stay.'

'Done! Only one problem though.'

'What's that?'

'De oysters, squid and quail's eggs is fine but I'm fresh out of bread.'

She chuckled. So it was settled. A tingly feeling surged down her spine. She had been bursting to press her naked breasts against his hard, muscled body since they met.

God, it's at least four months since I slept with Eugene. I'm glad I never stopped taking the pill.

Tiger's dick had gradually gone to a concrete hardness whilst on the phone to Yolanda. He had been fantasising for weeks about what he wanted to do to her. Sex had been okay with the couple of girls he'd had since he met Yolanda, but just satisfactory, nothing sensational. This was going to be the boom experience.

As soon as they walked into his Kensington flat, Tiger made his move. He backed her against the front door, taking hold of both her wrists and started kissing her very slowly and gently on her face and mouth, working his way down her body.

Christ, she smells nice.

Wow. Tiger. You're keen.

Yolanda managed to free her arms but couldn't move her body and when Tiger had worked his way to her breasts, slowly passing his tongue over her taut nipples. She couldn't stop herself quivering. It had been a long time since she'd felt like this. She felt the moisture between her legs ...mmmhh... and gently pressed her hand on his dick.

God, he feels good.

He had not felt so excited with a woman since the Monday night sessions with Esther and the odd one-night stand; the time he joined the mile-high club with a Brazilian flight attendant was high on his list... Then there were the two slappers in a Stringfellow's toilet... And the Italian babe in the local deli who got kinky ideas after seeing *Jungle Fever*.

Wow. She's so soft and warm. It was worth de wait.

He bent down, lifted her up in his arms and carried her into the main bedroom, placing her gently on the enormous four-poster. He kissed her on the forehead then all around her face, finally finishing on hot welcoming lips. They kissed passionately for several minutes with Tiger supporting himself with his outstretched left arm and caressing her with his right.

He slowly unbuttoned her blouse, unhooked her skirt and slipped it off before tossing it gently on the floor. He stood up and undressed slowly, watching her slender body with awe.

Shit, her legs are LONG.

He wanted to savour every moment. She tantalisingly peeled off her tights, placed them on top of the skirt then pulled the quilt back and got into bed still wearing her bra and panties. He stood beside her for a few seconds, his dick throbbing in her face, but she would not put it into her mouth.

'No. I'm not ready.'

'You soon will, Yolanda.'

She laughed.

'Do you have any condoms, Tiger? You know the saying - no glove, no love.'

Yolanda knew his type well. *Most rude boys like him are notorious bare-back riders.*

Slightly disappointed, but without saying a word, he went to get one out of a drawer beside the bed and fumbled with it before trying to squeeze it on. Too tight, he flung the condom away and got another one. This time it fitted. Just.

He hated wearing condoms.

You can't beat bareback. Fuck de dangers, you only live once.

Yolanda knew she had to be responsible, especially with a man with the libido of a rabbit.

He bent down and kissed her again, deftly putting his hands around her back to remove her bra. She lay there waiting for him to pull her panties down. She pulled him on top of her and their bodies fused together in mutual appreciation. Both gave out gasps of delight as they rocked slowly, gently back and forth.

'Jesus dread, dis is heaven. F'real,' he whispered softly.

'Oh, Tiger....yes, yes,' she smiled up at him. They had the most erotic experience of their lives around the room; in the bed, floor, chaise longue and against the wall in a marathon session of lust. Yolanda shook from those lovely tremors over and over again as Tiger explored every fibre of her soft, delicious body.

She was amused that he had a huge Gothic mirror on the ceiling above the bed.

Trust him to have that up there, the kinky bastard. God, I hope he's not filming us, like one of those pervy movie stars.

Tiger was a passionate and attentive lover. Yolanda could not resist his wishes the second time. She loved oral sex too. Tiger groaned.

Shit, this girl really knows what she's doing.

No woman had ever excited him so much.

Hours later, with condoms strewn around the room, they collapsed in a breathless, exhausted state as the early morning light began to creep through the window blinds. The smell of sex hung heavily in the air as they kissed and caressed each other, smiling and cooing and trying to avoid lying in the wettest patches. They laughed as they started playing a game of trying to manoeuvre each other onto the wet spots.

'Yolanda.'

'Yes.'

'Let's get married tomorrow?'

'Only if we can do it like that until we're eighty-five.'

'Bwoy, get me a trailer loada Irish moss, ginseng and manish water.'

'In that case, make it a hundred, Tiger.'

They laughed. He hugged her tighter, forgetting his own strength, until she shrieked with pain.

Yolanda called into work sick that morning.

He did not bother to go for his early morning run.

CHAPTER 11

SCRABBLE INSTEAD OF SEX

Three months after their initial meeting, Yolanda decided to rent out her neat two-bedroom flat in Maida Vale and move in with Tiger. They gelled like a Mills and Boon couple. A typical relaxing day would involve designer clothes shopping at Pie-Two and Pie-Four in Ealing Broadway, lunch at Cottons with a group of Tiger's close mates that usually included John Fashanu, Horace Notice, Frank Bruno and Al Hamilton. Yolanda sometimes took Tiger along to an afternoon showing of the latest black film at the Brixton Ritzy by Marc Boothe's Nubian Tales company.

Then it was more shopping at Bernard Hart's Lonsdale sportswear shop in Carnaby Street before drinks with PR consultant Kizzi Nkwocha, one of the best connected men in the field. Drinks with some of the boxing writers Tiger was friendly with at the Z Bar was an occasional treat for Yolanda as they always had amusing tales to tell. Colin Hart of *The Sun* usually had a great yarn about Muhammad Ali, Steve Bunce, the respected freelancer was an expert on Oscar De La Hoya and Steve Lillis who worked for the *Daily Sport* always had a witty one-liner.

Yolanda's friend Valerie John might invite them round to her palatial flat in Hereford Road, Notting Hill for dinner. Tiger loved Valerie's energy and enthusiasm. Even the staff she provided from her Maids to Order domestic help service were charming, likeable people. Valerie was always a warm, generous host and interesting characters were often popping round, like the eminent artist Elizabeth Rollins-Scott, computer wizard David Scott and the media moguls, sisters Deborah and Rosemary Bain.

Kendall Beaupierre and Andrew Green, the brilliant executives with ACN Communications, knew some interesting people too, especially Americans and caused a buzz in the street the day they brought Bill Cosby to Valerie's.

Media consultant Richard Adeshiyan always knew the latest news and he would pop in with old pals from his days at *The Voice*. When *The X Press* publishers Steve Pope and Dotun Adebayo were around laughs were guaranteed. Sometimes Valerie would throw a party and DJ Jerry Shillingford would drop the tunes. Served by Valerie's hired hands from Maids to Order, the parties would go on till the next morning.

Lee Henry, international playboy and owner of Rion Travel, was the best dancer. 'Man, you're dark.' Tiger said of Lee's moves. 'You really have some wicked moves, rude bwoy.'

Trish Adudu, the hilarious TV presenter, would often be at Valerie's and *New Nation* editor Michael Eboda might drop in too fishing for exclusives. Anthea Lee and Janise Elie, *New Nation's* best columnists made a point of passing round regularly to catch the latest gossip.

Music writer Lloyd Bradley was one friend Tiger was always pleased to see at Valerie's because they could talk endlessly about the history of reggae music. David Upshal, the celebrated TV presenter-producer, sometimes popped round. Every time Lennox Lewis turned up the whole neighbourhood would peer out of their windows. No wonder Valerie was a subject on the TV docu-soap *Paddington Green*.

Sometimes Tiger would take Yolanda somewhere incongruous for such a glamorous, educated woman, like to a KO

Circuit boxing session at the All Stars Club on the Harrow Road. He even occasionally persuaded her to join in a session and was amused as Yolanda puffed her way through padwork with the owner Isola Akay and struggled to do more than one press-up under the strict orders of Colin Tindle. Roger D would puff his way around the circuit with Llewella Gideon. As two of the funniest people on the comedy circuit they could always be relied on for laughs in the gym and give Yolanda plenty of encouragement.

Tiger was ecstatic. This was the first woman he had ever wanted to live with. Apart from the countless one-night stands and casual relationships, he had not had a main squeeze for a while. The last serious relationship had lasted about six months but it all came to an acrimonious end when she caught him playing away with her best friend. Tiger did offer to have a threesome but both of them turned him down flat.

The first time Yolanda was given a guided tour around his flat, her impression was that it was typical of a rich, twenty-something bachelor; functional and bland, but not very homely. State of the art gadgets in the modern kitchen that were barely used, marble and pine furniture in the lounge, but few decorative ornaments.

He's got nice taste, but it's missing that womanly touch.

It had three bedrooms, the main one en suite. One bedroom was fitted out with a multi-gym and the whole flat contained every luxury money could buy.

But the master bedroom. She was astonished!

A shrine to sexual depravity. How many oils, creams, vibrators and gadgets can one young man own? This guy's a perve.

It was not just the gigantic mirror above the bed, but the

pornographic books beside the adult videos underneath the TV and the massive painting above the headboard, depicting a couple copulating.

There was the obligatory white jacuzzi in the en suite bathroom, big enough for three people and more women's toiletries than his own. It included nail polish, foundation creams, oils for the jacuzzi, Fashion Fair products, Dark and Lovely hair lotion and Sof'n'free hair creams.

The toiletries were for when his female cousins and mother stayed over, claimed Tiger, tongue firmly in cheek. The magazine rack beside the toilet was packed with copies of *Skank* and soft porn mags specializing in black women. Yolanda was not convinced and pushed him in the chest. He pretended to be mortally wounded, but knew she was not amused.

All this shit has to go. It looks more like a brothel than a bedroom.

A week after she moved in, on impulse he took her to Anthony Gee's jewellers in Hatton Garden and bought a diamond encrusted twenty-four-carat gold ring for nine thousand seven hundred pounds. They celebrated their engagement at The Spot nightclub in Covent Garden that night with a few close friends.

'Bout time you settled down, Tiger,' Junior said. 'You were getting a bit wild with the pum-pum, star. Yolanda's cccrriss. Nuff man mus' hunger for dat. Believe! Don't even think about distressing her. Dat is *class* punany!'

'Junior, you is my key spar. Bona fide breddren. Hear me now. Dat girl is gonna have my pickney. All eight ah dem. Trust me. She's my soul-mate and future wife.'

Tiger and Junior had been through a lot together in their adolescence, including stints in detention centres and borstals. They shared girlfriends and had silly bets in trying to outdo each other when it came to chirpsing girls. Theirs was an unbreakable friendship, bonded by years of almost living in each other's pocket.

Unal was happy for Yolanda, but her enthusiasm for her best friend to settle down with this over sexed rude boy was tinged with caution; but she wasn't going to say anything for the time being.

As Spots was a favourite watering hole for celebs, the party was in full glare of the intrusive media.

Some weeks later, Tiger had almost forgotten Yolanda's volatility on their first meeting and did not realise how highly strung she was. He was soon reminded.

As they were relaxing in his flat one night, he said: 'You know, Yolanda, despite my name, me is a man dat don't like being used as a zoo showpiece. Know-ah-mean?'

'Yeah, you're not wrong. Yesterday I saw a snapper going through your dustbin. God knows what he expected to find. I should put one of those steel animal traps in there and mash up his fingers.'

'What about de other day when dat big-tittie gyal asked for a picture wid me at the R Kelly concert and de next day it was in *De Star* dat she was my new woman.'

'Are you sure you only took a picture with her?'

''Ow you mean, sugar. I was with de boys from de gym. You know dat.'

She looked at him warily.

'Stop asking dem suspicious questions, Yolanda. Would I be pictured with a gyal I'm supposed to be waxing?'

'I don't trust any man. Especially you. Your reputation goes before you, Tiger Crawford. I remember that story: TIGER

HAS MAULED THOUSANDS OF PUSSIES.

'Priscilla couldn't wait to get her paws on you, could she? Then there was Jemima and Hilary. That was in your debutante days, wasn't it? Was it their bodies you were after or their daddies' money? Then you went rootsy as I remember. Got a taste for the sistas. Delia, Paulette, Charlene and Lola, wasn't it? Then it was the media girls... Let's see, Greta Magee, Stephanie Cargill...

'Just cool, Yolanda. Just cool. I'm not in de mood. Who cares how many gyal I waxed? Who's counting? I was young, free, single and with nuff nuff corn inna me pocket and nuff gyal fe check. Every man mus' explore him sexuality and you see me? I just needed to get de most experience. Anyway, dem papers deh ah chat fuckery. It's more like twenty dan three t'ousand. You know dem nasty reporters deh always exaggerate dose banging stories.'

One thing he would soon realise was that she had tremendous self-esteem. She resented society's double standards; it was alright for a man to have lots of sexual partners, especially if he was rich and famous, but that was not on for a woman.

It niggled her that he was promiscuous and could be praised and admired for it, but if she behaved the same way would be classed as a slag. He called her a rampant feminist. She just thought she was a Nineties woman who took no shit from any man. It had already led to several heated arguments. One time Yolanda stormed out of a wine bar when a woman, evidently drunk, made a serious play for him in front of her.

She could never pinpoint if and when Tiger was unfaithful but she had a feeling, a woman's intuition, that he was not completely loyal. Apart from his suspected philandering though, he was a perfect partner, a passionate and thoughtful lover, good conversationalist and generous fiancé who was always spoiling her with presents.

'I'm just glad you didn't get someone pregnant nor catch AIDS or some other nasty disease. That was quite an achievement, going through all those women without getting at least one pickney out of it. Are you sure there's not a little Tiger cub prowling around out there, sweetie?'

Tiger sighed and tossed his head back in resignation. Sometimes Yolanda could be a tougher adversary than any boxer; she had a disturbing possessive streak.

He was not a sexual predator - anymore. In fact, late one night he asked: 'You want a game ah Scrabble?'

'Scrabble instead of sex. Tiger! What's wrong? Dick's fallen off? Or have you been playing away again?'

Not used to such a tirade, he patiently ignored her, getting the Scrabble board out and laying it on the grey marble coffee table.

'Gwwaann!' He flicked his fingers. 'See my word deh, Yolanda.'

The smile on her face vanished as she looked down to see B-I-T-C-H on the board.

A triumphant Tiger smiled and started adding up the score. 'Dat's twelve and it's a double word score. Twenty-four. Your turn sugar.'

He did not have time to look up and see the fury on her face, nor stop her reaching underneath the board to fling it into the air and scatter the tiles around the room.

'Don't you dare disrespect me Tiger. Don't forget who I am.'

She stormed out of the room and into the master bedroom and for the next five minutes he could hear her banging around, presumably getting ready to go out.

He switched on the TV and began channel surfing, unable to concentrate on anything.

Why does she always have to lose it? Gyal's a nutter.

'Don't wait up for me, you pig!' She shouted from the hall-way, before slamming the front door behind her.

Tiger shook his head in exasperation. Twenty minutes later, bored of the TV, he picked up his mobile.

'Milly? Yeah yeah. Y'alright? Good! Whatcha doing? Can I come round? Dat's right, no jooky jam. I just want some *social* intercourse and be intimate with your superior intellect.'

He laughed.

'I'm not chatting shit. No, Yolanda's away for two weeks on a modelling trip... Can I come round or not?... See you in half an hour.'

~

Sitting in the living room of Unal's flat in Caledonian Road, an hour after storming out of Tiger's place, Yolanda puffed heavily on a Silk Cut, feeling guilty that she was smoking, something Tiger loathed. Yolanda had known Unal since she arrived in London. They were like sisters, even though Unal was a Turkish-Cypriot and Muslim. There was no questioning Unal's loyalty. She even occasionally went to church at Kensington Temple with Yolanda.

Despite the cultural differences they got on famously through their mutual love of reggae and raving. Tall with long, naturally crinkly, dark-brown hair Unal had big, dark eyes and an instant smile that made her as much a target for lusty men when they went out together.

All heads turned whenever the two dressed up and made an 'entrance' at a function. Unal was a buyer for a large fashion house and was always jetting off around Europe on company business. Troubleshooting at their Monaco office made her an invaluable member of staff.

Yolanda thought Unal should be a fashion model but knew she was neither anorexic nor that vain. Unal's big ambition was to be an r&b singer. The British version of Mariah Carey or Whitney Houston. A well known and respected session singer, Unal always dreamed of the big-time.

Yolanda always knew she could rely on Unal who offered her as many cigarettes as she wanted. Tiger would not approve.

It's funny how he thinks it's alright to have a spliff when he's not in serious training, but I'm not supposed to smoke cigarettes. Double standards, or what? Men.

Calmer now, her mood had changed to one of benevolence towards her fiancé. The anger had dissippated with successive pulls on the pack of Silk Cuts.

'He bought me more silk underwear yesterday, Unal. I do love him. He's a rough diamond and he has his faults, but at least he's a winner.'

Unal was not impressed. 'He's just a typical man, Yolanda. Thinks he's a geezer, but really he's just like all the rest - a little boy, who only thinks with his dick.'

Yolanda nodded. But now she did admire his boxing prowess more than anything about him. His dedication to training, the four-mile runs in Hyde Park at six every morning, his attention to his diet and abstinence from alcohol and sex before fights. His only weakness seemed that he liked a regular puff - for recreational and therapeutic reasons he always claimed. An occasional spliff was the only vice she could see in him.

Sitting at ringside shouting him to victory had become an integral part of her life. His indomitable spirit in the ring had a sexual fascination for her; those hardened muscles rippling under the bright ring lights covered by a simmering coat of sweat with thousands of spectators bellowing encouragement, was a sensuous experience.

The controlled anger against an equally fit and tough opponent heightened the excitement. Tiger would always win, invariably by knockout and she knew that within a couple of hours they would be having the most exhilarating, passionate sex either had ever experienced.

Her nipples hardened thinking of watching Tiger in the ring as Unal handed her another brandy and Babycham. A slightly inebriated - and very horny - Yolanda climbed into a taxi, smiling to herself during the drive home back to his flat.

She stopped at an off-licence on the way to pick up some mints and chewing gum to hide the smell of nicotine on her breath. She was disappointed that he was not there to satisfy the aching sensation between her legs, but it did not matter.

When he comes in we'll make up like we've never made up before.

She fell soundly asleep before he arrived in the early hours and did not stir. But next morning, her itch was well and truly scratched.

CHAPTER 12

RESPECT DUE, RUDE BWOY

'Yo! Tiger! Respec' due everytime.' The brotha in the street recognised him from the media coverage and held his fist out to greet him. Tiger touched fists with his admirer. He loved walking down the Brixton Road where brothas hailed him. It took twice as long to get served in Stop Gap Caribbean take-away than it should because everyone wanted to chat to him and get an autograph.

'Breddren, me jus' love de way you lick down dat yout',' another brotha said. 'Mek sure you knock out dat pussy-claat bwoy Harrison.'

'Respec', respec',' Tiger said modestly. Keeping in touch with his roots was important to him. 'Me is not one ah dem man dat get rich and switch,' he often said. 'And I'll never 'ave a pickney wid anyone but a sista.'

After twenty-four contests he was in championship class now and earning excellent money, amassing over seven hundred thousand pounds in his first five years as a pro.

Ring earnings were supplemented by TV appearances and sponsorship. He even made a small fortune from the royalties when he rapped on a cover version of *I've Got the Power*, going down a storm on *Top of the Pops* in his tiger-skin shorts.

Of the many sponsorship deals Tiger had, his most unusual was to help promote the Chilli Hut curry house in Walthamstow, east London, famous for serving the hottest curries in Britain. The place was popular with black people. Samina Saeed, the globally renowned fashion editor, would take business clients and celeb friends there like Alexander McQueen, Saeed Jaffrey and Meera Syal.

Tiger often went to parties held by Samina at the Chilli Hut. Through her he met Jacko Ali, the Bangladeshi kick-boxing hero. Jacko Ali was the world lightweight kick-boxing champion and a huge celeb in the Asian community. There was immense mutual respect from the start and both would go to see each other fight. Tiger was always the guest of honour at Ali's shows, usually at the York Hall. Tiger joked: 'Jacko you've got t'ree good shots - de left jab, de right jab and de Punjab!' Tiger liked to tease Jacko about his name. 'Let's hope you don't fight like Michael Jackson and sing like Muhammad Ali.' Their connection gained Tiger enormous popularity with Asians and at Ali's shows, promoted by Jacko's company JKO Promotions.

Tiger built up quite a following in the Asian community and the successful entrepreneurs amongst them were always putting business opportunities his way. They regularly used the Chilli Hut for meetings. Tiger earned good money with Jacko promoting his kick-boxing shows.

Added to that were the many property deals. The best was when he bought two run-down houses in Kensal Green, converted them into four flats and sold them at a total profit of two hundred thousand.

By buying a luxury flat in Kensington, Tiger had managed to steer clear of the drug scene and street violence of the sleazier parts of south London. Most of his career earnings had gone on the quarter of a million the flat cost and the flash cars.

Since he was a novice pro Tiger had been sponsored by Richard Daley, an enterprising businessman who ran a sports management agency, Premier Sports and RD Properties, an

international property development company. Daley immediately saw Tiger's potential and did not hestitate to put his
money into what he saw as a sound investment. Daley -
wealthy beyond most people's dreams - had a presence. Not
tall or particularly big, nevertheless he exhuded confidence
and warmth. People were immediately drawn to him. A real
charmer.

Broad-shouldered and trim, he played Sunday league football occasionally, an ambition to be the greatest striker in
Manchester United's history long forgotten. He was always
immaculately dressed in Versace, had a magnificent house in
Farnborough and drove a four-point-six Range Rover and
seven-series Beemer. He employed thirty-two people, including most of his family and generously gave time as well as
money to black charities and good causes.

But he was not a pretentious man. As one of seven siblings
of Jamaican immigrants, keeping in touch with his modest
east London upbringing was important to him. Tiger liked
that.

'Tiger, you're going all the way and I'm proud to put my
money where my mouth is,' Daley said. The only time there
was conflict was on football matters. Tiger was a big Arsenal
fan.

'Respec' Richard. You're safe, even dough you're a Cockney
Red. No matter, it's easy to support a team dat wins for fun.
Winning de treble was a fluke, star. Which part of Manchester
did you grow up?' Tiger always had time for Daley. Of all the
sharks involved in boxing, he knew Daley was a diamond
geezer.

Life was sweet for Tiger, now he was seeing Yolanda.
Taneesha was history the moment he met her. He couldn't

believe his luck when they hooked up at the Motor Show.

'Mum, Naomi Campbell looks plain beside dis gyal,' he said soon after they met. They were inseparable. Well almost. He couldn't help enjoying himself with the occasional admiring female or two clamouring for a piece of him. He tried to be discerning but available women were everywhere, many not disguising their interest, even when Yolanda was around.

The only time he got worried about his womanising was when he inevitably picked up a sexually transmitted disease. Tiger phoned the two girls who could have possibly infected him and broke the bad news before going to the venereal disease clinic in Hammersmith. He was not bitter to either one. Contracting VD was just an occupational hazard as far as he was concerned.

Luckily, Yolanda had been in New York for a few days and was oblivious to all this. He was put on a course of antibiotics for gonorrhoea and advised not to have sex for two weeks.

Tiger counted his blessings when Yolanda returned and was on her period and the following week was too tired to press him for her t'ings. She did wonder though why he refused to share a bath as they usually did on a Saturday morning. She was also puzzled when he insisted on going to church with her soon after.

Little did she know why he lit a candle and kept muttering thanks to the Lord as he prayed.

~

'Tiger, can you please stop bulging your eyes in that girl's direction,' Yolanda said at Mary J Blige's after-show party at Equinox. 'What you talking 'bout, Yolanda? Which gyal?'

'Don't give me that innocent crap. That girl's titties are

pushed up so high they're almost earmuffs.'

The girl in question was a stunningly attractive brown-skin girl with short, relaxed hair, like Halle Berry used to wear. The tight, cling-on trousers she wore accentuated her strong, shapely legs. Her exposed waist showed a ring through the navel, which set his kinky thoughts racing. When Yolanda went to the toilet, Tiger made his move.

'Yo, I'm Tiger.'

'Tiger? Escaped from the zoo, have you?'

'Easy, easy. I've *never* heard dat one before. What's your name sista?'

'Cerez. And I'm not your sister.'

'Where you from Cerez?'

'Camden actually.'

'No. Nah bodder wid dat. Where your family dem from?'

'I was born in Finsbury Park but my parents are Brazilian.'

'Do you like Pele?'

'Who's he?

She laughed at Tiger's lame lyrics.

'You like football?'

'Not really, but I love Andy Cole. He's really cool.'

'Why don't you come to an Arsenal match wid me?'

She paused.

'Will your wife be there?'

'My wife. You mus' be mad. Dat girl's just a friend.'

'A friend. Didn't look like that to me. Looks more like your girlfriend. Where is she?'

'Gi' me your digits Cerez an' I'll bell you.'

'Okay, but the only balls I want to see are footballs. Right?'

'You gottit sugar.'

Tiger took her businesscard, pecked her on the cheek and

moved back to where he had been standing just as Yolanda returned.

'I saw you talking to that girl, Tiger.'

'Not me Yolanda.'

'You liar. I *saw* you.'

'Oh, she just wanted an autograph.'

'Liar. You better not be up to no good.'

'Gimme a break, will ya? What's wid dis jealousy shit, man? Can't I talk to any odder woman widout you accusing me of chirpsing her?'

'I know what I saw, Tiger Crawford. Shall we call her over and ask her what was said?'

'Go on den. Call her over.'

Yolanda glared at him and in Cerez's direction before storming off to the bar upstairs.

He breathed a sigh of relief.

The next Wednesday evening he picked Cerez up at Marylebone station. They never got as far as Highbury that night, but Tiger scored alright. At a friend's flat in St John's Wood.

Cerez was just one of a string of women Tiger played around with. He rationalised that until he was married, indulging in casual sex with plenty of more than willing partners was fine - as long as Yolanda didn't find out. But after the gonorrhoea incident he remembered to carry condoms.

He lived for the thrill of the chase. Honeys who already had a man were the greatest ego-boosters. He loved laying down lyrics on the sistas before waxing them. One of his favourite hunting grounds in his early waxing days was the perfume counters of department stores in Oxford Street. He would start at Tottenham Court Road and walk down to Marble Arch taking in Top Shop, Debenhams, John Lewis and Selfridges along the way.

The sistas were his main target but because he believed he was an equal opportunities schemer, he did not discriminate against other races. English, Mediterranian, Indian, Australian, Russian and American. There was no glass ceiling when it came to their slack behaviour. The United Nations would be proud.

Sometimes Junior would join him on the pussy-shopping trips and they always had a wild time. In fine weather they enjoyed sitting outside the Rock Garden in Covent Garden, honing their lyrics on passers-by. They once charmed a couple of American sistas fascinated by their false public school accents into entertaining them in their hotel rooms in Russell Square.

'Bwoy, Junior. I hope dis can las' forever. We're having the *most* fun.'

'Yeah. But don't let pussy turn you fool. Don't lose sight of being the best. Stay focused champ.'

'Nah bodder bout dat, breddren. Ain't no pussy can come between me and a worl' title. By the way, remember that Brazilian gyal I rubbed?'

'Nah, I can't keep up with all the punany you've dealt with, star.'

'Well, I bumped into her at Spots last night. And guess where yours truly ended up 'til five dis marning?'

'Saying prayers in Westminster Abbey?'

'Yeah right. Funny. I rubbed her down again at her flat in Camden, star. Bwoy, dat pum-pum was sweet, eeh!' They laughed.

~

They were sitting outside the Soho Brasserie with their drinks one fine spring day. Tiger was in a bubbly mood.

'Colly phoned me dis marning and him say we're going America dis summer fe train with some top Americans and I might get a fight in Vegas on a Don King bill.'

'Wicked,' shouted Junior, flicking his fingers. 'Bad, bad, bad, bad, bad, exposure.'

'S'right, rude bwoy. Can't get better exposure than a Don King bill.'

'Make sure Colly gets your sheckles sorted from King though, star. Dey say he teefs everybody who works for him.'

'I don't t'ink so, Junior. King's not as bad as the media coats him off to be. He's just smarter dan de white ones and dem hate him for dat.

Always trying to bring down de breddren. De man's cool.'

Tiger changed the subject.

'How's your dance shaping up, Junior?'

'Gonna be a ruff session star. Jah know. Got de ruffest revival artist on de bill. John Holt, Pat Kelly and Freddie McGregor all confirmed. Work permits? Sorted. Advertising? Sorted. Media profile? Sorted. Brixton Academy's gonna be ram for t'ree nights.'

Tiger was pleased for his friend. He'd worked hard at building up the music promotion company, *Hard Knocks Productions* that they'd formed together. Tiger's boxing commitments meant that he made very little physical imput, but Junior didn't mind, he loved running things and using Tiger as a front man.

'You've come a long way from being a sound system operator, Junior. Touch me.' Tiger held out his clenched fist. Junior took a sip from his hip flask containing Wray & Nephew white rum and coke.

'Respec' Tiger,' Junior fisted him back and added: 'Whole heap of jugglings had fe gwan fe get so far, only Jah know.'

'Yeah mon,' Tiger replied. 'Glad to see you meking some corn and not having to teef to make some change.'

Tiger felt Junior was as big a champion in the reggae field as he was in boxing. Just like him, Junior had steered clear of the drugs and the gangsta scene to get on in life. Many of their peers were dead, strung out on drugs or serving long sentences after going down that route.

But despite their circumstances and early brushes with the law, Tiger and Junior had carved out successful careers for themselves.

Junior used to sell records and CDs on a Petticoat Lane Market stall on Sunday mornings in his early days to subsidise his meagre earnings with the Supa Flex sound system, always arriving straight from an all night party.

'Ah we run t'ings, t'ings nah run we,' Junior chanted on the mike. 'Hol' up your hand if you want fe jam. Pam! Pam!' Ravers from all over London clamoured to the Flex dances.

Tiger thought the six members of Flex would last forever and was surprised when Junior told him he'd left them over a financial argument.

'I brought in all de corn but dem teef me blind,' Junior explained.

CHAPTER 13

DUMPING THE COLOURED CHAP

Yolanda was enjoying life. She had met this talented boxer who was on his way to becoming world champion. Every Sunday she walked to the Kensington Temple, dressed impeccably in a designer suit, she sang loudest and prayed hardest in appreciation of her blessings.

Oh Lord, please don't let him be one of those wort'less rude boys. Let this one have some ambition, substance and common sense. Please.

Regular church going was an important aspect of her life and she was fed up with praying so hard and living a good Christian life but not finding the man she felt she deserved. Tiger wasn't tall nor handsome but he fitted all her other criteria: black, solvent and no serious emotional baggage - he claimed. Ah well, three out of five was not too bad. And definitely, he had a fit body.

Pity daddy isn't still around. He could have given me some advice. Ah well. Tiger seems to have a good heart so I'm not complaining. Seems to like women too much though. But then again, what man doesn't. Especially a black man.

She knew that her fiancé had not been a model citizen in his youth, but now, in his mid-twenties, had matured from his rude boy teenage days.

Soon after they met he told Yolanda of his dodgy past and she admired him for his honesty and reformed character, apart from the occasional indiscretion with some willing punany, he was a New Man. Tiger was changed, but never an angel.

She should be t'ankful if all I do is occasionally wax some gyal. It's not like de gyal means anyt'ing to me, anyway. It's just a physical t'ing women can't understand. She could never give de works if I didn't trouble some outside pum-pum from time to time. I'm doing her a favour f'real.

Tiger knew that he could never justify being unfaithful to his fiancée but so as not to trouble his conscience too heavily, he rationalised that the fact that his father had returned to Jamaica when he was a small boy made him cautious to give himself wholeheartedly to anyone he loved in case they walked out on him again.

~

Yolanda loved her job as a PR executive with the sports marketing firm SPEX. Their clients included Premiership footballers, high profile boxers and the odd rugby player and cricketer. SPEX Marketing were the field leaders in promoting established and emerging sports stars.

She enjoyed the work and loved the social life attached. Getting propositioned by horny athletes whose libidos dominated their stunted intellects was an occupational hazard she took in her stride.

Tiger was a refreshing change; although he was no academic, he wasn't a simpleton. Articulate and charming, he never embarrassed her in public or took her for granted.

Yolanda remembered the American basketballer she dated briefly in New York who used to urinate in public all the time. Very tall and handsome with a big dick.

The only trouble was he liked drinking beer but had a small bladder and was always getting caught out. She shuddered when she remembered the time he got caught pissing in an alleyway by a fan who wanted his autograph and he had to wipe his hands dry on his jeans before signing. She dumped him after that.

She loved her work but was not completely comfortable with Simon, the managing director. He paid her well and virtually gave her carte blanche to pursue any sports celeb she wanted to secure for SPEX but there was always that sexual edge in the way he looked at her lecherously and touched her at every opportunity.

Simon, a tall, angular man in his late thirties, with his thick, auburn hair and rugged looks, thought he had more than a passing resemblance to Robert DeNiro.

'The only thing you've got in common with DeNiro is your big nose,' she laughed. He never mentioned the similarity again. Yolanda put him in the same category as all the other men who had tried to hit on her over the years.

She concluded from an early age that this was the norm because so many guys tried to chirps her as soon as she reached puberty; apart from in the usual nightclubs and social events, bus conductors, lorry drivers, road sweepers, traffic wardens and even policemen tried their luck on occasions.

Men only think with their dicks. Always. Some have no shame. Even trusted family friends old enough to be my dad have tried it on. And as for supposed friends of my boyfriends! Forget it. Those guys are fully fledged Alsatians, the stunts they've tried behind my man's back.

~

By the age of twenty-four Tiger was still unbeaten and had

won the British and European titles on the way. He went to Rimini to challenge Silvano Costello for the European title knowing that the partisan judges were bound to favour their man. Tiger ensured that he came away with the title, stopping Costello in the seventh round.

Even then Costello's handlers tried to rob him, claiming that Tiger hit their man when he was on one knee and defenceless. Tiger did throw a punch when the Italian was down but only caught him with a glancing blow. But it was enough to give the Italian camp cause to complain bitterly and their animated dissatisfaction led to Tiger and his entourage being bombarded with a hail of bottles and debris.

'You're not fighting in Italy ever again, Tiger,' Colly said on the plane home, itching for a cigarette but unable to on the non-smoking flight.

'Bwoy, Colly, I'm in no hurry to go back dere. Did you see the hatred in dere eyes? I just give t'anks to get out of dere in one piece.' Lonnie had been against him fighting there all along.

As European champion, Tiger qualified as a top ten ranked super-middleweight contender on the World Boxing Board ratings. He was just one fight away from a world title shot but because Colly was not in favour with the WBB officials for various trivial reasons, it would take Tiger a year and three more fights to get a crack at the world title.

~

In the meantime Dale, armed with his economics degree had resumed his boxing career.

'I want to be world champ, Archie,' he said on the phone. 'Can you get me a crack at the WBB title?'

'No problem, mucker. You'll need two or three fights to shake off the rust and by this time next year you'll be ready to challenge for it.

By the way, son. You know Crawford's going for the title too, don't cha?'

'Yeah. That's who I wanna meet.'

'Dale. Sorted. I'll get'cha a blindin' deal. Leave it to Archie.'

Dale had watched Tiger's progress with increasing jealousy during his time away from boxing. He hated all the attention and coverage his old nemesis was getting and desperately wanted to rekindle the old rivalry. University life was quite an experience but for sheer excitement it was nothing compared to boxing; the roar of an appreciative crowd, the back slaps and praise afterwards, being recognised in the street from TV and press coverage.

No drug or sexual activity could beat that rush of adrenalin for undiluted pleasure, as far as Dale was concerned. Archie suggested the new graduate change his ring name to 'The Professor' but Dale was quite happy with his old 'Silky Smooth' moniker.

Justin was not happy that his son intended to return to the noble art.

'What did you go to university for if you did not h'intend to use your superior h'education son? You've wasted your time and our money.'

'Dad, you loved me boxing when I retired. Seems like you've got a short memory.'

'Yes, I did h'enjoy you doing it but I was relieved when you did give it up and decided to h'improve yourself h'intellectually. I want to see you working in the city as a chartered h'accountant like your brothers, son.'

'There's plenty of time for that, but right now I want to see how far I can go in boxing.'

Justin's opposition only lasted until Dale started attracting media interest like before.

'Goodbye Dale. I couldn't possibly plan my future with a boxer, darling,' Daphne, his latest girlfriend said on the phone a week after he told her of his plans. 'What would daddy and his friends at the Rotary Club think? I know he would be fwightfully cwoss. A gal of my standing and bweeding cannot possibly be associated with someone who punches people in the head for a living. Good heavens. It's as bad as being a bus dwiver or bawwow boy.'

Dale was not too aggrieved. Daphne was too pompous, even by his own pretentious standards.

At least she isn't racist, despite all her snobbery. I suppose going to school in Kenya when her father worked there made her a little bit liberal.

Daphne phoned her father when she hung up from Dale. 'Daddy, I'm not seeing Dale anymore.'

'Really, why's that petal?'

'He's going back to being a boxer.'

'That's jolly good news, Daphne. I must admit the thought of a coloured chap in the family did not enthral your mother and I at all.'

'Will you buy me that flat in Chiswick now, daddy?'

'Of course, darling, now that Kunta Kinte is out of the way.'

Dale had become almost impervious to racial animosity in his three years away from the ring. He took Daphne's aloofness and her parents' indifference as merely part of their snobbery and totally dismissed the fact that they could be racists.

Little did he know that Daphne initially responded to his advances because he made her believe he had family connections with a wealthy Jamaican shipping family of the same name and their relationship could benefit her father's export business in the Caribbean.

There was also an element of sexual attraction with her bit of rough trade, but she always claimed that their relationship was based purely on an intellectual level.

'He's the first black man I've met who knew that the Gaza Stwip wasn't just Paul Gascoigne's football kit,' she was fond of telling her friends. 'He also weads Voltaire and Nietzsche, *The Financial Times*, and *The Times*, but I was appalled to see him weading *The News of the World* once.'

Dale enjoyed Daphne's sophistication and the fact that she claimed to be a distant relative of the Royal family on her 'paternal grandmother's side' was a status symbol, hence his pet name for her, Duchess.

They enjoyed weekends away at the family's cottage in the Pennines and went clay pigeon shooting in the New Forest. Dale thought he was totally accepted by Daphne's family. Little did he know that whenever he left the family house in Holland Park, her father had instructed the housekeeper to check that nothing had been stolen 'by our dark friend.'

~

Dale was in the Integrated Circuit wine bar in Covent Garden drinking with a friend when he noticed Yolanda across the room with a group of girlfriends. She sat near the bar and he headed across the room towards her.

'Hi, Yolanda. Or should I say Dora,' he said.

'Oh hello. I met you at...at...'

'Cafe Royal at last year's fashion show. You were called Dora then.'

'Oh that's my middle name,' she giggled as her friends smiled in unison.

'Anyway, how do you know it's also Yolanda.'

'Seen you nuff times in *The Globe*.'

He bent forward and whispered: 'Fancy coming out for a drink some time?'

She whispered back: 'Yes.'

'Really!'

He stood up smiling.

She beckoned him to lean down again and whispered: 'And I'll bring Tiger with me.'

He forced a smile, walked away immediately as he heard Yolanda laughing raucously with her friends at his expense.

Feeling humiliated, Dale left the bar and decided to head for Shane's whose company always cheered him up.

I hope he's not stoned though. Can't stand him snorting all the time. He won't listen to my advice to cut down.

As soon as Dale walked out of the wine bar he noticed three white men beating up a smaller black man in an alleyway. Dale thought the black man looked familiar and considered helping him out. He braced himself to run at the gang but weighed up the odds before turning and walking away.

~

Bobo Hendricks, world welterweight champion and Dale's former gym-mate hit back at the Murrays, two gangster brothers and a cousin from south London with every ounce of strength he possessed. After weeks of insisting that Hendricks agree to throw his next championship contest against their unfancied fighter, Roy Johnson, this was their final warning.

Mick Murray had a baseball bat, Doug a claw hammer and Stuart used a pair of knuckle-dusters. They were better known by their 'tools' of trade than their real names. Baseball, Duster and Hammer were heavily built six footers who had done some boxing themselves but were more refined in street fighting.

Hendricks put up some brave resistance with his feet and fists but was no match for the three tooled-up heavies. His fierce warrior instinct prevented him from fleeing.

Although he landed some good shots, at one point looking like he was going to overwhelm the thugs, Hendricks got systematically worked over; cuts and bruises everywhere, broken ribs, depressed cheekbone, fractured skull and a dislocated shoulder.

In a symbolic act of cruelty, Hammer and Baseball picked him up and Duster slammed both Hendricks' hands with a car door repeatedly. In case there was any doubt, his boxing career was definately finished. Hendricks had already passed out, enveloped in pain.

The sickening crack of bones breaking made all three Murrays laugh. They pushed him roughly onto a pile of rubbish, hid their weapons under the rubble of a nearby skip, dusted themselves down and went for beer in a pub across the road. They spent the rest of the night applauding each other's 'bravery'.

A couple who witnessed the assault phoned the police on their mobile. Four cars and two vans arrived as the Murrays were drinking in the pub. Two policemen waited for the ambulance to arrive whilst at least ten more went to arrest the perpetrators.

The cops walked out a few minutes later having put away their notepads, truncheons and handcuffs. The Murrays laughed. Retaining senior officers on their payroll had its advantages.

Bobo Hendricks lived. Just. He spent two months in intensive care and another year in hospital and rehabilitation. Roy Johnson fought for the welterweight title vacated by Hendricks and against all expectations knocked out his opponent in the fourth round.

The Murrays collected their six-hundred thousand pounds from strategically placed bets around the country and threw a big celebration for their champion.

Hendricks was confined to a wheelchair for the rest of his life. Tiger personally gave Bobo's wife and three kids ten thousand pounds and organised a benefit dinner that raised another twenty-three thousand.

Dale and Archie donated five thousand each although they could afford much more, especially Archie who had accumulated millions. They visited Hendricks only once in hospital and once at home, both times making sure the newspapers were there to record their visits.

The Murrays were into everything bent; drug trafficking, extortion, bank fraud and stealing top of the range cars to order were their principle rackets. They viewed their earnings from boxing as a nice little sideline.

Fixing fights was a classic case of turning the odds against the bookies, but they also liked managing and promoting fighters and matching two of their own boxers against each other so that they got most of the fighters' earnings in managers' and promoters' fees.

Another good scam was blackmailing referees and judges

by filming them with prostitutes they had supplied.

It also made fixing a fight much easier, especially if the boxer they had requested to take a dive would not play ball. Sometimes they might feel 'generous' and give a referee or other official a present like a cheap imitation Rolex watch or bundle of counterfeit twenty pound notes to entice them to favour their fighters.

If the recipient found out the present was bogus and object-ed, Duster had a way of persuading him to keep quiet. He simply brought out both knuckle-dusters and started clinking them together.

The Murrays loved being compared to the Kray twins, the Sixties gangsters who terrorised the underworld but became a part of the celebrity circuit until they were imprisoned for many years. 'Those slags were like choirboys compared to us,' they would say. Nobody ever contradicted them.

~

Tiger knocked out three more opponents as he marked time waiting for a WBB world title shot. He was becoming very frustrated at being frozen out for a chance at the big prize. It all changed the day an excited Colly came bustling into the gym dressing room waving a piece of paper about.

'Blindin' news Tiger. We've got the WBB title shot.'

'Wicked! Den I'll prove dat I am de best super-mid-dleweight in the world.'

'I've just got the fax confirming I've got the promotional rights. You're in there champ. Dale Harrison, March the tenth, Docklands Arena.'

'Colly, you're safe! Man, I'm gonna knock de shit out of that pussy-claat bwoy. Dis is my time. Mash him up like callaloo soup.'

'Yeah, Tiger. How does it go? We run t'ings, t'ings nah run we!'

The four other black boxers in the changing room roared with laughter when Colly broke into patois. They all gathered round to see the fax.

Beside himself with excitement, Tiger dressed quickly. They drove into Brixton and sat in the restaurant area of the Z Bar in Acre Lane and discussed the fight over plates of steamed fish, rice 'n' peas and plantain.

'You're getting four hundred and fifty big ones Tiger which isn't bad considering Harrison is only on three hundred gees.'

'How you mean, Colly? De title's vacant so de purses dem should be fifty-fifty, surely?'

'Yeah, but you haven't got Stretch in your corner, have you? The bastard's skimmed off his own whack as 'manager's fees and expenses' and that's all Harrison's getting.'

'De lickle bomba-claat. I just give t'anks for having you Colly.'

'Yeah, I look after you kid. You know if you win Don King is interested in putting you on the Julio Cesar Chavez bill in July. He likes your style and thinks the Americans will warm to you.'

'Bwoy, Colly, I'm gonna train like a demon for dis one. Christmas is out. Just pure training. Training in Florida? Bwoy, me just can't wait.'

'That's right. No expense spared for the champ.'

Running through the streets of Kensington and Hammersmith on Christmas Day, Tiger thought of the lovely meal he knew his mother was preparing. It would be his last act of indulgence for the next three months.

When he arrived at his mother's flat in Brixton and put the key in the front door, the smell of Iris's cooking made his nose tingle with anticipation. A luscious combination of classic English and Caribbean cuisine made him smile. A veritable feast awaited; roast turkey, cooked ham, curried chicken and fried snapper with all the trimmings; roast potatoes, steamed cabbage, rice 'n' peas, fried plaintain, corn on the cob, salad and broccoli.

Cassius was there with his wife Marcia. It was the first time the brothers had seen each other for months. Cassius' work as a draughtsman had taken him to Northampton, an hour's drive away.

They phoned each other regularly but as they moved in different social and professional circles they rarely saw each other. It was only on special occasions like this that they really spent time together.

Cassius and Marcia had been together longer than anyone could remember. They met at school as fifteen-year-olds and been inseparable since, so Tiger called them the Siamese Twins. Cassius resembled his younger brother strongly but was slighter built and had a lighter complexion.

He dressed well, but not as trendily as Tiger. Dangly earrings in each ear, heavy jewellery and baby locks certainly weren't for him. He preferred to wear his hair in the rather dated Eighties flat-top style, no jewellery, smartly pressed slacks and crisp white shirts rather than the jeans and designer tracksuits that Tiger favoured.

Marcia seemed perfect for Cassius; she had a typical fit sista's figure, curvy with wide hips that Tiger claimed were ready to produce an American football team. As there are around forty-five players in the average team Marcia was not amused, but she liked her brother-in-law all the same. He was kind and generous and even helped them financially to buy their three-bedroom semi in Northampton.

'So Tiger, you're going to take on Dale at last. Are you going to win,' Marcia asked naively.

'How you mean! You mus' be mad! I'm gonna spark him, Marcia. Lick 'im down in five. Believe. Dere's no way dat lick-le...'

'Tiger!' Iris interjected, anticipating profanity.

'Sorry mum,' he said sheepishly. 'Marcia, I'm gonna lick him down. F'real.'

'Give him some licks from me, rude boy,' Cassius added. 'The geezer's too blasted leery. 'Bout him 'ave a degree and shit!'

'Cassius Crawford, you mind your language, y'hear,' Iris admonished. 'Lawd ah mercy, is only pure bad word my children dem ah talk.'

'Sorry mum,' he said standing up from the table to walk round and kiss his mother, making a fuss of her. She playfully pushed him away.

'Mum, nobody likes that Harrison, he's a psuedo-black man. Tiger will be doing black people a favour by knocking him out. Like Ali did when he knocked out Foreman.'

'Nobody likes Harrison except the *Daily Herald*,' corrected Marcia. 'They love him, don't they? Black man from a middle-class family with a degree who only checks pork. They did a big two-page spread the other day trying to emphasise how easy it is for black men to get on in society. It's all bullshit.'

'Typical of the *Herald*,' chipped in Cassius. 'I wonder how many black journalists they've got there. I wonder how many are employed on the national newspapers, period? They're only trying to use an unusual black man as an example of how liberal and non-racist this society is. Bullshhhh...'

He looked guiltily at his mother who was clearing the table. Her glare made him feel nine years old again.

Tiger laughed. Marcia bent her head to hide her smile. It was always a pleasure to be around his family. They were never boring.

'By the way, where's Yolanda, Tiger?' Marcia asked.

'She gone ah Manchester fe spend Christmas with her family. She sends her apologies.'

Iris was not entirely disappointed. Although Yolanda had never said or done anything to upset her, Iris never really took to her. She felt that as her son was now a celebrity girls were more interested in the size of his bank balance than the depth of his character.

'Me ah tell yah,' Iris would say to her friends, 'how can a gyal wid such pretty, pretty fingernails do any 'ousework and care for 'er man? She t'ink sey she too heity-teity. Could'na wash a spoon!'

Tiger drove home in his slick Mercedes that evening feeling very happy. Everyone appreciated the expensive presents he bought them. Marcia got a gold bracelet, Cassius a Louis Vuitton briefcase and the best of the many presents he bought Iris was a burgundy cashmere coat.

'You can t'row away dat London Transport coat now mum,' he proudly declared as he watched her eyes boggle. Iris walked around for hours in it after everyone had gone and hung it on a wardrobe handle in front of her bed to admire it.

When she woke up in the middle of the night to use the toilet, before putting out the light, she stroked the coat lovingly before getting back into bed. 'Dat son of mine is a good bwoy.'

~

Tiger always found time at Christmas to do even more charity work than he usually did.

At one Barnados children's home he noticed a shy, black boy sitting quietly watching the other kids mob him. Tiger walked over and introduced himself.

The kid's name was Errol and his main interest was boxing. Tiger was astonished that Errol knew the name of every opponent he had fought, the venue and the result.

'You're my hero, Mr Crawford,' Errol said looking down at his own feet and thrusting his autograph book in Tiger's direction.

'Call me Tiger.'

'Yes, Mr... I mean Tiger.' Errol wore silver-rimmed glasses that gave him a bookish look. Errol was dark and solidly built like Tiger was at that age. Tiger quizzed the little pundit.

'What year did Muhammad Ali first win the world title, Errol?'

'1964, against Sonny Liston,' came the immediate reply.

'Respec' Errol. Nobody can test you on boxing facts. Now, who did Mike Tyson beat to become heavyweight champion in 1986?'

'Trevor Berbick.'

Rahtid, dis kid knows his stuff.

Tiger stayed for a couple of hours, enjoying the chat with his new friend, even missing a date with a woman he was trying to bed.

'What do you want to be when you grow up, Errol?'

'A boxing writer, so that I can go to see all your fights.'

'Well you better not write anything bad.'

When it was time to leave, Tiger stood up and looked down

146

at the boy's feet.

'What size shoes do you take?'

'Two, Tiger. Why?'

'Nu'tin. True sey, your feet favour pickney size.'

It took Tiger twenty minutes to leave because everybody wanted to get photos with him, including the staff. As he walked through the front door, he turned round and winked at Errol who smiled and waved back.

The next day Tiger returned with a pair of Adidas boxing boots for Errol. The look of delight on the kid's face was the best present Tiger had that Christmas.

~

Tiger held his dick in his hand as he spoke on the phone to Yolanda.

'Yeah, sugar, I'm missing you bad. Believe. Got a stiffy just t'inking 'bout you.'

'Don't be crude now Tiger,' she giggled, 'don't you ever think about anything else?'

'Only when I'm boxing. Even den I jus' wanna knock the geezer's brains in quick-time so I can get my t'ings.'

She laughed again.

'How's your modder, Yolanda?'

'Fine thanks, she sends her love and thanks you for the stereo.'

'Dat's okay. It's hardly a stereo though. Portable boxes like dat ain't got no t'ump. Dem speakers are more like tin cans. Enjoying yourself?'

'Yes, but mum's a bit sad. She still misses dad at times like this. They may be separated but there was still a strong bond. Mum says dad's brother lives near you. In Shepherd's Bush.'

'Oh yeah, what's his name?'

'Cecil.'

'Cecil what?'

'Cecil Ford.'

The realisation hit Tiger like a sneaky left hook - the type you don't see coming but which do the most damage.

'Cecil Ford. So your farder was Delton Ford, right?'

'Yes, Inspector Clouseau. Got it in one. Why d'you ask?'

'Ah nothing. I just remembered you told me your dad's name was Delton but you didn't mention his las' name.'

Tiger's dick went limp. He soon cut off the conversation and replaced the receiver slowly.

Delton Ford. It can't be. Please God. No. No. No....

He ran to the main bedroom wardrobe and pulled out the scrap book buried under a pile of old boxing magazines. Flicking frantically from one cutting to another, he finally found it.

He looked at it over and over hoping somehow it would magically go away.

He slammed the book shut and began sobbing uncontrollably.

CHAPTER 14

GET RID OF IT BITCH

'It was positive. The doctor confirmed it,' Constance sniffed.

Dale was dreading the news on Constance's pregnancy test result. He thought she looked pathetic and wished he had never bothered to sleep with her.

You weren't that good anyway. I was only interested in your dad's money.

'How did that happen, Constance?'

'How do you think it happened, Dumbo?'

'I mean, I thought you were on the pill.'

'Well I was, but that's not a hundred per cent. You must be firing some pretty potent stuff.'

They were sitting in the kitchen of her parents' elegant house in Stanmore. The harsh sunlight shining onto her pallid skin made her look older than her twenty-two years.

'What are you going to do, Constance?'

'Hah. What are *we* going to do, you mean?'

'Do you want to get rid of it?' he asked balefully.

'I can't say right now. I have to think it over.'

'How far gone are you?'

'Three weeks. I reckon it was the night we went out for a curry. Remember I got an upset tummy the next day? They say the pill can get flushed out in those cases.'

'Are you going to tell your parents?'

'No way. They'd flip. They want me to finish my studies and anyway, I don't think they could cope with me not being married and having a black baby with a boxer.'

'I thought they were cool about me and you.'

'Only to a point. You know how parents are with their only daughter. No man's ever good enough for them.'

Dale asked if they could move into the lounge where the light wasn't so bright.

On a good day, with plenty of make-up, Constance was an attractive, bottle-blonde with sparkling blue eyes. But her crooked teeth, discoloured by chain-smoking and plump figure did not really turn Dale on. Her main redeeming feature was her parents' money. Lots of it, from book publishing and running six mobile phone franchises.

Money would be no problem if they had the child, but being a father with someone he did not care for would be a bind. The only person in the world Dale really loved was himself. There was the fear of a shotgun wedding if she went through with it.

'I ain't doing that shit,' he mumbled.

'Doing what Dale?' she asked sidling up to him on the sofa.

'Nothing,' he replied curtly.

Irritated by her closeness, he got up.

'Call me when you make up your mind.'

'Don't go Dale, I want to talk to you. Please stay for a bit.' She burst into tears.

Instead of putting a comforting arm around her, he shook his head in annoyance and kissed his teeth.

'Sort yourself out, bitch. Get rid of it.'

Shocked by his callousness, she began crying hysterically.

'You bastard. I hate you. I thought you loved me.'

'Welcome to the real world.'

As he walked down the hallway to leave he heard her get up.

'Bastard! Bastard! Bastard!'

As he opened the front door he turned around for a last look just in time to see a marble ashtray whistling towards his face. He ducked. It thudded against the door and bounced harmlessly on the mat that ironically had WELCOME inscribed on it.

He took one step towards her to retaliate but saw such anger in her eyes and thought better of it. He opened the door, walked down the drive and quickly got into his brand new BMW. Without another look at Constance who was now standing in the doorway, he sped off.

Whilst he drove up from south London that morning he prayed that if she was pregnant she would say she was going to have an abortion.

He avoided all her calls for the next few weeks, always waiting to hear who was calling on the answering machine before picking up the receiver. He could always tell when it was her because the phone was slammed down without saying anything.

If she rang his mobile he pretended it was a bad reception and hung up. A few weeks later a letter arrived. Dale recognised Constance's handwriting and deliberated about opening it. Curiosity got the better of him.

Dear Dale,

You'll be pleased to hear that I had a termination last week. Mummy knows but daddy doesn't. She guessed what was wrong and I just had to tell her. There was a lot of tears. Thankfully, daddy hasn't found out. It would have upset him too much. He had a mild heart attack last year and we feared for his health.

Your behaviour was absolutely despicable. You are a very nasty person. I was prepared to go against my family's wishes and settle down with you and possibly marry you. Mummy was right, of course, black men are scared of commitment in relationships and can be totally irresponsible.

Although I don't hate you, I have no wish to ever see you or talk to you again.

Goodbye and good riddance, you bastard.

Constance.

PS I hope you get knocked out.

Dale was totally unmoved. He breathed a sigh of relief, tore the letter up, threw it away and never thought deeply about Constance again.

The fight with Tiger was only six weeks away and he wanted to focus on getting totally prepared. The media had already given this contest plenty of build-up. There were so many angles to cover, like the fact that they were former club mates in the amateurs and the obvious hostility between them.

At the first press conference to announce the match, Tiger had been polite and respectful but Dale, wanting to wind him up, announced that he was going to bet ten thousand on knocking Tiger out inside three rounds.

Tiger, having never been knocked down in a long amateur and professional career, was incensed. He claimed that Dale was the one who would get sparked. Dale retorted that Tiger was technically too limited to do that. Tiger said his rival had never met anyone remotely as fast or powerful as him. It was the usual banter.

'You've only fought geriatrics and stiffs,' Tiger shouted. The pressmen and TV crews laughed.

'Your opponents are so limited they don't know a left hook from a fish hook,' Dale retorted.

'At least none of mine needed an oxygen mask before they got into the ring,' Tiger said to more laughter.

The insults continued until Tiger lost his temper, rose from his chair and moved towards his tormentor. They were kept apart by their managers and trainers. The media loved it and next day the tabloids carried headlines like:

TIGER POUNCES!

TIGER TRIES TO RIP HARRISON APART!

UNLEASHED TIGER

It was great publicity. Promoters and TV executives rubbed their hands with glee as tickets sold faster than anticipated.

~

With four weeks to go both men were in good shape. Dale was in a training camp in a remote gym in Bournemouth and Tiger was enjoying himself in Safety Harbor, Florida.

Dale had never had a weight problem and was only five pounds over the twelve stone limit when he arrived at the training camp in early January, unlike Tiger who was thankful that Colly had taken him to a warm climate so that he could sweat off the twenty-six pounds of Christmas excess he had accumulated. Colly wasn't happy.

They sat in a coffee shop in the luxurious resort on their first evening; Colly admonished his young charge for his indiscipline.

'Tiger, this is the biggest fight of your life. I thought you was going to keep your weight in check.'

'Don't worry Colly, I'll beat that pussy-bwoy. Sorry, but I couldn't resist all de bun and cheese and coconut drops my modder cooks. Bwoy, you should taste her red peas soup. Wicked.' Tiger rolled his eyes in appreciation. Colly rolled his eyes in disapproval and puffed furiously on his roll-up.

'Right,' Colly said. 'There's two things you have to be wary of out here - food and women - but not necessarily in that order.'

'De food's no problem, you can't get Yard food round here. But Colly, have you seen the punany man! Crisssss. Titties and batty and t'ighs....' Tiger rolled his eyes again.

'And dem love de English accent. In de paper shop just now dis Sharon Stone type asked me to repeat myself just fe hear my accent. Dat's when I put on my best English voice, old chap. Speak real proper. Normally dose kinda blonde bimbos don't even want fe talk to a black man. When I drop dose 'how do you do madam' lyrics pon dem dey'll be wriggling out of de baggies faster dan an Exocet missile.'

'Hello there, is anybody home?' Colly waved his hand in front of the fighter's glazed expression. 'You can come back to terra firma now.'

'Do what?'

'Get back to reality, we've got a world title to win.'

'Ah nah nutin' Colly. Man can't train twenty-four-seven.'

'Twenty-four-seven?'

'S'right. Twenty-four hours a day, seven days a week.'

Colly shook his head in bemusement. 'You and your street talk.'

'Colly, de fight's a month away and dis is my first time in de States. You can't expect me fe live like a monk.'

'Sex drains a fighter's strength and resolve. You won't have the energy to even climb into the ring. I've a good mind to tell Yolanda.'

Tiger laughed at the hollow threat. Colly was always dropping that one on him, but would never do that, mainly because Tiger had put a few willing girls his way in the past.

'As long as I give you what you want in de gym, dere shouldn't be a problem, Colly. I'm de article Bonecrusher, remember. Busted more ribs dan Colonel Sanders. Nobody can match me wid running and I'm in bed by eleven o'clock every night.'

'Yeah, but who with? And when do you finally get to sleep?'

'Just 'cos I love my jooky jam, don't sweat me man. All work and no play makes Tiger a very dull boy. Ask Jack Nicholson. He was vicious in *The Shining*.'

'Okay, but Tiger, there are nasty diseases going round and one of them is a killer. I hope you're being careful.'

'Durex should make me a major shareholder. Remember - no glove, no love.'

Colly laughed. Tiger had an answer for everything. He was impressed with the fighter's new found maturity. Tiger was one of the hardest trainers he had ever known, but he liked to play just as hard as he worked. Colly knew Tiger was a serious party animal but never did hard drugs nor got drunk, although he had a fondness for champagne. Women were his sole weakness.

Tiger was at his peak now after eight years as a pro with an impressive unbeaten record of twenty-eight bouts. He was always in excellent shape, knowing that his lack of technique meant he relied on power and fitness to wear down and overwhelm opponents.

Against Harrison, a supreme stylist who had recorded only

eight knockouts or stoppages in his twenty-three contests, Tiger's brutal strength and immense stamina would be the vital factors for victory. Colly knew Tiger's weight would drop drastically in the time they were going to be there, but his insatiable appetite for women was his biggest worry; invariably black, pretty and big breasted.

Colly was amused at Tiger's confidence and knack of picking up girls. He was also amazed at his front. Like the time they went to a tribute dinner at the Bloomsbury Crest Hotel for Muhammad Ali and Tiger met the daughter of an ex-fighter.

Tiger put on an authentic American accent and claimed that he was one of Ali's London representatives.

He introduced her to the great man as if he really was one of his entourage and got him to have his photo taken with her. The girl was so thrilled that when Tiger invited her out the next night she agreed instantly. The rest of the seduction process was easy. The hardest part of it was remembering to keep the phoney accent going.

It did not take Tiger long to find a companion in Safety Harbor.

'Gee Tiger, are you really friends with the Duchess of York? Fergie is really popular here 'cos she's so human, unlike those other royals.'

'Sure,' Tiger smiled to Breeya, a beauty consultant in one of the nearby hotel's health salons.

'Tell me what her palace is like?'

'Oh, you know. It's like any other royal yard; big and old wid lots of butlers and servants.'

'Really? What's she like?'

Tiger carried on lying. He got a kick out of impressing nineteen-year-old Breeya. She had big, brown eyes - and breasts to match. Her full lips reminded him of Yolanda. He was not too keen on her shoulder-length weave-on but her fit body more than made up for that.

'Fergie's a big boxing fan, y'know.'

'You're kiddin' me.'

'Trust me, she's got all Tyson's fights on tape.'

'Wow!'

'Sure. She'd love fe come to de fights but being royalty she can't. Wouldn't seem right.'

He was amused by Breeya's gullibility and decided to take the joke further.

'Breeya, can I trust you with a very big secret?'

'Sure.'

'Fergie likes to get waxed by de breddren,' he whispered conspiratorially.

'No!'

'Takes it up the arse in orgies with two or three brothas at a time.'

Breeya put her hands over her mouth in shock. Tiger bent forward as if to tie his shoelaces but really to hide his smile.

Dis girl is seriously stupid.

He spent the next hour in the bar opposite his hotel convincing her that he knew The Spice Girls, George Michael and Tony Blair, so getting her back to his room was a cinch.

When he produced a condom she smiled and started wriggling out of her panties. Afterwards he went to the bathroom, leaving her asleep on the bed. Just as he finished showering and stepped out on the floor, the phone rang. Fearing it was Yolanda, he panicked. 'I'll answer it!' he shouted and as he rushed along the wet bathroom floor, slipped and fell awkwardly on his right ankle. 'Shit!'

He got up hobbling.

'Are you okay?' she said.

'Yeah, I'm cool.'

He hopped on his left foot, genitals bouncing around as he moved towards the phone. Breeya put a hand over her mouth. It was her turn to hide a smile.

'Yolanda. What y' sayin' sweetness? I'm missing you bad, man.'

'Tiger, in case you didn't realise, I'm not a man.'

'Easy. Easy. I thought dis was a love call. Ouch!'

'What's wrong?' Yolanda asked.

'I just hurt my ankle, slipping on de wet bathroom floor. It might be sprained.'

'Are you okay?'

'Shouldn't be a problem.'

'Make sure you get treatment. Tell Colly. Right?'

'Yes darlin'. How's t'ings?'

'Hmm. Nothing new. I'm missing you, Tiger.'

She paused waiting for a reaction.

'I'm missing you too, princess.'

'Ah, that's nice. Are you behaving yourself?'

'Naturally. I train hard and don't eat or drink anyt'ing I shouldn't.'

'You know what I mean, Mr Loverman. I just hope you're keeping your dick to yourself.'

'Ooh. Yolanda. Ah me you ah talk to, baby love. Bona fide one woman man.'

'Huh. One woman a day, you mean.'

'Just cool Yolanda. I'm living like a monk here. F'real.'

'Make sure you keep it that way.'

They exchanged small talk for a few more minutes until Tiger reminded her that it was after midnight locally and he needed to get some serious zeds.

'Just make sure you're sleeping alone, Tiger.'

He sighed. 'You can trust me Yolanda. Believe.'

'Hah. Good night darling. I love you.'

'Love you like cook food - I mean to the bone, Yolanda.'

He hung up.

Breeya was smiling.

'Who was that Tiger?'

'My modder,' he said sarcastically.

'You didn't tell me you had a girlfriend.'

'Cut de crap Breeya. You know de coo. You're not exactly short of male company yourself.'

She looked reflective for a few moments then pulled him onto the bed and kissed him passionately.

Wow these American girls are really forward.

Two hours later it wasn't just his ankle that was sore.

~

Colly was not pleased that Tiger was unable to run, skip and spar for three days because of his injury. Tiger's explanation that he slipped over in the shower was plausible but Colly felt there might be more to the story.

Apart from that setback, preparations in Florida went well. The night before they returned to London, Colly, Lonnie and a couple of sparring partners went for a few drinks before turning in early. Bored of male company, Tiger feigned exhaustion at ten and as he entered his hotel room he phoned Breeya. She arrived a few minutes later and they got down to business straightaway.

159

When they had finished exchanging body fluids, Breeya pulled out a sachet of weed from her handbag.

'I can't smoke dat. De fight's only two weeks away.'

Tiger decided not to have a puff and went to shower.

When he came back, the room was filled with the pungent smell of herb smoke. Unable to resist, he held his hand out for a pull on it.

'Are you sure, Tiger?'

He nodded and took it from her and pulled hard. He held his breath for a moment and exhaled slowly feeling a terrific swirling sensation coursing behind his eyeballs.

'Bwoy, dat's strong. Have you put anyt'ing else in it?'

'No,' she said timidly. 'It's sensi. Dexter, our Jamaican gardener grows it in his backyard.'

'Well tell Dexter we could do wid some ah dis in Brixton. De sensi trail seems fe stop at Heat'row and Gatwick. Dose corrupt custom officials keep the best puff for demselves.'

Breeya stayed the night. Tiger ensured she got up with plenty of time for him to get ready to check out. They kissed at the door.

'I'll miss you Tiger. Please keep in touch. You've got all my numbers.'

'I'll try, but bwoy, I'd like to come back fe check some more juicy pum-pum,' he squeezed her buttocks and ran his index finger along the crease of her backside. She pushed him away playfully.

He watched her round, wobbly backside wiggling down the corridor and regretted having to leave. He'd enjoyed the time in Florida. Like being on holiday.

CHAPTER 15

I'LL BOX YOUR EARS OFF

Dale's preparations were going well. Sort of. Apart from damaging a bone in his hand when throwing a left hook in sparring. The media's interest in this fight meant it was a sell-out weeks before.

Pundits favoured Dale's deft skills but many fancied Tiger too for his aggression and punching power. It was a genuine even-money contest.

The one million pounds that the newspapers announced they were earning annoyed both fighters as they were being paid considerably less. This type of hype only increased the pressure on them; expectations were heightened for each to win and the taxman was likely to give them a hard time.

Dale wasn't worried, his father's company accountant would deal with that - and probably make him pay only a nominal amount. Tiger felt confident with the very above board accountant, Howard Ellis managing his affairs.

Ellis, a tubby, balding man with clammy hands and bad breath, wore cheap suits peppered with dandruff despite his wealth. He liked to wear his half-moon, gold rimmed glasses on the tip of his nose peering over them imperiously when speaking to clients.

His air of superiority irritated Tiger but Colly had recommended him and Tiger was frightened of being chased for back taxes in the future as had happened to Joe Louis and many other great fighters in the past.

He was aware of the two million Grant Bailey, the former

heavyweight champion, had to hand over to the Inland Revenue a couple of years earlier. Tiger tolerated Ellis' bad personal hygiene and as far as Colly knew, Ellis's honesty was unquestionable.

~

The final press conference, three days before the fight, was packed in a huge conference room in the Dorchester Hotel. Crammed with reporters, TV crews, boxers, Boxing Board officials and every conceivable player in the sport.

The two sets of females supporting their respective heroes were easily identifiable by their dissimilarities. Dale's were white career types in smart, designer suits that one journalist dubbed Dale's Debs.

Tiger's girls were gold-toothed ragga devotees, dripping with heavy jewellery and fitted out in black or primary-coloured lycra from top to toe. The press called them Tiger's Titbits and they were led by the luscious Mayo, who was known as 'The Nubian Princess'.

'You won't be able to match my strengt' and power,' declared Tiger into a microphone.

'You won't be able to catch me, Crawford. I'll box your ears off like I did in the amateurs.'

'Dat was years ago, man and you still didn't beat me even den. You pussy. I used to lick you down den and I'll do it again on Saturday.'

'You're too stupid to catch me.'

'Cha, you ain't in university now. I've got de intelligence to beat you, dat's all I know.'

'Oh yeah. Qualifications? How many GCSEs have you got?'

'Twelve,' replied Tiger.

There was a stunned silence.

'You're joking, aren't you?' replied a clearly surprised Dale.

'Well you started it,' grinned Tiger to howls of laughter.

At the weigh-in the day before the fight, both fighters looked tense and refused to shake hands. Tiger was right on the twelve-stone limit and Dale half a pound lighter.

Tiger, who needed to starve himself to make the weight, devoured two bananas and gulped down a two litre bottle of water immediately after the weigh-in. By fight time he would be at least eight pounds heavier.

Tiger stayed in the Dorchester that night. Colly wanted to keep him away from the distractions of friends and well-wishers. It was also a psychological way of Colly making Tiger feel he was worthy of staying in the best hotels.

'You're the best super-middle in the world. There's no way he's gonna beat you.'

Archie insisted Dale stayed at his Hampstead mansion for the last three days. Dale thought this was a thoughtful gesture by his manager, not realising that by keeping the overall expenses down there was more profit for the promoter. It wasn't hard to guess who Dale's promoter was.

Archie sipped his whisky and mentally worked out how much he would earn.

At least one-point-two million, which is more than those two jungle bunnies are gonna earn between them. 'Andsome.

He gulped down his drink and poured another one in celebration.

Dale was worried. Things had not gone well in the last few days. Harriet, his latest girlfriend, refused to come to the fight. She hated boxing and feared that Tiger was going to seriously hurt him. Her anxiety only increased his own worries.

Dale enjoyed cultivating his brash and supremely confident persona but his stomach was churning the morning of the big day. He felt unrested although he had slept reasonably well. The day went excruciatingly slowly for him. He felt like a man awaiting the call to his execution. Meaningful conversation was impossible.

As he limbered up in the dressing room waiting to be called out he wanted to pee for the umpteenth time. Jack wouldn't let him. 'Calm down, son. You're going to be the champ.' He held a fist to his mouth imitating the ring announcer: 'And the NEW world champion - Dale Harrison.'

Jack picked up his trainer's pads and put Dale through some drills in preparation. The red leather gloves were the regulation eight ounces. Dale felt so strong after months of sparring with sixteen ounce gloves they seemed like rubber washing-up gloves on him. In the other dressing room, Tiger was going through the same routine.

~

Tiger hadn't felt so relaxed before any fight, amateur or pro. He was one hundred per cent certain he would finally overcome his nemesis.

Bwoy, me wanna beat the shit outta the pussy-claat bwoy. He'll never be de same again.

Tiger rattled off combination after combination with Lonnie on the pads as they warmed up in the dressing room. They heard the cheers as Dale, in long white shorts, walked out into the ring and braced themselves for the final call from the whip. As soon as Dale's theme tune *Minnie The Moocher* stopped, Tiger set off and as he marched out under the glare of the bright TV lights, he spotted familiar faces in the crowd, mostly friendly.

'*Hidee, hidee, hidee, hi!*'

'*Hidee, hidee, hidee, ho!*'

Three quarters of the twelve thousand crowd were cheering for him and he wasn't going to disappoint them.

No Retreat, No Surrender blared out and he spotted brothas and sistas dancing and shooting out two fingers in gun salutes as Tiger walked to the ring in spangly red shorts. Tiger was led out by Colly and put his gloves on his shoulders. Lonnie walked behind him. A group of security men circled the three. Two female flag bearers in red lycra outfits carried the Union Jack and the Jamaican flag ahead of them.

The cream of British boxing sat ringside. It was like a Who's Who of the sport and included Nigel Benn, Chris Eubank, Frank Bruno, Colin McMillan, Duke McKenzie, Gary Mason and Naseem Hamed. Lennox Lewis and his brother Dennis shook hands with well wishers.

Sports agent Ambrose Mendy handed out business cards to the City bankers at ringside with the view to yet another deal.

Top promoters Frank Warren, Jess Harding and Frank Maloney looked on. Claude, Tony, Simon and Daniel from *Boxing News* and Glyn, the *Boxing Monthly* editor, watched attentively. Richard Daley, Tiger's wealthy business associate, chatted to pressmen. Daley was his main sponsor now. Daley sat with his wife June who struck up a conversation with Michelle Edwards, aka Miss Lickshot, the *New Nation's* reggae writer, who had forged a friendship with Tiger through their love of the music.

White youths swilled beer, singing to the tune of '*Guantanamera*', 'One Tiger Crawford, there's only one Tiger Crawford, One Tiger Crawford, there's only Tiger Crawford.'

Yolanda had insisted that her friend Unal sang before the fight began. In her shimmering gold cocktail dress, Unal overcame her nerves to give a wicked rendition of *The Greatest Love Of All*. Hairs on the backs of people's necks stood on end.

The millions watching on TV were moved as well. It was a smart move, Yolanda desperately wanted to get her friend some exposure to pursue her singing ambitions. That performance would have spectacular results.

The fight lived up to expectations; in the first round Tiger pressed forward, slamming blows to head and body whenever he got close enough and Dale boxed beautifully on the retreat, peppering his opponent's face with sharp jabs and uppercuts.

Yolanda jerked her shoulder in sync with Tiger's punches, wincing whenever Dale landed a solid shot. Cassius bellowed encouragement as his mother buried her head in her lap, praying on rosary beads that both fighters would come out in one piece. On the opposite side of the ring Justin and his family sat watching in silence as Dale took more punches than they had ever seen.

Tiger's ankle was throbbing from the fall in the shower in Florida. The painkilling injections were not working. He limped back to the corner at the end of the round worried and sat on the stool a second had placed there. Colly had already climbed into the ring, a white towel draped over his shoulder. He too looked apprehensive.

'Ankle feels bad,' Tiger mumbled after Colly pulled out his gumshield. Colly smacked him hard on the side of the face before Lonnie, standing outside the ring stretched between the ropes and pressed a bottle of water to his lips.

'Don't fucking talk about that ankle again. You hear? This is a world title and nuffink's gonna get in your way. Least of all Dale fucking Harrison.'

Tiger spat out the water. He was surprised at Colly's sharp tongue. It was out of character. But he knew he was right.

'Keep pressing forward but watch his left hook. Remember to keep moving to the left. Goddit?'

'Come on, Tiger. Get your combinations going,' called Lonnie.

Tiger nodded as Colly covered his face with Vaseline then replaced the gumshield.

Dale was alarmed by Tiger's tenacity in the opening round. The couple of left hooks he threw did not land cleanly on his shorter adversary. Dale was worried by a sharp pain, like a mild electric shock, passing right up his arm when he threw the left. But Archie had instructed him to throw them as usual otherwise Tiger would know something was up.

The second, third and fourth rounds went the same way. Dale knew he was falling behind and could feel he was getting marked up around the eyes.

'Throw that fucking left hook like you mean it, Dale, other-wise you can find another promoter,' shouted Archie at the end of the fourth.

'But it hurts like fuck, Archie,' protested Dale.

'Just do it, you little shit. Or you're history.'

Dale went out at the start of the fifth and landed an almighty left hook to the top of Tiger's shining, sweaty head. The pain was indescribable for both. Tiger's bad ankle momentarily gave way as Dale groaned softly from the elec-tric currents coursing up his arm.

A tense Yolanda sitting ringside, turned away in horror fearing the worse. The crowd went mental; ringside radio and

TV commentators went into overdrive as the hairs on the back of their necks bristled. Pressmen scribbled frantically without looking down at their pads, cameramen clicked madly, sweat streaming down their temples.

Even the two ringside girls in one corner screamed excitedly. People who had bet with their mates on Dale were holding out their hands demanding to be paid there and then. The Murrays gloated at their wideboy friends for being so daft and backing Tiger. They stood to make two hundred thousand if Dale won.

'You hurt him bad, mucker. Don't lose the fucking initiative,' Archie bellowed at the end of the round.

The fast pace never abated as years of hatred, jealousy and resentment collided in the twenty-by-twenty-foot space. Dale's single punch success turned the tide, for a while. He was able to win the next four rounds simply by jabbing with his left and planting a well timed right cross on the oncoming Tiger's chin. Aches and excruciating pain throbbed everywhere.

'We love you Tiger, we do. We love you Tiger...' chanted his most loyal white fans as a rallying cry.

'Clap de lickle bomba claat coconut,' yelled a rude boy.

'Lick down de red bwoy Tiger,' shouted another.

'I know it's a cliche but this must truly be one of the fights of the century,' declared one TV commentator as a heavily pregnant cousin of Tiger overcome by the heat and pandemonium fainted behind him and slumped onto his back. Few people noticed as two medics escorted her and her husband away.

The commentator glanced over his shoulder to assess the commotion and without pausing continued animatedly: 'Not since the epic series between Sugar Ray Robinson and Jake La Motta have we seen such ferocity in the ring. I kid you not, this is *Raging Bull* revisited.'

Tiger summed up all his strength to finish hard and fast. His ankle felt like it was going to explode out of his boot but the thought of imminent victory was a great motivator. He noticed that Dale's left hooks were not as potent since that big one, nor as frequent. For the first time in the contest he was in trouble.

As they tired and the fight pace slowed, things got ragged. Tiger frequently pressed his hard head into Dale's face.

Tiger started talking to Dale in the mauls. 'Give up you bitch....Dem pussy-bwoy punches can't stress me...where's your left hook now, motherfucker?' The referee ignored the abuse.

Dale was incensed but could not muster enough strength for a meaningful counter-attack.

In the eleventh round, one head clash had blood streaming out of Dale's nose. Tiger felt it crack, stepped back and sneered. Outraged, Dale forgot the hurting hand and threw a left hook with the finesse of a drunken pensioner. He missed wildly. The crowd laughed.

Tiger sneered again, waded in and landed six body shots plus his own left hook. Dale stepped back stunned and disorientated, shaking his head to clear it as Tiger's fists flailed around him. The bell went for a desperately needed one minute respite.

The referee insisted they touched gloves for the start of the twelfth and final round. He had to forcibly make them.

Nobody watching in the venue sat for the last round. Stamping feet on the floorboards gave off a low rumble like impending thunder as the two gladiators threw venomous punches.

The final bell could not be heard and even when the referee intervened, they kept at it. Colly and Archie pulled their respective fighters away as the ring filled up with officials, wannabe celebs, security men and close friends and family.

Consensus was that Tiger had edged it but there were plenty of arguments for Dale. His marked face told the story after thirty-six minutes of astonishing violence. There were no knockdowns. Tiger had seemingly won seven rounds. But as they waited for the three judges' score, there was the Archie Stretch factor to be taken into account.

Archie had never disguised his allegiance to the World Boxing Board officials and unsubstantiated stories about him providing high-class hookers and expensive jewellery to the officials were rife. A decision in Tiger's favour was not a foregone conclusion.

The ringside press were unanimous; Tiger Crawford had won comfortably. When the ring announcer declared there was a split decision amongst the three judges, the crowd stirred, sensing the type of diabolical decision that occasionally blights the sport.

'They're gonna teef Tiger,' black supporters shouted. A deathly hush descended on the venue as the MC announced the decision.

'Judge Herman Stein of the United States scores one hundred and sixteen Crawford, one hundred and twelve Harrison.' Mass applause.

'Judge Ruel Fernandez of Puerto Rico scores one hundred and fifteen Harrison, one hundred and fourteen Crawford.' There was a tumult of boos, whistling and jeering. Pressmen phoning over their copy gave up trying to make themselves heard.

'Judge Julian Burgess of England scores one hundred and fifteen to one hundred and thirteen..' He paused. Both fighters held their breaths.

'And the NEW World Boxing Board super-middleweight champion is...TIGER CRAWFORD!'

An explosion of noise engulfed the venue as if the tannoy system had suddenly gone into the twilight zone. Tiger sank to his knees and clasped his hands as if in prayer. A distraught Dale did not acknowledge his victor in time honoured fashion and clambered between the ropes and headed towards his dressing room to a chorus of boos for his unsporting behaviour.

The Murrays had stood near an exit door anticipating the worse. They left without settling their bets.

Yolanda climbed through the ropes and pushed her way towards Tiger. They hugged tightly despite the sweat pouring down his body drenching her cream Nicole Farhi dress.

'You were great darlin'.'

'I've finally got de fucker outta my system,' he breathed in her ear. 'Bwoy dis is the 'appiest day of my life. F'real.'

'I'm so proud, Tiger.'

'We're gonna party big-time,' he said pushing his groin into hers.

She smiled as he was pulled away to give a live TV interview. After the interview it took an age to reach the dressing room as hordes of fans insisted on expressing their congratulations.

Dale took less than a minute to reach the dressing room. Supporters patted him on the back in sympathy but he was oblivious to that. He just wanted to get away fast.

Harriet stood outside the entrance to his dressing room. She had decided at the last minute to come and give moral support. She smiled lamely.

'What you doing here?' he snarled.

'I came to support you Dale,' she said meekly, bowing her head. 'But it seems you don't appreciate that.'

Dale looked over his shoulder anxious not to seem insensitive in front of Jack and Archie. The security man behind Harriet could hear everything but discreetly kept his back to them.

'Piss off Harriet,' he hissed. 'I'll call you tomorrow.'

She looked pleadingly at him.

'Go!'

She stormed past him in a huff. Jack and Archie said nothing.

Justin and his two other sons pushed their way through and entered Dale's dressing room.

'Never mind son, you'll beat him in the rematch,' Justin said weakly.

Dale looked so fiercely at his father, onlookers thought he was going to whack him. Dale bowed his head and sighed. A heavy silence descended on the room.

'You can still be a champion in the future, Dale. Just believe in yourself,' said his faithful mate Trevor who had bet three hundred on him winning and would have drawn twenty-five thousand from the bookies for all the stakes he placed over the years. There was disappointment in Trevor's voice but no bitterness.

Dale tried to thank him but the utter despair and feeling of humiliation made the words stick in his throat. His nose throbbed in pain. The doctor had confirmed that it was just badly bruised.

A while later they heard Tiger's noisy entourage filing past. Archie and Jack walked out. There was more money to be made with another fighter they had to attend to.

Dale gave his urine sample, showered and changed into his blue Fila tracksuit. He refused to answer reporters' questions, only giving BBC TV and radio interviews in his dressing room.

'I thought I did enough to get the judges' verdict,' he repeated over and over. 'At least one of them made the right decision... No, I'm not retiring... I'd like a rematch. I'll beat him next time.'

He left through a side door with his family, refusing to give any more interviews.

~

Tiger appeared in a conference room in the arena to rapturous applause from the media present, laughing and joking with them for ages. Flanked by Yolanda, Cassius, Colly and Lonnie, Tiger was in his element.

'De judge who gave it to Harrison left with a guide dog,' Tiger chirped, making everyone laugh. 'Nobody tol' me he was Dale's godfather... Colly said I might 'ave to knock 'im out just to get a draw. He was almost right!'

A reporter asked: 'Was he as good as you expected?'

'Nah, my modder's boxed me ears harder dan dat.'

'Will you give him a rematch?'

'Yes, but he'll have to wait,' he paused for effect, 'until I draw my pension.'

The banter went on until Tiger smoothed down the lapels of his Versace jacket and took Yolanda's hand. 'Excuse me ladies and gentlemen, me 'ave some serious partying fe enjoy.'

There was more applause as he left with Yolanda, Junior, Cassius and a small group of close-knit friends. Tiger, Yolanda and Paulette, Junior's girlfriend got into Junior's Mercedes and headed for the Brixton Academy where Colly, with total belief in his charge's ability, had organised a massive celebration party.

The party was kicking.

Supa Flex, London's number one sound, dropped exclusive dub plates and the PAs were provided by a host of big name artists, including Maxi Priest, Omar and Gabrielle. Moet & Chandon flowed by the caseload in the VIP lounge.

'Respec' Colly, you've done me proud tonight.'

'That's alright Tiger, I took the cost out of your purse.'

Tiger's face dropped until Colly broke into a grin. He hit Tiger playfully on the arm.

'Don't worry, this is my treat. The best forty grand I've ever spent.' Colly later told Tiger that he had written off the cost of the party as a legitimate tax expense so it effectively cost him nothing. Tiger did not mind. He reasoned Colly could have spent it taking his family on a trip to America and writing it off in tax that way. 'It was de wickedest night of my life,' he said. The three thousand people packed in the venue thought so too.

As Tiger mingled through the crowds he was closely pursued by Yolanda. 'I'm watching you champ,' she whispered ensuring that he didn't get too close to the hordes of women showering him with hugs and kisses.

Some offered more! When one nubile sista with more breasts on show than a plastic surgeon's stock room made her intentions very clear, Tiger found himself being whisked back to the VIP room upstairs where the women were at least a little more subtle with their advances. Everywhere he went the brothas offered him a clenched fist. The word 'respect' came with every acknowledgement.

Wayne Byrd, the lovable con man had somehow got into the VIP lounge. 'Respec' Tiger,' he said. 'Listen, I've been meaning to speak to you for ages. I've got this fantastic deal lined up with Nike. Guaranteed two million. I speak to Michael Jordan's people every week and they say they want you on board with him at Nike...'

'Not interested, Wayne. Sorry,' Tiger said firmly.

'Tiger. Breddren. I'm not winding you up. Believe.'

'What about dose bogus fifties you gave me when I was gonna turn pro?'

'Breddren. That was in good faith. Believe. Anyway, if you wanna walk away from a two million deal, it's your loss.'

'Dat's cool.' Tiger turned away.

'Oh, by the way Tiger,' Wayne's voice sounded desperate. Tiger stopped. 'I was talking to the prime minister of Jamaica this morning and he said if you won he would like to stage your first title defence in Kingston.'

'Kingston? Been dere loads ah times when I've visited Hampton Court and Teddington Lock.'

'Breddren, I'm serious. He wants to put it on and he wants me to co-ordinate it.'

'What's de prime minister's name, Wayne.'

'Erm...er...'

Tiger laughed and walked away, limping slightly from the painful ankle.

'Bona fide respec', Tiger,' said one admirer. 'Concrete respec' supa,' said the next. Several people offered him a pull on their spliffs but he was fearful of being observed. He soaked up the atmosphere.

I don't want dis to stop. Dis is it. A whole new era in my life.

His mother could not help herself but keep hugging him. 'Lawd ah mercy, my son, the worl' champion,' she kept repeating raising her arms up to the heavens.

Cassius helped Yolanda move him through the crowds.

Junior dropped them home as the early morning sun was rising.

Twittering birds seemed to be singing his praises. A couple of road sweepers spotted him and asked for his autograph.

'Blindin' fight Tiger,' one said.

'Yeah, you're a diamond geezer, not like that 'Arrison wanker,' said the other. Yolanda laughed, Tiger was ready to burst with pride.

Tiredness and inebriation eventually took its toll. Yolanda lovingly undressed him, shuffled him to the shower and steered him back to bed where he slept until late afternoon.

'Sweetness,' he called as he woke up.

'Yes champ,' she replied coming in and standing over him with a large glass of orange.

'I'm de champion of the world!'

'I know. And you're my champ as well.' She bent and kissed him.

'We can get married now, can't we?'

'Only if your head don't swell so much that it can't fit through the church doors.'

'Nah. I promise.'

She kissed him again.

Tiger took that as the cue for some serious jooky jam. As he pulled her towards him, her left breast popped out of her white bathrobe.

'No you don't,' she said, tucking it back in and wriggling free of his arms. 'There's about a million messages on the answer phone and I've already told Junior and a couple of others who called round to wait a few days because you're exhausted. There was supposed to be a press conference at the Dorchester this morning, but Colly cancelled it. It's rescheduled for tomorrow at eleven.'

He was still so elated he didn't really take in what she had just said. The thought of getting his t'ings was the sole thing on his mind.

'Just cool, we'll sort all dat out later. Now, 'ow about some jooky jam, sweetness?'

She was sitting at the end of the bed and turned round to see him, sitting upright, naked on the bed, arms outstretched. His sitting position wasn't the only thing upright. She felt so loving towards him that she stood up, slipped out of her bathrobe and onto his dick. The phone rang and was picked up by the answering machine for the next two hours as they refamiliarised themselves with their most intimate spots.

'Wooh, that was definitely worth waiting for Tiger.'

'Yeah, man.'

'How long is it since you made love to me, darling?' she asked.

'Must be about four weeks.'

'And when was the last time you had sex?'

He looked at her cutely. 'Hah, hah. Your lyrics are lame, sugar. Dis seed is exclusively reserved for de world's sweetest pum-pum. F'real.'

'Yeah and one day there'll be a black leader of the National Front.'

'You're too suspicious. Not all brothas are schemers Yolanda.

Believe,' he smiled.

'Hah.'

The phone rang again. This time Tiger went to pick it up. Yolanda pulled his hand away.

'Let's talk some more, champ,' which he knew meant that in this post-coital state she meant a serious discussion about their relationship. He sighed.

'Yes Yolanda, I do love you even though I'm now worl' champion.'

'How do I know you still love me? Look at the way those girls last night were rushing you. I'm sure you would have gone off with one of those ho's if I hadn't been there.'

'Yolanda, I love you like cook food.'

'What does that mean?' she shouted. 'Like ackee and salt-fish but not like bun and cheese? Black people really come out with some crap. You're always saying that but what does it really mean?'

'Yolanda, let me explain. Man can't live without cook food, you get me? He would die without it. Na true?'

'Well... yes.'

'Den it stands to reason that if I love you like cook food I can't live without you,' he said cheerily. 'And you. You are the jerk in my chicken, the rice in my peas and dumpling in my soup. Believe.'

She laughed in exasperation. Having a meaningful conversation about their relationship was nigh on impossible.

'So when are we getting married then, champ?'

'Immediately after my next fight. Let's see. I should box again around July. So maybe August. That's a good time. In

178

one of dose drive-in place in Vegas.'

He knew how she'd react and deliberately covered over his head. She picked up a pillow and bashed him with it.

'You can pull a girl off the street if that's your intention. We're having a big church affair, at the Kensington Temple or nothing.'

'Mum wants us to have it at her Baptist church,' he said cautiously.

'We're not getting married in Brixton! All the rude boys would turn up firing guns in the air and scare everyone off.'

The conversation continued on that level until Yolanda suddenly became melancholic.

'What's de matter, sweetness?'

'I won't have my father there to give me away.'

A huge wave of guilt suddenly shot down his back making the hairs on the back of his neck bristle.

'Yeah, dat's a pity.' He cuddled her awhile then got up and went into the bathroom to shower, leaving her lying glumly on the bed. The joy of winning the world title suddenly seemed totally unimportant and irrelevant. When he returned, Yolanda was still lying on the bed.

'I love you bad, Yolanda,' he said kissing her gently on the forehead. He cuddled her again.

'I know you wouldn't let me down, Tiger.' She hugged him in appreciation. He felt another wave of guilt.

Tiger spent the rest of the evening on the phone. Junior came round with some breddren with a box packed with champagne, brandy, Red Bull, Babycham, Dragon Stout, Red Stripe and Special Brew. There was also plenty of Supermalt and Lucozade. If Tiger and Yolanda intended to have a quiet night to themselves, those plans were dead.

179

CHAPTER 16

DESPICABLE BEHAVIOUR

Dale got drunk in his flat after the fight. His parents wanted him to come home with them but he flatly refused. He was distraught and all their irritating habits and patronising sympathy would have driven him mad.

Four cans of Foster's Export was enough to lull him into a deep sleep, still wearing his tracksuit. He couldn't be bothered to listen to his answerphone messages and ignored the knock on his front door of commiserating neighbours.

He woke up suddenly on his sofa and cussed when he noticed that an almost full can had spilt onto the Axminster carpet. The clock on the wall said three-twenty. He picked up the phone.

'Harriet?'

'Who's that?' replied the alarmed woman.

'Dale.'

'Oh Dale. You frightened me. It's the middle of the night. How are you, anyway? I came round and knocked a couple of times but you wouldn't answer.'

'I fell asleep. I'm alright. How are you?'

'Well, not frightfully anxious after the way you treated me.'

'I didn't exactly have a lot to be cheerful about, did I?'

'You still didn't have to be so beastly Dale.'

'Okay. Alright. Okay.'

They both waited for the other to speak.

'Can't you say sorry Dale?'

'For what?'

'For being so horrible. You really upset me.'

There was a long silence. She knew he never said sorry under any cicumstances.

'Are you coming round Harriet?'

'What's the time?'

'Three-twenty.'

'What! How dare you phone me at that time.'

'Come round Harriet. I'll let you in this time.'

She sighed softly.

'Please Harriet.'

There was a pause.

'I'll see you soon.'

He smiled and hung up. His ribs still ached and even smiling was painful, but at least Harriet was on her way to help relieve the pain. It took him several minutes to muster up the energy to overcome the ache in his ribs to answer the door when she rang an hour later.

'Nice to see you Harriet,' he smiled then immediately wished he hadn't as the left side of his face hurt again.

'Hmmph!'

She strode past him haughtily and sat down on a chair beside the dining table in one corner of the lounge.

'Make yourself comfortable. Sit on the sofa.'

'No thanks, I'm quite alright here.'

She crossed her legs revealing her thighs under her red viscose skirt. The room's coldness made her nipples stick out of her thin cotton top. Dale was getting aroused.

'Come here Harriet and we'll talk things over,' he motioned her to the sofa.

'I think you owe me an apology first Dale Harrison.'

'For what?' he snapped.

'Your behaviour last night was utterly despicable.'

'I'd just lost a world title fight!'

'So. You didn't have to treat me like that. Mummy and daddy were very, very cross when I told them.'

She glared at him.

'You still haven't said sorry Dale.'

He rolled his eyes in contempt and in a flat tone mumbled: 'Sorry.'

'And what else?'

'What else what?'

'And you won't do it again.'

She looked at him with her chin lowered and rolled her eyes as if asking him if he really meant it.

'Come and give me a cuddle, Harriet.'

She hestitated before standing up and walking towards him. He grabbed her and steered her backwards onto the sofa. He manoeuvred her onto her back and gently placed himself on top and kissed her with the right side of his mouth, the side not bruised and tender.

'Not so fast, Dale. I haven't completely forgiven you yet.'

She tried to push him off.

'Aah! That hurts,' he said clutching his chest with his right hand whilst still holding her down with his left arm.

'Serves you right.'

'What? Look, I haven't had a dip for weeks. *This is* what I deserve.' He forced his hand up her dress and inside her panties.

'Oww! Dale. You're hurting me.'

She wriggled, trying to get him off but he was too heavy and strong.

'Get off, you beast.'

'Shaddup, bitch.' He slapped her hard on the face with the back of his hand. She stopped wriggling and fixed her eyes into his cold face. She noticed the dark bruises and nose swollen from Tiger's relentless punches. His angry eyes had a fearful, demonic look.

'Don't struggle.'

Resigned to the inevitable, she stopped resisting. He yanked down her panties roughly then pulled out his dick through the fly in his boxer shorts and forced his way inside her.

She stiffened from the pain, gasping loudly. 'That hurts.'

'Just relax and you'll enjoy it.'

A surge of rage overcame her initial fear. He was looking ahead at the wall behind her as he pumped away, lost in his own world, oblivious to her emotions or discomfort. When he finished with a grunt a few minutes later she was already sobbing.

He rolled off her and went into the bathroom down the corridor to wash. Momentarily in shock, she lay there thinking about what had just happened, then picked up her panties, handbag and keys and ran towards the front door.

'You bastard,' she shouted as he came out of the bathroom. 'You won't get away with this. Never. You black b-b-b.... NEVER!'

Dale did not have time to react as she slammed the door behind her. He only had a towel wrapped around him so could not pursue her. He went to the lounge window and watched her get into her Golf GTI a floor below.

Popping his head out of the window, he shouted: 'I'm sorry. Okay. I'm sorry.'

She ignored him, backed the car into the street and sped off.

'Bitch,' he hissed. 'Bitch. Bitch, BITCH.'

CHAPTER 17

SETTING A BAD EXAMPLE

'How do you feel about being awarded Tiger's world title under these circumstances, Dale?' a reporter asked at the press conference. Dale sat beside Archie, Jordan and Cedric Fenton, the celebrity lawyer, at the top table in the packed room at the Marriott Hotel.

'Fine, 'cos I thought I'd won it anyway.'

'Actually, only you and one judge thought you had won it, Dale,' another press man said.

Dale shrugged. 'Everyone's entitled to their own opinion.'

'Do you think it's fair that Crawford was stripped of his title after traces of marijuana were found in his urine tests?'

'Of course. That's cheating,' Dale replied emphatically.

'But marijuana isn't a performance enhancing drug, quite the opposite, in fact,' another reporter said.

'It's still an illegal and banned drug,' retorted Archie. 'Think of the example he's setting to the kids. We've got to maintain moral standards in boxing.' The media corps chuckled at Archie's hypocrisy. Archie laughed the loudest, thinking they were laughing with him.

'Dat Stretch is a bomba-claat pussy-hole,' shouted Junior to Tiger as they watched on TV. 'A lickle sensi inna de system is no reason fe tek way a man's worl' title. Dem nah respec' you, star.'

'Yes, me breddren, me know dat,' Tiger said dismally. 'But dem ketch me red-handed. Even Colly couldn't work some runnings fe wriggle me outta dat shit.'

'Breddren, if dem did ketch dat lickle pussy-bwoy Harrison, dem woulda cover it up and 'im would ah keep 'im worl' title. BELIEVE.'

'Seen. But it nah run so. Me jus' haffe tek time an' beat 'im raas de nex' time.'

For the next few weeks Tiger was inconsolable. Losing the world title he had worked so hard for under these conditions was agonising. Yolanda had been great, putting up with his mood swings and dealing with the media. He was distraught. He was convinced that the marijuana would be out of his system in time for the fight. He suspected that Archie had paid someone to doctor the sample. But how could he prove it?

'It's not like I've done a Paul Merson,' Tiger repeated over and over. 'But him was addicted to drink, drugs and gambling. I just had one puff. *One puff.* De punishment don't fit de crime.'

The shame on his mother's face the first time he saw her after the news broke was almost as devastating as being stripped of the title, given a ten thousand pound fine and six month suspension.

The only reason he was getting an immediate rematch with Harrison was that the public outcry over his punishment was so strong. Few openly condoned him smoking herbs, but the vast majority thought it was unfortunate because he did not gain an unfair advantage.

The whole issue lead to a renewed wave of debates as to whether 'soft' drugs should be on the banned list and even raised a question in the House of Commons on legalising cannabis. Rastafarians had never been interviewed so much which led to enormous interest in the rasta movement and a new wave of recruits. Some liberal minded newspapers even campaigned for him to be reinstated.

Tiger became a recluse and only cheered up when he was given the all clear to train again in preparation for the rematch on September the fourteenth.

I'll beat you again, pussy-bwoy.

CHAPTER 18

GOOD NEWS AND BAD NEWS

Tiger took the spliff from Yolanda and pulled on it heavily. The local ganja was the best he had ever smoked. He breathed out noisily and looked along the beach and onto the gently undulating, blue-green sea, shimmering under the glare of the early morning sun. The leaves of the palm trees behind them swayed slowly in harmony with the gentle breeze.

Two fishermen were hauling in their net from the side of a small boat. A couple of luxury yachts slowly cruised past in the distance. The spliff, the tranquility and natural beauty that surrounded them filled the couple with a welcome serenity.

'Bwoy, dis is good,' he said looking at the joint admiringly. 'It's been a long time.'

'Yeah,' smiled Yolanda. 'Pity about the test.'

Tiger grunted. Dale was the last person he wanted to be reminded of.

'Dis is de life, sweetness. Montego Bay is so criss.... I just wish I'd beaten dat pussy-claat bwoy.'

'You're still a winner with me, Tiger,' she said gently. 'Anyway, we've agreed not to discuss it. Let's talk about more positive things, like the wedding.'

He sat up, sinking his elbows into the sand. 'Yolanda, really and truly I'm not ready fe tie de knot until dat belt is mine. It'll have to wait.'

'Don't worry about the world title, Tiger. I want to get married soon and start a family. You know that.'

'You don't have to be married fe have no pickney, Princess.'

'Come on, Tiger. You know how I feel about that. I may not be a good Catholic but I'm not going to have outside children. No way.'

'Heh, just cool, baby,' he said cowering mockingly. 'I've got to win dat title first. Know-ah-mean? Harrison's postponed our wedding day. De lickle bomba-claat.'

'Can you PLEASE stop using that foul language, Tiger. Let's just drop it for the time being, okay?'

Tiger stood up, picked up a handful of pebbles out of the sand and threw them angrily into the water.

'He's fucking up my life.'

'Calm down baby,' soothed a startled Yolanda. She rose and threw her arms around him.

'It's not the end of the world. You can go for another belt. Come on, relax. I don't want you to even think about boxing until we get home.'

She's right. There was no point in getting upset about it now.

Besides the WBB belt, he reasoned there was the WBO, IBF, WBA and WBC titles to go for, all theoretically world titles. Unfortunately for the purists, there were now as many as five 'world' champions in each division and lots of other 'world' bodies with their own champions.

The sport had become so fragmented because greedy opportunists created their own titles. These avaricious administrators formed their own 'world' bodies on a whim to gain lucrative sanctioning fees and TV revenues when fighters were matched under their jurisdiction. However, the World Boxing Board title that Dale held was considered with the World Boxing Council the most competitive and honourable governing body in the sport.

Tiger was cheered by the thought of his other career options. 'Dat's right, baby, I can go for another belt, win it, then look for a unification bout wid Harrison. I'll beat de fucker next time. Believe.'

'Hey! Calm down. Alright. You're on holiday now and we're going to have fun.'

Tiger's tension drained away as Yolanda began to stroke his face then started kissing his cheeks, eyes, nose and forehead. She knew exactly how to snap him out of his foul moods. Both were on their knees, bodies pressed tightly together. As his right hand touched her left breast lightly over the top of her bikini, she pulled away.

'Not here, Tiger,' looking round to see if there was anyone around. A middle-aged couple in deckchairs were watching disapprovingly.

'Let's go,' she said pulling him up. 'Last one back to the hotel pays for tonight's dinner,' she shouted, sprinting away.

'Hey! Cheat! Come back!'

Yolanda raced towards the hotel lobby a hundred metres away. Tiger allowed her to reach first. He grabbed her around the waist in the foyer and they laughed loudly, attracting curious looks from staff and guests.

They were a stunning couple; Tiger's hard, muscular physique attracted wistful glances from older women and admiring looks from younger women in the time they had been there.

Yolanda's curvy, trim figure had caused more than one man to be reprimanded by his wife for staring too long at this vision of loveliness.

That night in their hotel room, all the frustration and anger was exorcised from Tiger as he made love with a gentleness and intensity that belied the fierce image he so pervasively cultivated.

She lay seductively, still in her pink lace panties on the bed as he came out of the bathroom after showering. He bent over, kissed her gently, took hold of both hands and asked her to stand up beside the bed. He silently peeled off her knickers, stopping on the way down to kiss her little dark triangle, neatly trimmed for her bikini line.

She gasped with ecstasy as his tongue worked his way into her wet pussy. He stood up and pushed her onto the bed rolling his probing tongue over her nipples before working his way back down again.

She spread her legs and as he entered her she moaned, grabbing his buttocks, trying to force him to move deeper and faster.

'Not so fas',' he smiled. 'You mus' wait for de love TKO.'

'Come on, baby. Don't tease.'

'How much you want me?'

'I want you bad. Please. Come on.... Yeah.... Yeah....Ride that juicy pussy rude boy... Oh, that's good. Yeah baby... That's it... Yeah...'

Wow, Tiger, you're the best, darling. The original bad-boy lover. You can really FUCK.

They stayed in their suite for the rest of the day. He phoned for room service and ordered two chicken rotis for himself, a callaloo dish for her and lots of Ju-C soda. They did not bother to leave the suite for dinner. More room service brought a huge selection of seafood, yellow yam, green banana and mangoes for dessert.

After another long session of passionate intimacy, Tiger lay awake beside Yolanda, listening to her soft breathing as she slept contentedly. He could not sleep despite the exertions of the day.

Am I ever gonna be a worl' champion? Harrison leads a charmed life. Yolanda's right though, I should go for another belt. Colly had better get me a good match for my comeback. Some American journeyman, but not one of dose idiot Mexican roadsweepers. Someone who'll give me a good work out before I go for another worl' title.... Wonder what Junior's doing? Hope his business is running right.. After tax and deductions, dere should be five hundred and fifty t'ousand more in my account after de Harrison fight. Won't be able to earn dat next time tho!

He eventually fell asleep, but was restless and fidgety, turning over repeatedly. The demons were lively that night, preying heavily on his mind.

Harrison... worldtitle... Yolanda... wedding... Bad Night... money...

The next day he was awakened by Yolanda's voice on the phone beside him in the bed. She hung up the receiver, turned and kissed him.

'Good morning darling. I just rang the office. Everything's fine.'

'Yolanda, you're on holiday, man. Chill, alright? Stop phoning your work. Dose people take steps wid you, man. Even five t'ousand miles away they've got you working your ass off to run t'ings. Dat nah right.'

When he was in one of those moods, she just adapted her unruffled approach. 'Look, Tiger, I just wanted to make sure that contract with Adidas came off, okay.'

'I earn enough for both ah we,' he answered tetchily. 'You don't have fe work so hard for dem idiot-man deh.

'Oh, shut up Tiger, you know I value my independence. Ever since my father died, I've always fended for myself. I eventually want my own PR company and this is part of the process. Anyway, fingers crossed, the Reebok deal will come off too and help me land some bigger deals. I'll never be a kept woman. I'm not one of your little star-struck tarts you know. Who have you been dealing with lately? Sonia, Trudy, Paulette, Marcia?'

'Just cool, man. Just because I've been photographed wid a woman in a club, dat don't mean I'm rahtid waxing her.'

'That's not what The Globe reckoned. They caught you with your pants down, didn't they sweetie? What was the headline? ... *BUSTY BELINDA TURNED TIGER INTO A PUSSYCAT*... now do you recall?'

'De bitch lied.'

'We're not BITCHES. Are we dogs? No! Men are the dogs. You're the ones that fuck anything that moves. You piss anywhere you feel like, burp and fart all the time. As for cleaning a toilet! Forget it... Anyway, how come she mentioned the mole on your backside then?'

'Junior must have told her,' Tiger protested. 'He's always telling de fans dem my personal business.'

There was an uneasy pause before he tried to change the subject.

'Come on, princess. You know where we're going today? Dunn's River Falls. Dat barman last night said he'd take us dere for a hundred American.'

Tiger jumped out of bed and opened the balcony's shutters. 'It's a beautiful day, baby. Let's go. Marcus said he'll meet us at two.'

~

Yolanda finished her lunch half an hour earlier than Tiger who was tucking into his third plate of ackee and saltfish. She waited patiently, reading *Waiting To Exhale*.

'Hey! Haven't you finished? You'll be a heavyweight by the end of this holiday if you're not careful. Big enough to take on Lennox Lewis.'

'Relax, baby. Colly said to enjoy myself and forget about boxing completely. Why you nah have some more. Vicious. Come on, you're not modelling anymore. Want to make a comeback? Come on, you won't get fat. You could never be one of dem mampy gyal dem dat have to wear tent-size baggie.'

Yolanda smiled then winced and turned her face away as Tiger tried to put a spoonful of food into her mouth. She knew she still looked good. Her curvy five foot ten inch figure was still in perfect shape. She had put on ten pounds since her modelling days but was curvy now instead of what Tiger considered as magga.

'I have no intention of modelling again. The only good thing about it was the money. Naomi and Tyra were the only genuine ones amongst them, but I don't want to go back.'

'You was the horniest, sexiest t'ing on the catwalk.'

She giggled. 'Shut up Tiger, don't be so coarse.'

'Oh, don't!' he mocked. 'As if your shit don't stink.'

'Tiger!' she exclaimed, looking around quickly to ensure no-one heard.

He popped his last piece of fried dumpling into his mouth, burped loudly and got up to leave.

'You're so disgusting.'

'Yeah, but lovable wid it.'

193

'I don't know about that,' she smiled evading a lunge for a kiss.

Nearly an hour after the set time, they were still waiting for the driver in the foyer of the Harbour View Hotel. The subject got on to Tiger's dad.

'Bwoy, I can't wait to see him tomorrow,' he said.

She rolled her eyes in mock ridicule. 'Why do you love him so much? He abandoned you all those years ago. He doesn't deserve such a loyal and loving son.'

'Shuddup Yolanda. We've gone over dis time and time again. Dad couldn't cope in England. You get me? He was a master carpenter but when him arrived in London he had to take all de fuckery building jobs dem nasty white people wouldn't do. It destroyed him. Bruk 'im heart. Dat and de climate. He had to get out odderwise he would ah gone mad - or frozen to deat'.'

'Yes, but he left you, Cassius and your mother to fend for yourselves. That wasn't fair.'

'Dad always said fe look after yourself first. Dat's a good philosophy. Bwoy, him took nuff hard knocks. NUFF. All kinda man use fe take steps wid pops all de raas-claat time. Anyway, he didn't leave us destitute. Left nuff, nuff corn. Dat Milton is one conscious farder. Big respec'. Him always did two jobs, saved hard, whatever he could and provided well for we. It kept us going for years. Two-twos, I was an ignorant lickle rude bwoy, but I straightened myself out, got some education, turned pro and done well.'

'*Did* well, Tiger.'

He kissed his teeth at her impudence.

'And Cassius is a draughtsman, so we've turned out alright. Anyway, dad never beat mum or chased gyal. He liked a drink and a bit of gambling, dat's all. Normal black man runnings. Him did need some relief in dat existence. I wouldn't call it a life. Just an existence. You get me?'

Yolanda pulled out her nail file as she always did when losing an argument and started grooming them furiously.

Marcus eventually arrived. A tall, thin man in khaki shorts and a white string vest, smiled engagingly, displaying a set of shiny gold front teeth before explaining away his lateness.

'Sorry 'bout de time, boss, but de pickney was sick and me 'ad fe tek 'im to de doctor.'

'Okay Marcus,' Tiger smiled, unconvinced. 'It doesn't matter. Let's go.'

They walked out to the courtyard and when Yolanda saw their transport, her jaw dropped.

'I'm not getting in that. It's a death trap. It doesn't look like it could get down this driveway without breaking down. Look at the baldness of the tyres.'

Tiger looked grimly at the battered open-topped Hillman Avenger, circa 1971 and had serious misgivings too.

'Marcus, you did tell me sey you had a criss car, star.'

'Yes boss. It 'as never let me down. Trus' me. Me baby-modder sey me spend more time wid it than wid 'er.'

Tiger shrugged and started to get in. Yolanda stayed put. After half an hour of coaxing by the two men, she eventually got in but not before negotiating a reduced fee. Yolanda always got a deal on everything.

They had a bumpy ride but got there and back safely thanks to Yolanda putting a speed limit on Marcus of twenty miles per hour.

Highlight of the trip for Tiger was not climbing up the waterfalls but stumbling on a record shop where he bought a stack of Studio One LPs for a fraction of the British price.

'Do you know how long I've been trying to get dis Gregory Isaacs LP, Princess? *Front Door* is his best LP but it sold out in London and was never re-pressed. And I've never seen dis Dennis Brown LP, either.'

Yolanda feigned a yawn. She preferred hip hop and swing-beat.

~

'Hello dad. Good to see you, man,' Tiger said, hugging his father tightly.

'Good to see you too, son,' Milton replied, tears welling up in his eyes. 'And you must be Yolanda,' grabbing her with one arm whilst keeping a tight hold of his favourite son.

'My, you're beautiful,' he exclaimed, looking her up and down.

'Tiger's a lucky man.'

'Hello Mr Crawford,' she said warmly, kissing him on the cheek. 'It's nice to meet you too. Your son's always talking about you.'

'Milton. Call me Milton. It's nice to meet you too, darlin'.'

The squat, dark Milton took them into the small, tidy kitchen in his modest two-bedroomed house in Bull Bay, a few miles east of Kingston, and brought out a bottle of Wray & Nephew overproof white rum.

He had put on a few pounds and lost more hair since the last photograph Tiger had seen, but he looked well in his red Hawaiian shirt and smartly pressed blue cotton shorts.

'Dad. It's too early in de day.'

'You're not in training now, son,' he said pouring two large glasses. He took a sip then reached into the fridge and brought out a jug of soursop juice.

'This is specially for you, Yolanda.'

She smiled and sipped it slowly, refusing Milton's offer for a shot of rum in it.

For the next three hours, Yolanda sipped the soursop, watched and listened patiently as father and son bonded, catching up with events. Milton occasionally asked Yolanda about her work and background, but was really only interested in what Tiger had to say.

Yolanda was at ease and enjoying the banter but there was only one topic that disturbed her when Milton asked: 'Are your parents Jamaican too, darlin'?'

'My mother is Dominican and my father was Bajan. He died when I was thirteen.'

'Oh, sorry to hear dat darlin'. What happen to him?'

'A car accident, apparently. I'm not sure what happened, my parents had split up then. I was living with my mother in Manchester.'

There was an uneasy silence before Milton turned to his son.

'How's your modder, son?'

'Yeah yeah. Mum's safe. Still works on de tube. Tell her sey she don't haffe work anymore and I'll take care of her, but she won't listen. You know dem way deh? How independent and stubborn mum can be?

'She always sey dat my big pay days won't last for ever. I know dat, but I've banked nuff, nuff corn in my last six fights. No mortgage, my flat's paid for. My only extravagance is my cars, one hundred and sixty thousand pounds worth. Only a fool-fool bwoy could squander all dat. Not bad for a sout' London ruffneck, eh?'

197

Milton slapped his sons shoulder in approval. 'You mus' be the richest man in H'inglan', son.' All three laughed.

'When I retire in a coupla years dad, I'll have nuff pension and insurance policies fe keep me secure forever. You get me? Dunno about serious investment dough. Property is only worth investing in as a long-term project at de moment. I'm looking around for some repossessed, run-down places in de suburbs fe buy cheaply, do up and rent out.'

'Dat's good son. Jus' don't do nuthin' rash with all dat money. Man can turn fool when 'im get rich so.'

Then turning to Yolanda, he added: 'I hope you marry dis lovely lady soon, Tiger, before someone snatches her away.'

'Milton, I was telling Tiger the same thing the other day,' Yolanda laughed.

They tucked into a meal of chicken and salad Milton had prepared, steadily sipping away at the white rum. Yolanda loved seeing them together. She liked to see the gentle, child-like quality in Tiger that always came over him when he talked to people he really loved and trusted. People like his brother, Cassius, mother Iris and Junior.

Milton loved to hear about Tiger's career. He had always been a keen boxing fan and his chest visibly puffed up with pride when he talked about his son, 'de worl' champion' even though he was technically robbed of the world title.

As they were leaving, Milton pulled out a grubby sealed envelope from his back pocket, gave it to Tiger and said: 'Give dis to your modder son. Tell 'er dat I'm sorry I don't write more often.'

'I've got something fe you too, dad,' he said giving Milton a white envelope.

Milton opened it and his eyes bulged when he looked at the

wad of money. He slowly counted out all twelve thousand in fifties. 'Tiger, dis is too much. You already 'elp me pay for dis 'ouse and put some good money away inna me savings. Me nah need dis. Really.'

He handed the envelope back.

Tiger pushed it back into his father's chest. 'It's yours. Enjoy. Give some to Uncle Taggy, Auntie Merna, Ma Sonia and my cousins in Portland. Dey'll appreciate it. Anyway, I would ah given dem some corn, but true sey me don't have time to reach over dere.'

A slightly embarrassed Milton looked down at his feet and mumbled:

'T'anks son. May de Lord God bless you.'

All three hugged once more before the couple got into the car and waved goodbye as Yolanda steered their rented Honda Prelude down the dirt track onto the coastal road back to Kingston.

'Mek sure you marry her soon, Tiger,' Milton shouted as they pulled out of sight. Yolanda wondered why Tiger only spent a few hours with his dad when he was in Jamaica for two weeks. When she finally asked, he just replied: 'Milton needs his space.'

She didn't push the point.

In reality, Tiger was still slightly resentful that Milton had left them when he was a kid. He had an ambivalent attitude to his father's departure. He could understand why he went, but then again, wasn't it a form of desertion?

Had he not left us I wouldn't have got into all that trouble.

The holiday served its purpose. Rested and rejuvenated, worries at home were almost insignificant after a while.

They even found time to play Scrabble on his travel board.

That was the only time they argued, when Tiger tried to use Jamaican patois. 'So what if it's not in de dictionary,' he said. 'Everybody know's dat word. Trust me.' Yolanda was not easily persuaded.

During a game, she got a call from an excited Unal.

'You know that American promoter who saw me singing on the boxing show and said he can get me work?' gushed Unal, 'well, you know we thought he was bogus? Think again sista. I'm joining Stevie Wonder's gospel chorus. I went for an audition for the European leg of his world tour and Stevie loved me. Yolanda, I'm gonna be a star!'

'I wanna be your manager,' Yolanda shrieked back. 'Don't sign anything until I get back girl.'

'He's also interested in producing my songs and thinks I could make it as a solo artist.'

'I hope you don't forget your friends when you get there, Unal.'

'Sure. You can be on my payroll. Chauffeur or housekeeper?'

They chatted until the units on Unal's ten pound phonecard ran out.

Yolanda was so excited for her friend.

The following Monday, they were due to return home. It had been a thoroughly relaxing break and neither of them felt like returning to the pressures of London life.

Before leaving for Norman Manley Airport, Yolanda phoned her office as Tiger played Patience with the cards and listened to a Gregory Isaacs tape on his personal stereo.

'What's de matter, Yolanda?' Tiger asked, taking his headphones off as she walked towards him, her face creased with worry.

'Tiger, I've got some good news and some bad news. The good news is that we've got the Adidas contract. The bad news is that Dale is Adidas's latest client. He signed a three-year contract yesterday.'

Tiger just grunted and replaced his headphones. He would deal with this latest Dale episode when he got back.

On the plane home Tiger stayed quiet, only thinking about the first time he met Dale, ten years earlier. He despised him then but hated him now with a vengeance.

Not only has he teefed my worl' title, he's now going to be professionally involved wid Yolanda. She's got to pack dat job up.

Yolanda wondered what she was going to do.

There's no way I'm going to resign. Dale's not going to push me out of the job I love.

As the plane taxied on the Heathrow runway eight hours later, Yolanda was adamant about what she was going to do.

I'm just going to treat him like any other client.

Tiger was still seething. He hadn't slept a wink during the entire flight.

CHAPTER 19

WHO FORGOT TO DUCK?

The whole country was gripped with big fight excitement. For weeks the TV stations were running previews of the revenge battle, billed as 'Up Close and Personal'. When tickets went on sale they sold out in two days. Touts were offering them at huge mark-ups. A pair of five hundred pound ringside tickets were going for six thousand. The cheapest ones, thirty pound, were going for three hundred. Police feared big crowds would gather outside the venue and try to storm the entrances and issued a warning not to come to the ground if they did not have a ticket.

Boxers hoping to get on the undercard were pleading with their managers to get them a fight. Ring-card girls from around the country were offering sexual favours to whoever they needed to for a chance to work on this one. Editors of newspapers who had never previously shown any interest in boxing were ordering executive boxes for corporate enter-tainment. Drug dealers, pimps and prostitutes grasped the opportunity to earn some extra revenue from overseas boxing officials over for the fight.

Betting shops were taking record amounts for a boxing match with Dale being the slight favourite. The fight was even the main story in the national papers all week, for once knocking football off the back pages. Even Posh and Becks did not get a mention that week. At the press conferences Dale was his usual cool self, with an agitated Tiger providing most of the best insults.

Consensus was that this was the biggest fight for years and that was confirmed by the fact that American boxing writers had made the trip across the Atlantic. The Americans thought so little of British boxing that for them to come over for this meant it was a significant contest in the scheme of things. Even Don King was present at ringside.

As the bell rang to start the fight, twelve million households in Britain tuned in with ten times that figure in global audiences. Archie Stretch smiled at the thought of earning more from the TV revenues than the two fighters put together.

~

'Come on den, pussy-bwoy, I'm ready for you dis time,' mumbled Tiger through his gumshield.

As the bell went, he shuffled to the centre of the ring, hands aloft and landed a terrific left hook on Dale's chin.

The force of the blow wobbled Dale's legs and in an instant reflex action, the crowd of thirty-eight thousand stood and roared excitedly.

What the fuck was that?

Dale blinked repeatedly, surprised by the force of Tiger's first shot.

Another big left hook whistled just in front of his forehead.

Shit, Tiger's really up for this one.

Dale snaked out his trademark left jab as Tiger rushed towards him. But instead of smacking onto the bridge of his opponent's nose as intended, it flapped into thin air as Tiger deftly slipped the punch and landed a right uppercut on the point of his opponent's chin.

Dale wobbled again, his senses scrambled. Another roar of excitement burst through the warm autumn night's air.

A lot of money was riding on Tiger and the partisan crowd sensed an early night's finish and a satisfying time enjoying their winnings.

Christ, where did that come from? Tiger wants this one bad.

Tiger, five inches shorter and with a far shorter reach, was using the right tactics again.

You ain't leaving with my title dis time. Dat belt is MINE.

He sneered at Dale, black gumshield exposed to emphasise his contempt for the champion. Yolanda smiled as she remembered meeting Dale at a fashion show and in a wine bar when she rejected him.

Dale managed to survive Tiger's relentless advance by staying on the back foot and flicking out his authoritative jab.

Dale finished the round well, landing a right cross flush on the side of Tiger's head as he settled into the fight and found his range.

'Come on Dale, you're the fucking champ remember,' Jack, his trainer said, as he sat on a stool, gulped heavily from a water bottle before spitting out into a bucket held up to him by a second.

'He's making you look bad. Get your jab working and look to land the uppercut as he comes in. DON'T let him take control.'

'Okay, Jack,' nodded Dale still smarting from the unexpected onslaught and stung by Jack's verbal attack.

Dale added by way of justification: 'He didn't start that fast last time.'

'Well go with him. Don't let him take the initiative. Hold the centre and use your jab.' Jack flicked out his left hand in demonstration.

'You let him dictate the pace too much last time. SO DON'T

204

FUCKING DO IT AGAIN!'

The trainer rubbed Vaseline into his face roughly then whacked Dale on the backside of his red satin shorts as he walked out for the second round. The crowd applauded, anticipating another sensational round. They were not disappointed.

Any time Tiger Crawford stepped between the ropes, a guaranteed X-rated, full-blooded tear-up was on the cards. He was adored for his frenetic, all-action style, based on pressure and wearing down more tactically astute and skilful opponents.

A hero to the south London rude boys, coachloads of gold-toothed, Versace-suited young men and lycra clad babes in micro skirts always made up a vast proportion of his supporters when he fought. The air filled occasionally with cries of: 'Big-up Tiger, rude bwoy from time!', 'Hol' it down, Tiger!' and 'Respec' to the max, Supa!'

At least three thousand black people within a three mile radius of Brixton had converged onto the pitch at the Selhurst Park football ground in Norwood, to roar him on. Racist members of the Powerguard security firm around the ground had already christened Tiger's followers the 'Coon Platoon'.

Dale had little success in the next three minutes as Tiger pursued him with steely determination.

This is one hateful motherfucker. He's like a serial killer.

He felt Tiger's fierce stare burning into his face.

The memory of their last match had become an obsession that time could not possibly heal. Avenging that injustice was Tiger's sole ambition in life.

You lickle blood-claat. I beat you den an' I'll do it again. Dis is MY time... I'M de people's champ.

Yolanda watched from ringside. She had drawn lustful attention from adoring men when taking her seat earlier wearing a figure-hugging black dress and matching short jacket.

Tall and curvy, relaxed hair pinned up high in French roll fashion, complemented by delicate diamanté earrings that gave her a regal look. She sat with Samina Saeed and Jacko Ali, two of Tiger's close friends. Ali was now a regular training partner and an integral member of Tiger's camp. Hundreds of Asian supporters were in the stadium through Ali's involvement. He had sold thousands of pounds worth of tickets to the kick-boxing fraternity.

The shades on top of Yolanda's head accentuated her glamorous image. The pearl wine lipstick on full, sensuous lips and her large, piercing brown eyes made her stand out from all the other good-looking women there.

Amongst all the bottle blondes her dark features were a stark contrast, there was no denying she was the most gorgeous.

Wolf whistles and raucous applause greeted her entrance from the lager louts in the cheap seats. For sheer stunning beauty, she outshone all the TV and film celebrities, Page Three models and hopeful bimbos sitting around ringside.

'Come on Tiger, you can do it this time,' pleaded Yolanda, occasionally putting her hands over her face when the action got too brutal. Every time Tiger was hit she winced.

It was no better when he was landing punches. Even when he meted out the punishment, Yolanda was anxious. *This is barbaric.*

Dale was starting to find his range. 'Stop eating his jab, Tiger,' shouted his brother Cassius, sitting beside Yolanda.

'Bob and weave Tiger. Slip the jab. SLIP THE JAB!'

For the next three rounds Tiger boxed with a ferocity and resolve that few seasoned pundits had ever seen. By the ninth round, he was so far ahead on the three judges' cards, it was only a matter of staying upright to ensure he got the twelve round points verdict.

Dale had started as odds-on favourite on the strength of his superior skills, but Tiger was making nonsense of the bookies' and media's prediction of a comfortable win for the champion.

'Okay, Tiger. Just carry on what you're doing and you should be alright,' said Colly in the interval between the ninth and tenth.

Lonnie added: 'For Christ sake, don't do anything rash.'

Tiger nodded.

The tenth started like the rest, with Tiger pressing forward, preventing Dale from using his superior technique and reach. Round by round he had felt Dale's resistance slowly ebbing, the champion's arms tiring from all the venomous punches he received. Even when Dale blocked Tiger's clubbing blows, the effect on his arms was painful.

The adrenalin coursed through Tiger as he stepped up the pace. Dale, eyes swollen, nose bleeding, possibly broken, had all the hallmarks of a badly beaten opponent. Tiger smiled thinking how the vain Dale would worry about his looks and probably seek surgery on his nose.

Another sweeping left hook landed flush on Dale's jaw but this time instead of absorbing it and mounting a counterattack, his wiry legs buckled. Sections of supporters chanted: 'TIGER! TIGER! TIGER! TIGER! TIGER!'

The whole stadium stood up in unison, sensing a knock out

finish. They were right.

As Tiger pounded away to Dale's cowering body looking for the final payoff punch, he suddenly remembered that fateful night. The Bad Night. The night of the accident when another defenceless man was at his mercy.

Shit. What a time to have dat flashback.

In the split second he lost concentration Dale seized his chance and in desperation smashed a right cross that started from the tip of his toes and worked its way through his body, to explode flush onto the side of Tiger's face. The crowd gasped at the astonishing turnaround.

Referee Benny Stevens counted animatedly, holding up a digit in front of Tiger's face with successive counts.

'Three...four...five...'

Groggily he rolled over onto all fours and tried to haul himself up. But his body disobeyed his scrambled thoughts.

'Six...seven...eight.'

The crowd bayed for the People's Champ to get up. Only a tiny percentage of ringside observers and TV viewers were on Dale's side.

No amount of encouragement could help him beat the count though.

'Nine...OUT!'

Stevens waved the bout over before grabbing the staggering Tiger and steadied him against the ring ropes. A dazed Tiger stared into the glaring lights above already sobbing.

'You lost your concentration, Tiger,' Colly needlessly stated in the dressing room after. 'What a time to fall to a fuckin' sucker punch.'

'Yeah. Just cool, Colly, you've made your fuckin' point,' mumbled Tiger. The left side of his head was still throbbing

208

from the force of the knockout punch and his vision was still slightly blurred.

'I forgot fe duck,' he added wryly.

Their dressing room was typical of a loser's - eerily quiet. Yolanda, Cassius and a group of close friends and family watched silently. Noisy celebrations from Dale's room, further down the corridor, exacerbated the situation.

'You seem to be okay,' said the doctor after examining Tiger, 'but you have to go to hospital for a full checkup. You know you'll be under a mandatory forty-five day suspension after that knockout.'

'Don't worry 'bout dat, doc,' he said. 'I'm okay. I was going fe have a long break anyway.'

Yolanda sitting quietly on a bench nearby, got up and hugged her fiancé as the doctor packed his stethoscope back into his case.

'You're still my champion Tiger,' she said softly.

'T'anks sweetness,' he said, picking up an empty vial and walking into a toilet cubicle.

Tiger gave his urine sample to the doctor to be drug tested then beckoned the security man at the dressing room door to allow the waiting media corps to come in.

A group of well dressed men filed in solemnly. Tiger steeled himself. He did not enjoy the attention of the media at the best of times.

'Did you see the punch coming, Tiger?' kicked off Phil Harper of *The Globe*.

'What do you think?'

'You had him in trouble and you were on the verge of putting him away up to that point though, weren't you?' added the unruffled Harper.

'Yeah, but he found the punch that mattered,' came the bitter reply.

The verbal sparring continued until questions turned to whether Tiger would be retiring now.

'That's enough, gentlemen,' interjected Colly. 'It's too early to discuss Tiger's future plans. He has to go to hospital for a checkup now and then he's going to have a long rest.'

Colly shooed the reporters out and shut the door.

Meanwhile, in Dale's dressing room, the atmosphere was markedly upbeat. Media men jostled to get their microphones and dictaphones in strategic places. Smart suited young men and excited girls in skimpy skirts also vied for Dale's attention.

His mate Trevor was joyous as he waved his betting slips. 'Thirty-two grand. I'm fucking rich! Rich. Rich. RICH!' He gave out cigars like Bill Clinton celebrating another sexual inquest victory. The bookies had refused to pay out when Dale was awarded the world title the first time because they judged that he won it by default.

'I know it was close but I always thought I could find the punch to turn things around,' claimed Dale through swollen lips as he nursed an ice pack on his left cheek. He wore dark glasses and a thin plaster covered his nose.

'My superior technique was always going to pull me through,' he insisted defiantly when one reporter questioned his tactics.

'Here we go again, more porkies,' whispered one reporter to another.

'The fucker would never admit that he was going to lose.'

Yolanda walked ahead of Tiger down the corridor towards the waiting ambulance, stopping out of curiosity when she reached Dale's doorway. He noticed her over the horde of media men and slowly smiled before winking at her. It was more a sneer than a greeting and Yolanda knew it.

'Bastard,' she mouthed at him and walked back towards Tiger. As the beaten fighter reached Dale's dressing room, he unexpectedly turned and walked straight in.

The media corps separated to allow the furious looking Tiger access to his conqueror anticipating another, this time unscheduled, confrontation.

Yolanda called out softly: 'Tiger, don't.'

Tiger stood in front of Dale who had already clenched his fists in preparation to land a left hook. It was not needed.

Tiger's face lightened then to everybody's astonishment he embraced Dale. 'Respec' due Dale.'

Onlookers breathed a huge sigh of relief.

'Great story,' one hack said to another as he scribbled furiously.

'Yeah, I hope our snapper's got a shot of this,' said another.

Dale went to hospital immediately after he broke away from all the well-wishers. The doctor's post-fight examination had passed him fit even if he looked pretty mashed up. Justin took him into casualty where the broken bone in his nose was painfully pushed back in place. Most boxers prefer to leave their nose busted, as a sort of badge of honour to show their warrior status. Not Dale, he was too vain.

~

The newspaper headlines next day criticised Tiger mercilessly.

News of the World:
MAULED!

Harrison tames the Tiger

Tiger Crawford paid the price for a moment's loss of concentration and got mauled in an astonishing tenth round turnaround against arch-rival Dale Harrison, at Selhurst Park last night...

Sunday Mirror:

SUCKER PUNCHED!

Harrison turns Tiger into a pussycat

Tiger Crawford went roaring in but left with a whimper after sensationally losing the WBF title rematch to Dale Harrison by a tenth round knockout at Selhurst Park last night...

The Sunday Times:

TIGER TAMED BY HARRISON

Crawford's lapse painfully exploited in act of desperation

Never in the history of prize fighting has a moment's lapse of concentration so exposed the vagaries of the sport as witnessed at Selhurst Park last night. Claude 'Tiger' Crawford, winning by a handsome margin and on the verge of a tenth round stoppage, will forever rue the moment he moved in to excecute the coup de grace to only fall victim himself to a Dale Harrison counterattack, that not only detached him of his senses but deprived the tenacious challenger of the WBF title ...

A rueful Tiger read the headlines with increasing anger. 'What de fuck dem ah chat 'bout? I'm not chinny, de pussybwoy just got lucky, t'rahtid,' he shouted to Yolanda.

'I know baby,' she called from the next room, 'but now the bastards want to write you off. You're not going to retire are you?'

'No way. Dale Harrison ain't seen the last of me. BELIEVE! Me nah ramp nex' time. Well, y'see me? Ooh. Next time me jus' t'ump 'im down. BELIEVE!

CHAPTER 20

THE GLOBE HATES BLACK PEOPLE

'Hello Dale.'

She offered her hand.

'Hi Yolanda.'

They were in Simon's opulent office at SPEX. Simon knew the situation between Dale, Tiger and Yolanda but this contract with Adidas was too big to allow personal conflict to get in the way.

'I'm not asking you to roger him darling, just keep the old PR wheels rolling nicely along, that's all,' Simon said. 'You won't need to see or speak to him often after the first meeting.'

Yolanda felt like hitting her boss, but had to admit that he was right. Harrison was a high profile client, the most famous SPEX had handled and there was too much money and prestige attached.

She also knew that the ruthless Simon would sooner lose her than Harrison. Nevertheless, the animosity between Tiger and Harrison compelled her to hand in her notice on the day Dale arrived. After all that had gone down in the two fights, it was inappropriate to stay at SPEX.

Tiger was furious that Simon had been so tactless and taken the contract, but since when did making money have anything to do with principles? At one point he wanted to go down there and beat the shit out of Simon but thought better of it.

Simon was the sort of boss who did not ask his employees

to do things, he simply ordered them to. Rumours abounded that his cut-glass accent was not entirely due to attending Harrow public school, which he always claimed.

He only went to Harrow for a year before his parents transferred him to a state school nearby because they couldn't afford the fees. Simon always gave the impression he attended Harrow before going to university. Kingston Polytechnic actually, but he maintained that he attended Surrey University.

Yolanda remembered the time he was caught out by an ex-Surrey University graduate puzzled that he didn't know Simon although they were there supposedly at the same time and both studied political history.

Simon suddenly looked at his watch and remembered a non-existent 'important meeting' he had to attend. A tall, angular man with a ruddy complexion, Yolanda laughed when his face turned a deep red that matched perfectly with his silk tie.

Dale was out of character from his dour public image and a real charmer. Some of the giggly shop assistants in adjacent offices knew he was coming and kept popping in. Normally Simon would never tolerate that and shoo them away, but the thrill of signing his first big name client was too much for his ego.

Yolanda found herself absorbed by Dale's winning ways and noticed for the first time he was much taller than she originally thought. His smooth face hid all signs of his brutal profession, a total contrast to Tiger's which had become far more shop-worn in the time since she first met him.

Dale's bruises always healed quickly. The only trace of permanent damage was his nose which was slightly indented halfway down from where Tiger had damaged it in the second fight. He intended to have surgery when he finished his career.

There was still an air of arrogance about Dale as he sauntered around the offices that she found slightly repugnant.

He's not as down to earth and approachable as Tiger. Bit too self assured and slimey. Looks good though in those slacks. Armani I'd say. That shirt looks like a Boss number and the jacket is definitely Kenzo. At least he knows how to dress. He smells good too. Nice aftershave. Long fingers. Almost like a woman's. Smooth knuckles. Not gnarled and protruding like Tiger's. Doesn't look like a boxer at all. Should be a basketball player. Could be Michael Jordan's twin.

'After you,' Dale said allowing Yolanda to get in the black cab first on the way to the press conference at the Roof Gardens, Kensington. They exchanged small talk but it was mostly Simon who spoke to Dale.

The press conference got under way with people still discussing the ironic triangle in whispered tones with sly glances. Yolanda was careful not to be photographed near Dale. Apart from one time when she returned from taking a phone call and inadvertently walked past him, she did not go near him. It was at that split second that a freelance photographer took a shot. *The Globe* ran it the next day.

TIGER'S GIRL FINDS HIS RIVAL PURR-FECT

Tiger Crawford went into a beastly rage when he heard that his fiancée Yolanda Ashley is now working with his arch-enemy Dale Harrison. Tiger let fly for a third time, in an unscheduled fight against bitter rival Harrison in the lift of the Roof Gardens in central London when he unexpectedly turned up at the press conference to launch Harrison's new £1 million

Adidas deal...

Tears rolled down Yolanda's face as she watched Tiger read it and drop the paper onto the kitchen table.

'*The Globe* hates black people, Tiger. Especially successful ones. If you had any doubts you know the truth now.'

'Dis can't go on, Yolanda. Jah know. I hate dat man wid a vengeance. Either you resign or I done wid dis relationship.'

'Calm down, Tiger. This is purely a professional relationship. Anyway, I've got good news for you.'

'Eh?'

'I'm leaving SPEX.'

'You are?'

'I was going to leave anyway. Got fed up with Simon's bullshit. Gerald Stokes, managing director at Panache Modelling, has asked me to head his PR section. More money, perks, travel. It's a much better deal. I wanted to stay in sports PR but Dale's arrival has forced my move.'

Tiger stood up and hugged her so tightly she started screeching. 'Oh baby love,' he said. 'I never doubted the strengt' of our relationship for one minute. Believe.'

'Hah. You was threatening to end it all just now.'

'Me know dat. But true sey you ah dig-up from SPEX now, everyt'ing cool again. Seen?'

'Yes Tiger,' she smiled patronisingly.

'When are you leaving baby?'

'I handed in my notice yesterday so it'll be in four weeks' time.'

'Fine, but keep away from dat lickle batty bwoy in de meantime.'

'Is he gay? I don't think so.'

'He looks like a raas-claat batty bwoy, even dough dem picture 'im wid 'oman. Nuff ah dem man deh pretend dem like pum-pum but really only stab shit.'

'Don't be so coarse,' she slapped him playfully on the shoulder.

They laughed together for the first time in what seemed like ages.

The tension and disappointment of losing the rematch and Dale working with her had played heavily on their minds. Now everything would turn out fine.

Tiger took her to San Lorenzo's as a special treat. They met Al Hamilton there, founder and organiser of the Commonwealth Sports Award.

Al promised to take them over to his next awards ceremony in South Africa. Tiger liked Al because he never stopped trying throughout the years, despite all the setbacks to get the Commonwealth Sports Awards internationally recognised. Al was a hero in the black community and had strong links with boxing, having guided Frank Bruno in his early days.

Now things were taking off for Al he was happy for Tiger. Bruno was the guest of honour in Uganda one year and Lennox Lewis was Al's star name in Accra, Ghana the previous year, so it was a great honour for Tiger.

~

Simon was not happy at losing his star executive.

'I'll pay you five thousand more than Panache,' he pleaded.

'No. I've made up my mind, I'm going. You've never fully appreciated what I've done for this company and Harrison's arrival was the final straw.'

'Final straw? I didn't even know you were unhappy. This is awfully inconvenient.'

217

'Inconvenient? How do you think I feel? I don't know whether it's because I'm black or a woman - or both - but Gerald Stokes respects me. He has done ever since I met him on the modelling circuit.'

'Hah. He just wants to get under your knicker elastic darling.'

'I don't think so. He's gay.'

'A faggot! You want to go and work for a shirtlifter!'

'There's nothing wrong with being gay. He's a very charming and decent human being actually. And he doesn't make crass sexist statements like you do.'

Simon paused to think, swivelling round in his leather chair behind his art deco, mahogany desk and twiddling a Mount Blanc pen.

'Dale will be disappointed,' he said slowly.

'What?'

'Dale will be sorry to see you go.'

'What are you talking about Simon?'

'Dale said he was looking forward to working with you.'

'Really? Why?'

'Because he's heard that you are the best in the business.'

'That's funny. I never got that impression. The total opposite, in fact.'

Yolanda was not convinced. She knew Simon's strokes. He would say and do anything to get his own way.

'He was pleased about working with you, Yolanda.'

'Why?'

'Because he felt you had the wrong impression of him.'

'Well I wasn't exactly ecstatic knowing that I was going to work with him and I don't care what he thinks I think of him.'

Simon paused.

'Never mind. That's history now. You'll only have to meet him one more time. We've got a photo shoot at Wembley Stadium on the fifth of next month.'

'Fine. Please ensure I have my P45 when I leave.'

She stood up and offered her hand to him. He took it reluctantly.

Back in her office, Yolanda thought about the conversation.

How dare he try to make me stay using that stupid ploy. The little shit. I'm glad I'm getting out.

Dale was in a pensive mood, excited and pleasantly surprised at how stunning Yolanda was. His scheming mind went into overtime.

She's gorgeous. No wonder Tiger hooked up with her. But he's a doughnut. Unlike yours truly. Bit hostile today, but I can't blame her after what's gone down between me and Crawford. Fit body, man! Titties to die for. Pity she's with a low-life has-been. He ain't saying shit. Crawford's taunts are out of order. I'm not a coconut just because I prefer white girls. I'm sorry, but they've got more class than those council flat, gold toothed, baby mothers. And you can get on faster in life and be more accepted with a white partner. Everybody knows that. Now Yolanda, she's pure class. The most impressive black woman I've ever met. She's got looks, personality, intelligence, contacts... Better than any white girl I know. She deserves to hook up with me. We'll make the perfect celeb couple...

CHAPTER 21

DON'T FEEL SORRY FOR ME

'Do you like it, darlin'?' Gerald asked Yolanda. Her new office was not only bigger and better furnished than her old one, but it was more plush than Simon's too. The wooden desk looked antique, there were rows and rows of filing cabinets, a TV and video, coffee making machine, state-of-the-art computer and pine bookshelves. There was a discreet drinks cabinet in one corner, a fridge and an air-conditioning unit.

'It's very nice,' she said suppressing her delight.

'Fine. I didn't want you to think we were slumming it with Panache,' he said kissing her on both cheeks in typical luvvie fashion. 'We want you to be happy here sweetie.'

Yolanda really admired Stokes. For a camp, shortish, Jewish man with a pock-marked face, he was a real battler. He had secured many of the big names in modelling and was obviously intending to move into different fields, hence the reason he hired Yolanda, for her sports contacts.

At first Yolanda felt overwhelmed at Panache. Her contemporaries were mostly older men far more experienced in PR. Stokes quickly helped her overcome her misgivings and within a few weeks she was a confident operator.

She had settled in nicely at Panache when an unexpected phone call came. Siobhan, her PA, took the message. 'Yolanda, when you were in the meeting Dale Harrison called. He asked you to ring him back. Said it was urgent.'

'Harrison! What does he want?'

She closed her office door behind her, picked up the phone

and dialled the number.

'Good afternoon, SPEX Enterprises,' the receptionist said.

'Hi. Can I speak to Mr Harrison please?'

She was put through.

'Hello Dale, it's Yolanda.'

'Oh hi. Thanks for ringing back.'

'What can I do for you Mr Harrison?'

'Oh, I just wondered how you were getting on at your new place.'

'What has it got to do with you?'

'I'm sorry that you left SPEX because of me.'

'Don't feel sorry for me. Please. I can take care of my own destiny.

Okay? Bye!' She hung up before he could reply.

How dare he, the little shit. Trying to patronise me. Cheeky bastard.

The phone rang again.

'Yolanda,' said Siobhan. 'It's Mr Harrison again.'

'Tell him I'm in a meeting all afternoon.' She slammed the phone down again without waiting for a reply.

The next day her office phone rang and as Siobhan always vetted her calls, Yolanda picked it up without a second thought.

'I hope you're not in the same meeting, Yolanda.' Dale's voice startled her.

'How did you get past my PA?'

'I told her I was the president of Nike and I wanted to surprise you.'

'That's not very nice.'

'Sorry, but I just had to speak to you.'

'What about, Harrison?'

'Nothing in particular. I just wanted to know you're okay.'

'Well I'm fine. Now can you just leave me alone.'

'Sure, but would you like to have dinner to discuss it.'

'I'd rather have dinner with Saddam Hussein.'

'I happen to know that he's busy for the next two months.'

'The answer's still no! Now piss off!' She slammed the receiver down angrily.

What does he really want from me? After all that's happened between him and Tiger how could he possibly think I'd be interested in him? He's not serious.

Dale was fuming. He could could not cope with rejection. He decided not to go to the gym and went round Shane's instead.

Dale was happy with the Adidas deal but was willing to waive that for one night with Tiger's fiancé. Inspired by Robert Redford in *Indecent Proposal*, he had become so obsessed with her, he would willingly forfeit the million pound deal for a one-night stand. Yolanda had all the physical and mental attributes and the fact that she was Tiger's woman made her the most desirable woman in the whole world to him.

He phoned her every few days at the Panache office until it became a standing joke amongst the secretaries. Yolanda steadfastly refused to speak to him but did not tell Tiger what was going on, mainly because she feared his reaction.

Three weeks after his first call, she finally told Siobhan to put him through.

'Hi Yolanda. Thanks for speaking to me at last.'

'What do you want Dale?' she hissed.

'I just want to sort things out between us.'

'Sort what things out? We never had anything to sort out in

the first place.'

'The fact that there's all this hostility floating around.' He paused.

'Can we meet and discuss it? It would mean a lot to me. I promise you I won't be out of order.'

An exasperated Yolanda found herself almost imperceptibly whispering 'yes' but regretted it as soon as she said it.

~

They met at an Italian restaurant opposite the Richmond Odeon a couple of nights later. Yolanda wanted to be far away from the West End, where they were more likely to be spotted by the paparazzi or telltale gossip columnists. Dale was already there when she arrived. He wore a polo neck top and casual leather jacket. Heads turned as she glided towards him in her brown Gaultier trouser-suit.

Dale apologised for all the animosity that had gone down between him and Tiger and regretted that they had not been friends.

'After all, we black people in the spotlight should be getting on better.' She thought that was a strange thing to say considering he had such a bad rep with the black community.

'Why don't you tell that to Tiger, Dale? To his face.'

'Nah. He can be really ignorant when he's ready. And I'm not prepared to deal with the anger just yet. Too much aggravation. Anyway, it wouldn't be good for my image. The press feed off our mutual hostility.'

'Is that all?'

'Well I must admit that I've always been intrigued by you.'

'Oh yeah,' she smiled. 'What do you mean?'

'Well you're so attractive, if you don't mind me saying so.

And well educated and I just wondered what the attraction was to Tiger?'

'Our relationship is none of your business. But if you must know, he's a wonderful man. Lots of charm. Ragamuffin? Yes, but he has a heart of gold and treats me right, unlike a lot of black men I know.'

'What about... his indiscretions?'

'Other girls? He doesn't cheat on me. I know that. The tabloids just print lies about him, just because he has a lot of female fans. He's a good man.'

Dale did not contradict her but she knew she hadn't convinced him.

'Tell me something, Yolanda. What do you really think of me?'

'Not much.'

'What do you mean?'

'There's not a lot to say about you, is there? No-one knows much about you. You're really arrogant but people respect your boxing ability but they don't like you very much, unlike Tiger. Everybody loves him.'

Dale just shrugged and was silent for a while.

They spent the rest of the night talking shop; the Adidas deal, sports promotion and gossiping about people in the industry.

At the end of the night, Dale insisted on paying the sixty-two pound bill. Yolanda got the impression he was seriously tempted to take the thirty pounds she offered him had she insisted.

Outside the restaurant he asked her to come out for dinner with him again.

'What for? We've said everything necessary. Shall I bring

Tiger next time?'

'What a great idea. We can reminisce about the good old days when we used to punch the shit out of each other in the gym.'

'I don't think so.'

She held her hand out to shake his. He took it and pulled her towards him and kissed her on the lips.

Yolanda pulled herself back and slapped his face. 'You pig!' Two curious Italian waiters watching through the restaurant's window turned and pretended to busy themselves tidying tables. When they saw the couple move away, they rushed to the window to see what they would do next.

'Sorry, I got carried away by your beauty,' Dale muttered only slightly embarrassed. That stunt had always worked in the past.

'Well don't try it. You're getting far too bright, Dale Harrison.'

She walked around the corner to Richmond Bridge and saw a black cab across the road and tried to flag him down. The cabbie took one look at them and drove on.

'Racist pig,' she fumed.

'Come on, I'll give you a lift home.'

'You can drop me off at Richmond Station.'

She was silent in the short drive to the station's taxi rank.

'Good night, Dale. Do me a favour and don't ever bother to call me again,' she said getting out of his car.

He just smiled as she climbed into a black cab and lit a cigarette.

CHAPTER 22

HONEST, YOU CAN TRUST ME

'Miss Ashley, I think it's in your best interests to meet me, very soon.'

'Just what are you talking about Harper?' Yolanda insisted.

'It's too delicate a matter to discuss over the phone. Can I come to your office, say this afternoon at three?'

'No. Meet me at six at the Slug and Lettuce pub in Long Acre, beside Covent Garden tube.'

She spent the rest of the day wondering what Harper, Fleet Street's finest sleaze merchant was going to come up with. He was *The Globe's* best known scandal writer and she knew it could only be bad news.

'What do you want Harper?' she barked at him as she sat down. There was no need to exchange false pleasantries with such a heinous character.

He epitomised all the bad perceptions of tabloid journalists. His crumpled suit looked like a Mr Byrite reject. Obese with acute halitosis, he looked incapable of maintaining any friendships, let alone having a relationship with a woman. She did not take his hand when he offered it, knowing from past experience that it would be hot and clammy.

'Thanks for meeting me, Miss Ashley. Can I get you a drink?'

'No, now what is it Harper? You said you had something very important to divulge.'

He picked up a battered leather briefcase, opened it and pulled out a cardboard folder containing old newspaper cuttings that had turned yellow with age.

'I know you won't like this, Miss Ashley, but I thought it was in your best interest to be informed.'

He looked at her as she started reading them and a smile cracked from the corners of his mouth as tears began running down her cheeks. They were cuttings of her father's death, years before.

'Why have you given these to me Harper? It brings back such terrible memories.'

'I'm sorry to have to tell you this Miss Ashley, but the driver was someone you know very well. You know the reports didn't name the driver because he was too young to be named?'

'Yes. Do you know who it was, then?'

'It was Tiger. Claude Tiger Crawford. Your fiancé killed your father.'

Yolanda plunged into a numbing state of shock.

'There must be some mistake. How could it be? How do you know, anyway?'

'Lots of journalists have access to this sort of information.'

'Are you absolutely sure, Harper?'

He pointed out a police charge sheet and some court appearance documents. There was no refuting the information.

'On my honour, Miss Ashley. You can trust me.'

'Can I keep these?'

'No, they're *my* copies, here are yours.' He handed her a large brown envelope.

'One thing that puzzles me,' he added. 'How come your surname is Ashley and your father's was Ford? Did you take your mother's name?'

'What do you think? Idiot!'

'By the way. If you want to go public about how your fiancé

killed your father, I'm sure we can arrange a big fat fee on a Monday morning front page splash. I can see the headlines now: "Love rat Tiger killed my dad". Part two would be "How I made love to the man who killed my dad".... The story's got legs. It'll run and run.'

Yolanda picked up his pint of beer, threw it in his face, gathered up her bag and walked out without another word, clutching the envelope. On the tube home there was only one thing on her mind. Vengeance.

CHAPTER 23

THIS ONE'S FOR DAD

Phil 'Hatchet' Harper was despised by virtually every journalist who knew him. Loathed by the celebrities he exposed and sneered at by the public, he remained undaunted. Earnings of over one hundred thousand pounds a year helped steel his resolve. As a child he was always overweight and resigned himself to being fat and disliked from the age of thirteen.

An incredible ability for writing imaginative stories in English classes earned him top marks in creative writing. At school he was unpopular, not just for being fat and useless at sport but because he had a tendency to tell tales on schoolmates to curry favour from teachers. A career in tabloid journalism was an obvious choice. At thirty-four he was earning more from his kiss-and-tell exposés and sleazy revelations than journos twenty years older.

Fingers and teeth nicotine-stained by chain-smoking Marlboros, a rasping cough and fifty-inch waistline were the legacy of years of self abuse. No-one was too precious to be a Harper victim, making him the ideal bearer of bad tidings, hence him having no qualms in telling Yolanda about Tiger.

Legally the media were not allowed to reveal Tiger's name in the accident because he was a minor at the time, but as far as Harper was concerned stirring things up could lead to some juicy stories.

Anyway, he didn't like Tiger.

Cocky, illiterate black bastard. Too leery by far with all that jewellery and flash cars.

He was just as envious of Dale.

The only man to regularly beat me at poker. Took six hundred nicker of me last time. Bet the little coon was cheating, I'm sure.

Harper was pleased Dale had told him about the accident and he got immense pleasure telling Yolanda. He did not like her either.

Wouldn't mind fucking her though. Only black minge I've had were hookers.

He resented seeing young black people doing well so anything he could do to bring them down was *doing a favour to all decent minded white people.* With that sort of philosophy Harper's attitude made him a model disciple at *The Globe.*

The fat man's reputation went before him. He once approached a Tory MP who was a staunch boxing abolitionist for an interview on whether it should be banned. Mindful of Harper's tendency for exaggeration and misrepresentation, the MP gave him short shrift.

'I adamantly refuse to co-operate with disreputable people like you, Mr Harper,' the MP told him on the phone. The furious hack planted a totally fabricated rumour amongst Labour Party members that the Tory MP was a member of an international paedophile ring.

The rumours abounded and the member of parliament, confidence and nerves shattered, eventually resigned. A broken man, he suffered a nervous breakdown and never worked again. Harper was unrepentant. Quite proud in fact.

Seeing Yolanda sobbing made his day and was another entry for a proposed book *Falling Stars: How I Exposed Celebrities.*

When it came to evil, Harper felt a kindred spirit in Dale.

Still in the pub, his stubby fingers had problems tapping out the numbers on his mobile phone.

'Dale? Phil here. It's done. Told her.'

'Well done Phil. I owe you big-time. How did she react?'

'Whad'ya expect? Bawled her fuckin' eyes out and stormed off.'

'Nice work Phil. This is our secret, right?'

'Gotcha, Dale. I'll keep schtum as long as you do.'

'Thanks pal. Keep in touch. Let's go Stamford Bridge some time.'

'Yeah, right. They're playing Liverpool in a fortnight.'

'I'll sort out some tickets Phil.'

'Nice one. See ya.'

Both were very pleased with themselves – a good job, well done.

~

Yolanda noticed that the light in Tiger's flat was on as she entered the block. She had cried uncontrollably in the toilets of McDonald's before regaining her composure and walking home. Now she was ready for him.

As she opened the front door she could hear him flicking over TV channels in the lounge, as usual.

'Hi baby,' she called going into the bathroom.

'Yo, princess!' he replied.

She stripped off in the bathroom, had a shower and washed her hair before wrapping a towel around herself and walking into the bedroom. As she rubbed cocoa butter over her legs, Tiger walked in, startling her.

'Wha'appen. You nah come in and hail me.'

'Oh, I've had a terrible day and got a bit of a headache. I just want to get my head down.'

'Yeah, and you must get your head down on dis,' he held his groin and smiled.

'Don't be so crude Tiger. You know I hate you talking like that.'

He kissed his teeth and walked out.

'Must be PMT or sump'en,' he muttered.

But didn't her period finish last week?

Yolanda was thankful that he wasn't going to trouble her. She put on a pair of panties and a T-shirt and climbed into bed. Sleeping was impossible as she turned Harper's words over and over in her mind. *Tiger Crawford...killed your father. Tiger Crawford... killed...*

The bedroom door opened and the light from the passage filled the entrance of the room. She heard him undress and toss his clothes on the chaise lounge and walk into the bathroom.

She heard him pee then shower and brush his teeth, her sense of dread increasing as the minutes passed. She closed her eyes, pretending to be asleep as he got into the bed naked and snuggled up to her.

'Princess. You sleeping?'

She didn't answer but felt slightly repulsed by the semi-stiffness of his dick between her buttocks. She pushed him away gently.

'No Tiger. I think I'm coming on.'

'But it only finished de odder day.'

Shit. Trust him to remember that. He seems to have a computerised memory of my cycle.

'Well, I've got a stomach ache.'

'You want some Rennies?' he asked, genuinely concerned.

'No. I'll be alright. Just need some sleep.' She turned and kissed him on the forehead.

'Goodnight, Tiger.'

'G'night.'

She turned away and lay there until a few minutes later she heard the low rumble of his snoring. Before long he was in a deep sleep. She sighed with relief.

As dawn approached and the sunlight filtered slowly through the thin gaps of the bedroom blinds, Yolanda still hadn't slept a wink.

Harper's words still ran constantly through her mind. *Tiger Crawford... killed your father. Tiger... killed. Killed... Killed... Killed.*

She slowly climbed out of the bed. He stirred and turned towards where she had been lying. She thought he was going to wake up but within moments he was snoring deeply again.

She crept to the kitchen at the end of the hallway and pulled out the eight-inch kitchen knife she used for cutting meat. Looking at it and running her gaze along the blade, surreal thoughts filled her mind. *This is one type of flesh you've never cut into before, Mr Knife.*

Yolanda tiptoed back and stood on his side of the bed looking down at him, the quilt draped across his backside. Her heart pounded so fast and loud she thought he would hear it and wake up. Lying on his stomach, his broad back made a perfect target. Despite the early morning chill, her hands were sweaty and her face felt flushed. The knife felt like a lead weight in her hands as if the handle was suddenly encased in an invisible concrete block.

'This is for dad, you bastard.'

CHAPTER 24

LET'S GET IT ON!

'No-one laughth at my lithp, thith is serious business,' announced Chris Eubank to a posse of youngsters sitting around him. Sixty kids bordered the ring as Eubank spoke on the canvas. He was giving a motivational talk to a group of nine to sixteen-year-olds at the newly opened Miguel's boxing gym in Brixton under a scheme run by the local police to build better relations with local kids.

The former WBO middleweight and super-middle champion had for once left his monocle and jodphurs home and looked fit and businesslike in a conservative grey suit.

'I'm from the inner-city too,' he added. 'I grew up in Peckham and lived in Stoke Newington. I know what it's all about.'

Having been a tearaway in his youth, an accomplished thief in West End stores, he was fully aware of the temptations to go off-track. Mesmerised, the kids listened intently and woe betide anyone whose attention wavered as Eubank admonished them for doing so. Tiger leaned against a wall, grinning. He looked at Eubank's agent, Ambrose Mendy, and he smiled too.

'You must enjoy the power and beauty of your youth,' Eubank added during a rambling yet still fascinating account of his life. 'Sing, laugh, it's good for your soul. Don't waste energy on jealousy.

'My father taught me four things in life; respect the policeman, teacher, doctor and find yourself a trade to make a living.' He managed to do three and even trained as a secretary, but unruly behaviour led to him being sent to live with relatives in New York to sort him out. That's where he found focus and discipline and took up boxing seriously.

He then recited a poem about 'integrity, honesty and not quitting - that's the first rule of boxing' and advised them to study Rudyard Kipling's classic poem *If*. It met with blank expressions but they got the gist.

'Throughout my sixteen-year career in boxing I trained every day, even Christmas Day and my birthdays. I wanted to train harder than my opponents who I knew were only training six days. It's hard to put into practice and too easy to be stupid and do drugs. Don't follow that route. Education is very important. Make sure you do your maths. You're getting paid in kind right now with your education. You don't know that. The money comes later.' Tiger applauded and everyone followed.

'As a kid I did not take autographs from boxing stars because I truly believed I would be as good or better than them one day,' continued Eubank.

He wound up to rapturous applause then allowed a question and answer session before Tiger finished things off.

'My advice to you is stay off de streets and channel your energies positively,' intoned Tiger. 'Boxing as an amateur gave me a whole heap ah good t'ings. I travelled abroad, met some bonafide people. It's good for de police to invite me an' Chris to make dis presentation.'

'Anyone here fancy getting it on wid me?' Tiger joked. 'Get your gloves on an' let's get it on!'

'These young people are part of a four-week summer action play scheme run by the police,' said a breathless Tania Follett as the two ex-champions signed autographs. 'At Miguel's we believe we can build better relations between the police and the community by using the gym as a focal point and using boxing as a tool to empower youngsters. This is the first steps to making these inroads.'

Errol, the Barnados kid Tiger had befriended, was there. 'I've learnt how to punch and move and it was great meeting Eubank and Tiger,' he said to a reporter from the *Croydon Advertiser*. 'I was inspired by what they said,' another kid beamed. 'When I grow up I wanna wear kriss garms like dem,' said another.

Tania helped organise the event with gym owners John and Steve Sims. She was the first woman to get a manager's licence from the British Boxing Board of Control and was a good friend of Jackie Kallen, the renowned Los Angeles-based manager and the only woman ever to manage three world champions. Kallen, in London on business, looked on with interest. Kallen was with PR consultant Charlene Russell who specialised in showing American visitors around London.

'I've always been into boxing and seem to have a vocation for it,' said Tania. 'It's great that Chris came down on such short notice and for no payment. He just came to help the cause in Brixton and for the kids. They shouldn't be closing so many youth clubs in Brixton, they are so badly needed. The youth leaders are the role models, not necessarily our famous sportsmen.

'We know drugs and violence are everywhere. All we ask is that they leave anything they're involved in at the door when they come in here.

'These kids have problems and need discipline and we're trying to build better relations with the police. Boxing gets bad press but the sport does so much for charity and good causes.'

Danny Williams and Audley Harrison, two of the most talented prospects in Britain, helped Tiger advise the kids on keeping on the right track. Promoter Anthony Gee gave out miniature boxing gloves with Miguel's Gym logos on them. Mendy, generous as ever, handed out ten-pound gift tokens to use in Sports Pages, the West End specialist bookshop.

John and Steve were proud of their gym, named in memory of their late father. It was a progressive place that included a VO2 Max-testing machine that gave boxers regular cardio-vascular checks. They ran regular kick-boxing and women's boxing classes and the downstairs area was kitted into a high-tech fitness centre.

Tania, a bubbly thirtysomething leisure centre manager by day, worked at Miguel's in her spare time. Being a woman in such a male-dominated sport was tough but she was inspired by Jackie.

Tania shooed the kids out of the gym to give Tiger a break from signing autographs and having his photo taken. He feigned exhaustion by wobbling at the knees and wiping his brow. He sat down on a ring apron and Tania introduced him to Jackie.

'I like the way you fight, Tiger,' she said. 'Anytime you're in LA please look me up. Here's my card.'

'T'ank you ma'am,' he answered taking the card. 'My breddren in de States say you run t'ings over dere.'

'Hah! You better ask Don King that,' she smiled. 'Let's just say I'm doing okay.'

Tania left the two in deep conversation as she went downstairs to ensure the kids had left the building. John and Steve were supervising a group of amateurs in one corner. Eubank had already dashed off for a civic reception in his honour in Brighton.

Tiger and Jackie talked for ages about boxing and although she was blonde, white, Jewish, American and a generation older, they struck up a mutual respect. She invited him to train at her gym in LA anytime he wanted, free of charge.

'T'ank you Jackie. And in de few days left in London I insist on taking you on a tour of my favourite Caribbean restaurants. My treat.'

The next few days Tiger took Jackie, Charlene and Tania for meals at the Z Bar and Stop Gap in Brixton, Posh Nosh in Tufnell Park and his two Camden Town favourites, Mango Room and Cottons. Tiger tricked Jackie into liking Dragon Stout, the strong Jamaican stout. Jackie was virtually teetotal but he told her it was a non-alcoholic malt. She loved it but it wasn't until she started getting tipsy and looked on the label did she realise it was nine per cent proof!

Tiger was fascinated by what Jackie had achieved in boxing; as a journalist, PR woman and having worked with Tommy Hearns and Manny Steward in the Kronk gym. She was also a bestselling author and a Hollywood movie of her life was in production.

They had fun eating out and even found time to visit the Chilli Hut Indian restaurant in Walthamstow to have dinner with Tiger's friend Samina Saaed. Jackie so enjoyed the chicken tikka that she considered starting a Chilli Hut franchise in LA.

Tiger took Jackie to watch his friend Jacko Ali defend his world lightweight kick-boxing title at the York Hall. Jackie was astounded by the support Jacko attracted. She had never seen two thousand predominantly Asian people at any sort of boxing show and could see the value of promoting him in LA where there is a huge Asian community.

She was so impressed with Jacko's second round knockout that she became his manager and he signed a four-match deal worth a six-figure sum to fight on shows in Las Vegas and LA. Jacko was thrilled that at last he would get the chance to prove himself against the best Americans.

Kwame McMillan, Jacko's fitness instructor, was included in the deal. Kwame was famous in London for his ability to fine-tune even the fittest sportsmen for competition and Jacko insisted that the former Grenadian soldier who had won Strongman contests in America but was best known for his Afrobics classes, was part of the package.

Before Jackie left, Tania arranged for her and Tiger to tour local Brixton schools to give motivational talks. It was a huge success and covered by local papers and news reporter Deborah Bain on GMTV.

When Tiger waved Jackie goodbye at Heathrow Airport he knew they would meet again.

CHAPTER 25

NO TIME FOR COMPASSION

Harriet could not get Dale out of her mind. Everywhere she went there was a constant reminder of the evil way he raped her. Boxing on TV...BMWs...the LSE...Thornton Heath. She had lost a lot of weight and could no longer sleep. As depression set in, her timekeeping at work became increasingly erratic and inevitably she got the sack.

Her family and friends worried for her and her mother begged her to get psychiatric advice although Harriet stubbornly refused to say what was wrong. Harriet tried to confront Dale once, waiting for hours in her car for him to come home.

When he finally arrived, laughing loudly with a tall blonde girl, he just gave her a steely look and walked inside not looking over his shoulder. Harriet tried to phone him several times but the answer-phone was always on. The one time he did answer, she was so taken aback that she hung up in panic and cried for hours.

She considered going to the police and even walked into her local police station but immediately felt too ashamed and intimidated to go through with it.

Harriet eventually had a nervous breakdown.

~

After date-raping Harriet, Dale got on with his life as if nothing had happened. When it came to heartless bastards, he was a champion.

He did not even consider it rape anyway. Just rough sex. After all, hadn't the same thing happened to Tyson? Dale thought he should never have gone to jail for that.

There were no guilty feelings. Harriet didn't warrant that. His new girlfriend, Clarissa, was the epitome of the perfect woman and he had no time nor compassion to spare for Harriet; Clarissa was a twenty-three-year-old natural blonde, with model looks, a *Vogue* fashion consultant with a fat salary and great prospects.

Her family were well connected and accepted him with no reservations. Clarissa never got to find out about Dale's more sinister side but she quickly realised that he was a mean and demanding man.

'Darling, Roger at work said he saw you in one of those Soho lap-dancing clubs. I told him he was mistaken. It couldn't possibly be you Dale, I told him. It wasn't you, was it? You know how some people think black people all look...' She didn't finish the sentence.

'We don't all look the same, Clarissa. You're right, it wasn't me. Wouldn't be seen dead in one of those depraved places.'

'But darling he reckoned he saw you later in a card school in one of those King's Cross after-hours pubs. I said that was impossible but he insisted.'

'Look, I don't even know how to play poker. Let's drop it, okay?'

She could tell by his tone that the subject was closed.

'Sorry, darling. Sorry. Come on, let's go, the restaurant booking is for eight.'

They had an expensive Italian meal in Belgrave Square and as usual Clarissa paid. Last time Dale forgot his wallet.

The previous time he was waiting for some sponsorship

money to come through. This time he was a bit short because 'a big tax demand was on the way.'

Despite his meanness, Clarissa entertained his every sexual demand. She was certainly the most adventurous partner he'd encountered.

For such a prim and proper image she had some wild ways in bed. 'Likes it up the arse, y'know,' Dale would tell his mates at the poker school. 'And she sucks my dick at every opportunity. Even did it in the toilets at San Lorenzo's.'

Dale had very little respect for Clarissa, which is why he had no scruples about divulging all their sexual activities. The best story he liked telling was the night of his twenty-fifth birthday party.

They went for a meal at Giovanni's in Knightsbridge with a group of friends. The Bollinger and brandies had taken their toll by the end of the night and Dale was barely conscious when a couple of his mates carried him into the hotel suite Clarissa had booked as a special treat, stripped him and left.

A while later Clarissa, wearing only a white, lacy bodice was standing over him. She had turned off the light and he could barely see her shadow in the room's darkness.

'Dale, please wake up darling, I've got a special present for you.'

She peeled back the duvet and took his limp dick into her mouth. Even in his drunken haze, that was enough to bring it to attention.

Just when he was getting really stiff, Clarissa stood up. He heard some shuffling about the room then suddenly Clarissa's mouth was back playing the human harmonica. Only her touch and technique was different.

'Happy birthday darling,' Clarissa called from the end of the bed as she put a soft lamp on.

A startled Dale looked up to see Clarissa's friend Jenny wearing only bra and panties sucking away on his dick. Jenny, a well-built raven-haired stunner, looked up and winked. He smiled. She had the body of a Gladiator. Fit and shapely. He had often fantasised about getting it on with her.

Clarissa unhitched her undies, straddled him and placed her pussy an inch from his mouth.

'Here's your desert,' she said pressing her pubes into his face. Dale did not resist. A few minutes later, the girls swapped positions. Jenny moaned with delight. 'You fucker, you fucker, you fucker...' she groaned over and over.

A few minutes later, Dale was pressing his dick into Jenny doggie style as Clarissa stood by the bed having her nipples sucked. All three swapped positions as he performed sexual feats of endurance never experienced before. After two hours they tumbled into the bed in a heap of sweat, semen and body fluids.

'Happy birthday, Dale,' Clarissa cooed but he was already asleep. Jenny smiled too but it wasn't sexual satisfaction that sweetened her.

~

Shane was expecting a visit from Dale.

The fucker said he'd be here by midnight. Where are you Dale? I need you, man. I've run out of Charlie - again and the dealer won't give me anymore credit. Don't need much money. Just a couple of hundred to keep me going. Till tomorrow. Who am I kidding. The fucker's not coming. Hasn't been for weeks. I need a score. Fast.

Shane pulled out the well-thumbed business card he had

been looking at for weeks and phoned the mobile number on it.

~

Dale liked Clarissa a lot, but he couldn't help thinking of Yolanda constantly. He phoned her several times but she refused to take his calls. Clarissa and the other girls in his life were okay for the moment but Yolanda was his real target. She became an obsession and he often waited in a cafe opposite her workplace just to watch her going home.

You're mine, bitch. Tiger's history now.

CHAPTER 26

DON'T LIE TO ME

'Yolanda, what's de matter?' Tiger asked. Her sobbing had woken him. She was sitting on the chaise lounge crying. He thought it was strange seeing a kitchen knife on the floor in front of her.

'You killed my father, you bastard!' she blurted out.

'What are you talking about, Princess?'

'Don't lie to me. DON'T LIE TO ME! I know the truth. You *did* kill my father. I've got proof.'

He was quiet for a while, trying to work out what to say. He had rehearsed a thousand times what he would tell her if this situation arose but never come to a satisfactory decision. One thing he did know, there was no way of bluffing his way out of this one.

'Bwoy, me nah know who told you, but yes, it's sorta true.'

He slipped out of bed, pulled on his jeans and grabbed a sweatshirt from a dressing room drawer.

'What do you mean *sort of*?'

'I was a kid. A feisty yout'. Lickle rude bwoy joyrider just looking for t'rills. It was an accident pure an' simple. I never meant fe run into him. BELIEVE!'

He told her exactly what happened, the race with Junior in the other car and the fact that her father seemed in a dazed or drunken state.

She blew her nose, stopped crying and continued sniffing.

'Why didn't you tell me, Tiger?'

'Bwoy, I didn't know until recently myself who you were.

Believe. It was only when you said Cecil Ford was your uncle that it all clicked into place. An' it was hardly information I was gonna volunteer, was it?'

'But you knew I would find out sooner or later.'

'I was gonna tell you when de time was right. I promise you.'

She looked suspiciously at him.

'What's dis?' he asked picking up the knife. 'So you was gonna jook me dead inna me sleep, eh?'

Her eyes averted from his to the floor.

'I'd better sleep in a suit of armour from now on.'

'Don't you *dare* joke about this.'

'Sorry.'

There was a long silence.

'So ah wha' gwan now?' he asked.

'It's too soon to say for sure, but I know one thing...'

'What?'

'I have to move out.'

Silence again. He knew he couldn't stop her.

'But I love you Yolanda.'

'And I loved you too, Tiger. Until this. It's cast a whole new perspective on things.'

'But you didn't even know your farder. Your parents split up when you was a baby.'

'That doesn't matter. I'm still living with the killer of my own father, whichever way you look at it.'

They talked for hours. Yolanda phoned in sick and Tiger missed his morning run, just like the first night they made love. This time things were very different.

She slept at Unal's that night and for the next fortnight until she found a large flat to rent in Lauderdale Road, Maida Vale, just around the corner from where her own flat was being rented out. She often bumped into John Fashanu, the ex-footballer turned entrepreneur and United Nations representative, who had an office nearby in St John's Wood.

Yolanda did not tell Unal exactly what happened and just allowed her to believe she caught him playing around again.

'Don't worry, Yolanda, there's this gorgeous black designer we regularly use,' Unal said. 'And guess what? He's not gay! When you're ready, I'll introduce you.'

Yolanda smiled, humouring Unal. The last thing she wanted right now was a new relationship.

'Come to Monaco with me tomorrow. It's just for four days. You might meet a rich film director. You'll be the new Angela Bassett... and you'll give me a singing part in it... and I'll be a big star too...'

Yolanda laughed. For such a seemingly sensible, professional woman, Unal allowed her dreams to run away with her too easily.

To his credit, Tiger insisted on her keeping the expensive engagement ring. She took it off and placed it in a jewellery box on her dressing table. Depressed and lonely Yolanda virtually stopped eating. She lost some weight and started looking gaunt.

Unal often came round to try to lift her spirits but after she had left Yolanda would end up crying herself to sleep at nights. The news of their break-up was a green light for admirers to try their luck. Yolanda was surprised at how many of Tiger's so-called friends were hitting on her, including Junior. 'You know the coo, darlin',' he would say. 'Life must go on.'

They started pestering Yolanda for dates but she was not

interested and had to change her phone number twice to get rid of the pests.

Some months after the split, she picked up the phone at work and her secretary, Siobhan, told her that Mr Harrison was on the line.

What does he want?

'Put him through Siobhan.'

'Hello Yolanda. How are you?'

'What can I do for you Dale,' she said frostily.

'Oh, I just wanted to make sure you'd settled in okay at Panache.'

'Piss off!' She slammed the receiver down.

He's gloating about me and Tiger breaking up. Bastard.

The next afternoon Siobhan walked into her office with a large bunch of pink and white carnations.

'Looks like you've got another admirer, Yolanda. He must have spent a fortune.'

'They could be from a woman client, Siobhan.'

'Sure and one day I'll be the manager of the England football team.'

They laughed as Yolanda smelt the beautiful flowers then opened the card attached.

'Well?' Siobhan enquired as Yolanda read the card.

'Well what?'

'Come on, Yolanda. Who sent them?'

'It just says 'Silky'.'

'Silky? That's a funny name. Nothing else?'

'Nothing else, Siobhan.'

'That's funny. Do you know who it is?'

'Haven't got a clue.'

Yolanda tore up the card and threw it in the bin. Siobhan

laughed and walked out. That was normal behaviour for Yolanda.

The next morning Dale phoned again.

'Yolanda.'

'What?'

'Before you put the phone down on me again, just tell me if you liked the flowers.'

'What flowers?'

'Come on, you knew they were from me.'

'I get flowers all the time Dale. Bye.'

'Wait a minute. Wait, wait, wait.... Are you still there?'

'Yes but you'd better make it quick.'

'I just wanna say that I've been thinking about doing some modelling. Lots of footballers and other sportsmen are doing it now and I want you to give me a chance on the catwalk.'

'Our books are full for men. Bring me a new Naomi or Claudia and I'll be interested. Bye.'

She hung up.

He rang back.

'At least let's meet up to discuss it, Yolanda.'

'Why Panache and why me Dale?'

'I liked the way you handled my Adidas contract at SPEX and if I'm going into modelling I'd like you to sort things out for me again.'

'No. Not interested. Now don't call me here again otherwise I'll call the police. There are laws now for stalking.'

She hung up without waiting for a reply.

Dale didn't ring again but the next morning a letter arrived that looked more personal than business.

Dear Yolanda,

Please do not tear this letter up as abruptly as you slammed the phone down on me. Just hear me out. I know because of Tiger you have hostile feelings towards me, but you've never really given me a chance to set the record straight. I am not a demon. Tiger and I do not get on, everyone knows that. But there is no reason why we cannot be professional colleagues and possibly friends.

I do genuinely want to do some modelling as I know I cannot box forever. Ideally, I want to run a modelling and sports management agency in the long term. You are the most knowledgeable and experienced person I know in these fields and would appreciate any help you can give.

Can we possibly meet for a business lunch in the near future? If I don't hear from you by Thursday of next week I'll know you're not interested and will not bother you again.

Yours sincerely,

Dale.

PS I'm not happy with SPEX and Adidas are looking for a new agent. Know anyone capable?

She read the letter four times, punched his phone number and address into her electronic organiser, tore it up and threw it away. By Thursday of the following week she hadn't rung him. She waited until three weeks later and rung his mobile.

'Hello, is that Dale?'

'Hi, who's that?'

'Yolanda.'

There was a pause.

'Yolanda! You've given me a shock. I thought you weren't gonna get in touch.'

'This is strictly a business call, Dale.'

'That's cool. What made you change your mind though?'

'I needed time to think and believe working with you can further my career, that's all. So don't start bigging up yourself.'

'Okay. You call all the shots. Can we meet up soon?'

'How about next Tuesday or Wednesday for lunch.'

'Can't do Tuesday but Wednesday's good. How about we meet at one at Vincenzo's, an Italian restaurant behind Harvey Nic's?'

'Fine by me.'

'Okay. See you Wednesday at one, Yolanda.'

~

Walking to Vincenzo's, Yolanda was pensive.

What does he really want? Surely he's not looking for an affair! How dare he. After what's gone down between Tiger and him. Surely not. Well he ain't getting this pussy. Never.

She had deliberately dressed down in slacks and loose fitting casual shirt, minimum make-up and hair pinned back in her best librarian fashion.

Dale looked very handsome in the restaurant's dim lights.

He looks better with his hair clean-cut. That Eighties flat-top was so dated. They look like Calvin Klein jeans. Don't think much of his top though, even if it is Versace.

He offered his hand and she took it but was not prepared for his next move. He pulled her gently towards him and kissed her on the cheek.

'Don't get fresh with me, Dale.' She glared indignantly but he just smiled.

'Sorry, but you are very beautiful.'

'Cut the crap otherwise this meeting's over before it even

starts.'

He did not say or do anything out of place throughout their lunch; he had pasta, she chose ravioli and they both drank mineral water. When the bill came, she insisted on paying half 'to keep things on a business level'.

She agreed to represent him but insisted that the details of the contract wasn't leaked to the media. 'They're gonna find out anyway but in the meantime I'll have a word with Simon at SPEX so that he'll front it for as long as possible,' she said.

'Won't he mind, considering you don't work for him anymore?'

'Nah. Simon's been begging me to come back ever since I left so this will just give him hope that I'm coming back.'

'Yolanda?'

'Yes.'

'Why didn't you phone me sooner? When I didn't hear from you I thought you weren't interested.'

'I'm a businesswoman Dale and you're quite a catch.'

'Really?'

'Not in that sense. Don't get too bright.'

'But after what's happened between Tiger and me...I know you're not with him anymore, but ... but... surely there's still... how can I put it? Emotions.'

'Tiger and me are finished, as you well know. God, the papers had a field day when they found out. That bastard Phil Harper got the exclusive... Tiger's history and I'm an independent black woman, free to speak and do what I want with whoever I want to.'

They shook hands outside the restaurant and agreed to speak in a week's time when Yolanda had made preliminary arrangements.

Yolanda was preoccupied with thoughts of Dale for the rest of the day.

He seems nicer than before. But he was bound to pour on the charm, slimey git. The lech, I could feel him looking at my backside when I went to the loo.

Dale had only one person on his mind for the next few days.

What the hell did she see in Tiger? Stumpy. Ignorant low-life. I did her a favour getting Harper to give her that information. Got to do a James Bond now and turn on the deadly charm. Nice lips. Perfect for a good blow job. Well, there's only one way of finding out.

CHAPTER 27

A LITTLE MISUNDERSTANDING

Tiger was woken by the high-pitched sound of the TV screen. He had fallen asleep on the sofa again, fully clothed. Bottles of Bollinger, Remy Martin and cans of Special Brew strewn around the room made his stomach churn.

His denim shirt and silk waistcoat were soaked with sweat and clung to his body. His jeans were wet too, only it wasn't sweat. He groaned, staggered to the bedroom, stripped off and entered the shower where he stood for half an hour trying to rid himself of all the nastiness he felt internally.

I've got to pull myself together. Dis isn't de life. It's months now since the break up. All dat punany Junior hooked me up wid were just ho's. Yolanda? No more jooky jam. Why? No-one can change the past and no-one can bring your father back. You didn't even know him anyway. Women can be so stubborn. She never answers my calls or letters. Colly and Lonnie keep phoning, but I'm not ready to box again. Can't get my head round dat shit right now. Don't need to box anymore if I don't wanna. Got nuff sheckles put aside. Junior's all-dayer next week should net me another two hundred grand. He says he'll pay back that two hundred grand he owes Hard Knocks Promotions from runnings that never run right in de past. Says record producers who owe him big dollars are gonna square up after de show.

~

Helping organise the Sweet Love open air concert in

Finsbury Park with Junior had helped divert his mind from Yolanda. Thirty thousand people paying twelve pounds each were anticipated for the reggae event of the decade. Top notch artists like Buju Banton, Dennis Brown and Beenie Man were booked. The only thing that could spoil the day was the notorious British weather.

The concert billed to start at three'o clock inevitably began two hours late. Besides that, it was a great success as the sun shone all day. There were no serious incidents of criminal activity or rioting, which disappointed the hostile legion of police, tooled up in full riot gear intent on justifying their oppressive presence with a good ruck. Children with their parents looked curiously at the hard faces of the police and wondered what they were doing there at such a peaceful event.

'Daddy, that policeman looks very cross,' one little girl said.

'It's called racism, Taneka,' he replied.

'Racism? What's that? Is it like cancer, daddy?'

'Worse than that, darling. More people die from racism than any form of cancer. Heavy-handed policing and institutionalised racism kills just as painfully as cancer. Look at how many black people die in police custody. The police make up excuses, get let off after what they call an inquiry and the perpetrators get off literally with murder.' Tears appeared in the corner of the little girl's eyes.

Tiger noticed that Junior was edgy on the days leading up to the Sweet Love concert. Tiger thought it was just nerves but found out the real reason at the end of the night. Junior disappeared. So had all the box office takings.

Artists, musicians, roadies, sound systems, security staff and administrators all had to be paid. It was only because

Tiger was a famous boxer that he didn't get attacked by a disgruntled mob.

Fists are no match for bullets though and there were some ruffneck ragga DJs who had performed earlier on who were in no mood to be cheated out of their money. Packing guns as negotiating tools was *de rigeur*.

Tiger was so sure that this was merely a misunderstanding he gave assurances that he would pay out of his own pocket. the following day when the banks opened, if the situation wasn't resolved by then.

'Cool noh!' he repeated over and over. 'Junior's my breddren. Bona fide spar. Him nah cheat 'im breddren. Dis is just a lickle misunder-standin'. Trus' me.'

He was carrying a few thousand pounds and paid off the most vociferous demands. He stayed up all night trying to pacify everybody, went home to shower and change then waited for the banks to open at nine.

Two cars full of angry men seeking payment and revenge had gone looking all around London at addresses where Junior might be, but he had disappeared off the face of the earth. Somebody broke into his empty house but saw no sign, although they didn't think to check if his suitcases were still there.

A total amount of two hundred and sixteen thousand in bankers' drafts had to be made up to all the creditors by Tiger. It took him three weeks to pay off all the other debts, amounting to another eighty-two thousand of his funds. Junior had deferred payment on virtually everything until after the concert and gone off with advertising and TV payments.

He had evidently planned his moves for months. It was only then that Junior's ex-Supa Flex partners told Tiger the real reason why he left the sound.

'Bwoy, we had to get rid of him star,' one of them said. 'He appointed himself treasurer but was systematically teefing the takings. He's probably gone to Chicago or Detroit where he's got some family. Nobody's sure where he's ended up, t'rahtid, but someone will ketch him raas one day. Trus' me.'

Tiger was only so willing to honour the debts because he correctly assumed they could be written off in tax expenses. When he phoned his accountant it was on answerphone. So he phoned his tax office to ensure everything was running smoothly. There was another shock.

'What de fuck you mean I owe you a substantial sum?' Tiger asked over the phone. 'How much?'

'two hundred and seventy-nine thousand, eight hundred and four pounds and eight pence...'

'Wait. What the FUCK you ah talk 'bout?'

'Please refrain from using that offensive language, Mr Crawford.'

Tiger took a deep breath and spoke through gritted teeth. 'Dere must be somet'ing wrong wid your computer. I'm up to date wid my taxes. I paid dem weeks ago.'

'Our records show that you're not, I'm afraid. We received a ten thousand pound cheque some time ago from a Mr Ellis with a promise for further payment soon.'

'Ellis, dat's my accountant. I gave 'im de cheque for two hundred and seventy-nine t'ousand ages ago.'

'Well it hasn't been paid I'm afraid sir. And there is an outstanding amount of over four hundred thousand from previous years.'

Tiger felt his stomach churning, as if someone was punching him from inside. The last time he heard from Ellis was when he received a letter saying he was going on holiday for awhile but not to worry because his taxes were up to date.

Enclosed with the letter was a receipt from the Inland Revenue for the full amount of taxes owed. Tiger later found out that the receipts were forgeries, as they were for other bills he had entrusted Ellis to pay. Ellis had got a clever forger to produce the receipts.

Being a white middle-class chartered accountant, married with three kids, Tiger thought he was totally trustworthy. It turned out that when Ellis went on holiday, it was on a one-way ticket to Thailand with his secretary who was also his mistress.

He'd left his wife and embezzled Tiger's money to start a new life in Thailand.

Ellis has taken steps wit' me t'rahtid. I've been shafted by my own fuckin' accountant, like when Sting got turned over by his accountant for six million. Luckily for Sting he was rich enough not to feel dat six million too tough. But me? First Junior takes steps, now Ellis. Please God, dis ain't happenin'. Junior was my key spar. We never, ever had a serious brush wid each other, yet when I give him some responsibility and trust, two-twos he skanks me out of a whole heap ah corn. People say he's in America somewhere. Well he can run, but he can't hide. I'll find him. Lord knows I WILL FIND HIM.

The Inland Revenue demanded - and got - their money from Tiger. It was either that or prison. From the callous deception of Junior and Ellis he eventually found himself with less than one hundred thousand in the bank from almost two million earned. Tiger vowed that he would get revenge. Any plans to hang up his gloves had to be shelved now.

I'll have to fight Harrison again.

Ellis eventually returned voluntarily from Thailand, home-sick for his wife and kids after he fell out with his mistress who rejected him when his money ran out. It turned out that for years he had fed a gambling habit with clients' money but the more he lost, the more he stole. He set off to Thailand to win a fortune and claimed he intended to repay everybody in full, including Tiger.

Ellis was declared bankrupt and because of his background, with previous good character, only received a two-year prison term. With parole, he would be out in a year. Tiger groaned at the light sentence. There was nothing he could do and he would never got a penny back. Short of beating the shit out of Ellis, revenge was pointless. Even then Tiger would only find himself in prison.

He'll probably only serve twelve months. Some of my bred-dren get longer dan dat when de police pull dem up for having criss cars, rough dem up and dey defend themselves. Some get even worse - and two-twos lose their fucking lives. Look 'ow much black man get killed in police custody and nobody gets punished, t'rahtid. Look at de Stephen Lawrence killers. Walking free. White justice. Hah.

~

'You don't need Harrison again, Tiger,' Colly said firmly. 'There's bigger fish to fry. We'll get you your money back in no time.'

Tiger kissed his teeth. 'When I t'ink of all de punches and sacrifice I made fe make my dollars, Colly, it hurts big time dat I ain't got shit now.'

'You're not a pauper, Tiger,' Colly reasoned. 'Just put it down to experience. Still got a hundred gees ain't cha? Your flat is paid for and the motors and pension policies are safe. Just got to build up your cash reserves again. I've been talking to Lance Daniels and he wants us to go out to Vegas for a fight. He's offered four hundred grand.'

'Dollars or pounds?'

'Dollars, so say about a quarter of a million sterling.'

'How much does Daniels get out of it Colly?'

'Dunno, why?'

'If he's offering us dat I bet it's worth double.'

'Maybe, but who else can we go with?'

'Don King, of course.'

'What! Are you crazy? We'd never get a decent deal out of him.'

'Nah. I don't agree. Phone him and sound him out at least. Don's a cool breddren. He don't take steps. De man's sharp as a razor. I told you before, it's the white media dat disses him. He says he's made more black men millionaires than any other employer in the world. And it's true. De press hates King 'cos he runs t'ings. You get me? He's no worse dan any other white promoter. I wanna do business wid him.'

Colly shook his head in resignation and got up to leave Tiger's flat. 'Glad to see you in training again, Tiger, you fat bastard. Looked like an Easter egg when you came back.'

Tiger smiled. 'Had a lot on my plate recently, Colly. T'anks for sticking by me. You're safe.'

'You mean I'm not dangerous?'

'Piss off, Colly, you Cockney geezer.'

Tiger threw a training shoe at him as he walked through the door.

~

Colly sounded really excited when he phoned Tiger a week later.

'I just spoke to King.'

'Go on.'

'And he wants to top Lance's offer.'

'How much?'

'He wouldn't say on the phone but he sounded serious. Said he'd intended getting in touch with us for ages but always got distracted. Wants to meet us when he comes over for Stretch's bill at the Albert Hall next week. Looks like your career's on the up again, Tiger.'

King's six hundred thousand dollars far exceeded their expectations. It also included a promise of a WBC world title shot if Tiger won.

Tiger had met King before, but only had a chance of exchanging pleasantries. Sitting in his suite in the Dorchester, the big man with the frizzled hair seemed less intimidating in slacks and open-necked shirt, than when he was courting media attention in that booming jive style.

'I succeed because I have the necessary ingredients of wit, grit and bullshit,' King declared. 'I am the greatest promoter that has ever lived. I never cease to amaze myself - and I say this with the utmost humility. There's only been three really giant promoters in our lifetime; Michael Todd, PT Barnum and yours truly.'

A self-made man after serving time in prison for manslaughter, his estimated wealth in *Forbes* magazine was at least three hundred million dollars.

When in a light moment Tiger asked him why he was always getting investigated by the American government, King was forthright.

'I'm a victim of trickeration. I think I'm destined to be investigated until I die.' King always landed on his feet but the way Tiger saw it, white promoters were the real sharks.

Tiger had always been impressed with King, from his earliest memories. He could recite his life story from his early days as a numbers operator in Cleveland, Ohio without taxing himself.

'Don, you're the livin' entrepreneur!' Tiger laughed. 'Tell me 'bout yourself.'

'Hey!' bellowed King. 'Have you got a coupla days?'

He started telling them his life story when the phone rang and he was called out to sort out some important business.

Tiger knew enough about King to tell Colly all about the great man on the car journey home. Tiger was aware of King's shortcomings but realised that there were few other options in big-time boxing. Tiger told Colly that many who worked with King and severed their business relationships often resumed the association.

'Colly, you've gotta admit whatever his faults, King has been the biggest reason why boxing is such a high profile sport now that generates million-dollar purses. Respec' to the max to de man.'

The day before they were due to fly out, Lance rang with a counter offer of seven hundred and fifty thousand dollars and then faxed the contract. Colly phoned King to explain the situation and he said he wasn't prepared to top Lance's offer but was still willing to promote Tiger. So it was settled, Tiger would fight for Lance but King was seriously interested.

~

His financial future sorted, Tiger concentrated on getting the personal side safed up too. He tried contacting Yolanda but she didn't want to know.

'No way. Fuck off, Tiger. I hate you. If you ring again, I'll call the police.'

Whilst training in Las Vegas for his first fight for Lance, he met Charmaine Betts, a cable TV chat show host from Los Angeles at a Bel Air film launch for the latest Denzel Washington movie.

Dark-skinned, short and curvy with neatly plaited shoulder-length hair, wearing a pink Chanel trouser suit, she stood out even amongst the many celebs around.

Her huge, absorbing eyes, engaging smile and bubbly personality made it instantly clear why at twenty-four she was already being touted as the new Oprah.

Tiger was not only impressed with Charmaine's glamour, but by the fact that she wasn't besotted with Denzel.

'So what are you doing here if you're not?' he asked.

'Get real brotha, I'm just trying to get him on my goddamn show. Think of the kudos. My ratings will shoot into the stratosphere!'

'You can have me pon your show instead.'

'Fine, but what do you do that could possibly overshadow Denzel Washington?'

'I'm gonna be a world champion fighter.'

'Yeah right. And I'm gonna be the President of the United States.'

When Charmaine eventually checked Tiger's credentials, she was impressed enough to put him on her show.

'Good evening and welcome to the Charmaine Betts Show.

Tonight we have on the show Spike Lee talking about the social messages in his films...' Raptuous applause with a sprinkling of boos.

'And Magic Johnson on life in retirement from basketball...' More cheers'.

'But first we have the crashin', bashin' boxer from London, England... TIGER CRAWFORD!' Luke warm applause with comments of 'Who the hell's this?' and 'English? What's a white man doing on this show?'

The hostility soon evaporated as Tiger appeared and proceded to charm and entertain the crowd.

'You guys don't t'ink dere's any black people in England,' he said. 'We're not all tea-drinking City gents in pin-striped suits wearing Union Jack boxer shorts.' They laughed.

'Believe it or not, black people run t'ings in sport and entertainment,' he added in his best English accent that occasionally lapsed into Brixton-street. 'But like black people here, we are under-represented in the most important aspects of public life, politics and the media.'

Some brothas in the audience started whooping in appreciation.

'Tell it like it is, brotha.'

'You KNOW what time it is, Tiger!'

Charmaine was delighted and egged him on and he charmed his way through the next ten minutes. They gave him a standing ovation and one excited woman was so excited that she ran down to the podium to kiss and hug him.

'Girl, BEHAVE,' shouted Charmaine pulling her away. 'I saw him first!'

The crowd roared. People started jumping around. The whole place was in pandemonium. It took a full five minutes for them to settle. Spike Lee and Magic Johnson paled in comparison.

The ratings did so well from his appearance, such was America's intrigue by this articulate black Englishman, Tiger and Charmaine kept in contact. So ensued a transatlantic romance. Tiger had finally got Yolanda out of his system.

Well almost.

Thoughts of the Bad Night still came haunting back.

CHAPTER 28

LET'S KEEP IT PLATONIC

'Thirty grand Dale or *The Globe* will run the pictures on Monday,' said Phil Harper. 'You know I don't fuck about.'

Dale had seen the three-in-a-bed pictures but still couldn't figure out how Harper had taken them. Little did he realise that hard-up Jenny had arranged for a secret camera to film their passionate encounter for twenty thousand pounds. Dale was so fearful of tarnishing his image of respectability, he withdrew the money from his bank as soon as he could.

Dale saw it as just an occupational hazard for keeping his image as spotless as possible. There was no point in involving the cops because it would only get out.

He felt like left hooking the smug Harper as he handed over the package in the tea room of a West End hotel, but knew it would only make matters worse. Dale just hoped Harper would stick to his word but there was no telling when he might blackmail him again or release copies of the photographs.

Dale handed over the package of money, collected the photos and negatives and turned to walk out.

'Oh and Dale.'

Yes!' he hissed turning back to look at the fat, blotchy face.

'We know something else too. Bit of a misogynist ain'cha?'

Harper waddled away. After a few strides he turned and smiled.

'Oh, and have a nice day Dale.'

A furious and confused Dale walked out of the hotel. He did

not have to wonder too hard at what *The Globe* had next in store for him and just prayed that it didn't get out.

He spent the next two hours in a coffee bar in the King's Road before pulling out his mobile.

'Why don't we discuss it over dinner?' Dale said.

'Fine. Where and when?'

'How about tomorrow. I know a very nice Thai restaurant in Bayswater you'd like.'

So as not to look too pushy he suggested meeting Yolanda there.

'No. I expect to be picked up when I'm taken to dinner.'

He was pleasantly surprised and took her address and home telephone number. He picked her up at eight the next evening and they spent their time together not just talking about business affairs but about their personal lives for the first time.

In the months since their first lunch date Yolanda's hostility had melted to a warm friendliness. She found herself looking forward to speaking to him on the phone and the occasional meetings. At the restaurant the only taboo subject was Tiger. They found they had a lot of common interests; astrology, the cinema and swingbeat.

'I'm Leo, July twenty-ninth,' Yolanda said.

'The lion,' he said. 'Very apt. You can really bite someone's head off when you want to.' She smiled.

'I'm Scorpio. October twenty-second, so I'm on the cusp and I have some Libran tendencies I think.'

'A well balanced Scorpion, eh?'

'Something like that.'

Dale paid the bill and when they walked outside he stood in front of her and kissed her on the lips.

'Why did you do that?'

'Because I've had a wonderful evening. Thank you Yolanda.'

'But we only had a meal together.'

'It was very nice all the same. You seemed to switch off the business persona for the first time and relax for once.'

She smiled and shrugged her shoulders.

'Where to now?' he asked.

'Drop me home. I've got a long hard day tomorrow.'

When Dale pulled up outside her flat he switched off the ignition.

'Don't get any ideas, Dale.'

'What d'you mean?'

'There's not going to be any romance here.'

'Don't big-up yourself Yolanda, I'm just being sociable.'

'Oh, is that what you call it!' she giggled. 'Being sociable. The flowers, lunches and now dinner.'

'Yeah. We must have a harmonious relationship.'

'As long as it remains platonic, that's fine, Dale. Goodnight.'

As she leant over to peck him on the chin, he turned his head and kissed her again on the lips, then lurched back cowering as if anticipating a slap.

She smiled. 'You fool. G'night.'

He phoned her the next day at work to thank her for a very nice evening.

'When can we do that again, Yolanda?'

'Not for a while, things are very hectic here.'

'Why don't I come round and cook you a meal instead. My spaghetti bolognaise would show up any Italian chef's.'

Pause.

'Let me think about it.'

Two weeks later Dale arrived at her flat with all the ingredients for the meal. They sipped champagne to celebrate the improved Adidas contract Yolanda had helped negotiate as well as the good news that he had been invited for a catwalk session for Kenzo at the Milan fashion show.

The mix of relaxed conversation and copious amounts of Moet took their inevitable toll and when Dale kissed her this time she did not resist. It was months since she last had sex and the mood and circumstances were right.

As Dale entered her he smiled to himself. He thought back to the night as a youth he was in a card school, playing poker at the back of a shabeen and Delton Ford noticed he was cheating.

Dale started fighting with the semi-drunk Ford and although he was only seventeen his boxing skills and faster reactions allowed him to beat the shit out of Ford until it was broken up. Ford staggered away, ashamed that he'd been roughed up by a young boy.

Tiger's car probably only grazed Ford. Dad found out through the cops he plays golf with. One was an assistant commissioner. Forensic evidence shows two cars hit Ford but they nailed Tiger. Nobody knows, that I came round the corner in a VW Golf , almost immediately after Tiger had run Ford over and I ran Ford over again. They could not trace the killer's tyre tracks to a specific driver. They charged Tiger with his accidental death because it suited them. Lucky for me. Ford, the drunken, cheating fucker. He'd won six hundred and forty off me and I was mad. That was my Christmas money he fucking took. Tiger did me a favour. I wonder if Yolanda would be giving up her pussy if she knew the truth?

Dale smiled.

Tiger. What a dopey bastard. If only he knew... And that drug test. I'm sure Archie paid the medics to doctor his sample. Tiger was such a plum he didn't realise that the spliff was probably out of his system a long time before the test.

CHAPTER 29

ONLY IN AMERICA

Tiger loved the fastness and gaudiness of Las Vegas, the gambling capital of America. Here everything was twenty-four-seven entertainment. Literally any form of pleasure could be acquired at any time of the day. You could even get married in a booth at any ungodly hour.

Living there was no problem for a twentysomething champion athlete with an insatiable appetite for women and partying. Charmaine would take the forty minute flight from Los Angeles every Saturday morning and leave on the Monday morning to record her shows.

Sometimes he would go and spend the weekend at her apartment near Beverly Hills, but she normally would be at his place. They would go to the celebrity parties or to a casino, maybe go dancing or to a restaurant with friends. He loved it. During the week Tiger enjoyed the company of the many female tourists visiting America's most depraved city.

Vegas was a magnet for low-life, tricksters, hookers, pimps, dealers, the weird and the insane. High rollers thought nothing of blowing millions in one weekend in Vegas, and when they tired of gambling, there was always an available woman or drug dealer to supply them with alternative entertainment.

Corrupt high-ranking government officials who had embezzled state funds and government resources were the most welcome. They had no conscience.

Tiger fitted in well in Vegas. Never lacking in confidence, his fit body - and when necessary, best English accent - were babe magnets.

He had a strong affection for Charmaine, who bore a striking resemblance to Yolanda, but after his experiences with Yolanda, he was not in a hurry to fall in love again.

Bwoy, dat Yolanda really and truly fucked me up. Jah know. I did really love dat pum-pum but t'ings nah run right. I suppose killing her farder had a lot to do wid dat. Nice to be away from all dat shit. Vegas is cool, man. Nuff t'ings a gwan inna dis mad city. Punany everywhere. But, really and truly, punany is ten a penny. No point in having a trailer loada girls when you don't have no corn. What me want is another world title. I just hope King's at my next fight.

Colly was staying with Tiger in a spacious two-bedroom apartment that Tiger was renting for the last three weeks before he made his American debut on the undercard of a low-key boxing bill at the Las Vegas Hilton. Colly's contacts in Vegas had swung it for Tiger and he was determined to make a go of his career there.

Word was that if he impressed against Tyrone 'Damage' Drake, an ex-world champion in the twilight of his career but still dangerous, King was prepared to put him on the next Holyfield bill. Tiger got a pleasant surprise; this fight was the final eliminator for the World Boxing Federation super-middleweight title and if Tiger won he would get a crack at the world champion next.

Tiger trained at the famous Johnny Tocco's gym every day at three o'clock. He would turn up early at the gym to watch the legendary Manuel Hernandez.

Tall, handsome and articulate, he was America's classiest boxer at the last Olympics, winning a gold medal in style. Nicknamed the 'Golden Boy' for obvious reasons, Tiger liked studying him train. Hernandez had a huge entourage and a legion of fans - mostly Mexican-American women - watching his every move.

Tiger felt a little inadequate in Hernandez's presence as his entourage consisted of just Colly, Lonnie and a couple of local sparring partners.

'At least dere's no pressure on me like Manuel's got,' said Tiger wistfully to Colly. 'But Colly, he earns millions. I'd swap my pressure for dat kind ah package. F'real.'

'Don't worry, Tiger, you'll soon be in that purse range. You never know, if Manuel comes up in weight, you might get to fight him. He's taller than you and he's struggling to make middleweight and wants to move up to super-middle eventually. He's so tall for a ten-seven fighter and he could jump up to the twelve stone division, no problem.'

'No chance, Colly. I'm too dangerous for 'im. He just likes dem pussy-bwoy matches. Trust me.'

Nevertheless, the dream of fighting the legendary Hernandez somewhere down the line was a great motivator. Dale Harrison was history, as far as Tiger and Colly were concerned.

~

Yolanda phoned in sick for the next week as she came to terms with the night she slept with Dale. She felt repulsed about the whole thing and hated herself for succumbing to his slimy charms and showered constantly, psychologically cleansing herself of his spirit. She phoned Unal and arranged to meet her a couple of hours later to ensure she would not stay in and mope.

Yolanda felt as if she had been raped then shivered as she

273

remembered his cold eyes when he was waxing her and wondered why she found herself imagining him raping someone. She puffed heavily on yet another Silk Cut.

How could I have slept with HIM of all people? That piece of shit. The deceitful bastard. I fell for the oldest trick in the book. God. Why? This doesn't make sense. Tiger's emigrated and that creep's still here. Won't be hearing from Dale in a hurry, especially after that story in The Globe. Funny, I didn't think he was that type. Good job he wore a condom. I really told him where to go the other day when he rang. Tiger is a good man. Unal reckons I should forgive him, but no way. He killed my father. But it was an accident, after all...

On Sunday, Yolanda went to the Kensington Temple with Unal who had been very supportive, and sung and prayed her heart out, begging for forgiveness. She left feeling a little better and they went to lunch in a trendy restaurant with some other friends in nearby Portobello Road.

~

The Globe headline said it all:
WORLD EXCLUSIVE:
BOXER DALE IS
MY GAY LOVER
WORLD champion boxer Dale Harrison enjoyed nights of passionate gay sex with a secret lover for five years.

Bisexual Harrison spent torrid nights of wild gay sex at his lover's flat in Shepherd's Bush, west London.

Shane Barrett, a 26-year-old session musician admitted to The Globe that Harrison enjoyed bedding women but could not resist having a sordid gay affair with him.

Full story: pages 2,3,4 &5

The newspaper continued with extensive quotes from Barrett about the relationship, supplemented with photos and video footage taken of Harrison leaving the flat with Barrett. The evidence had been taken six months earlier but the paper did not run the story until Shane was desperate for the eighty thousand pound balance of the hundred thousand he was promised.

Phil Harper smiled and rubbed his hands with glee as work-mates grudgingly patted him on the back.

This should get me the deputy editor's job at least.

'Congratulations Harper, that must be number thirty-four whose life you've fucked up,' said one colleague unable to conceal his contempt.

'Thanks, Martin. Glad you're keeping count,' retorted Harper smugly. 'It's forty-two actually.'

'I never knew Dale Harrison was a nosher,' said another colleague.

'Yep. He's a nosher alright. Confirmed shit-stabber, James,' laughed Harper. 'Undercover shirtlifter.'

Dale took the phone off the hook at his parents' home but that didn't stop media people coming round. They kept ringing his doorbell and knocking and a squadron of photographers and TV camera crew were parked outside. Luckily, his parents were away on holiday. He packed his passport and some clothes into a holdall, ran the gauntlet of media men and jumped into his BMW.

He headed for Gatwick Airport, intending to go anywhere he could find. At traffic lights on the way to the airport he avoided eye contact with other motorists but could feel their eyes on him and occasionally could see out of the corner of his eyes people pointing at him and laughing.

He booked a two week trip to Tunisia and waited impatiently the three hours for the flight, looking rather curious with the hood of his Adidas top pulled over most of his face in the departure lounge. That did not stop people recognising him though. He could see people pointing at the newspaper and at him. The embarrassment he felt was mixed with anger at Shane but mostly at Harper for running the story.

On the plane there were more sniggers and when a brazen teenager approached and asked him to autograph *The Globe's* front page.

'Fuck off before I knock you out,' shouted Harrison to a mix of astonishment and amusement.

When Tiger heard the news the next day, he was elated.

'Serves de blood-claat batty bwoy right,' he said to Colly. 'I knew he was a fraud from de day I beat him up in de gym. Now de rest of de world know say he's a nasty, lickle bum bandit.'

Tiger sailed through training after that. Niggling injuries were ignored, there were no weight worries and his confidence soared immeasurably. He was given another boost when a week before the fight the World Boxing Federation announced that the reigning super-middleweight champion had relinquished the belt and Tiger and Drake would be fighting for the vacant title.

Drake was built like Tiger, short and stocky. It made things easier for Tiger as he was used to tackling far taller, longer-limbed opponents. Drake was powerful but slow. Tiger found him easy to hit and after six rounds was well on top. It was no surprise when Drake's corner pulled him out with a supposed damaged shoulder at the end of eight rounds.

'And the NEW WBF super-middleweight champion of the

world...,' he paused for effect, 'Tiger Crawford!' announced the MC as an official wrapped the huge, gaudy red plastic belt with gold gild around his waist.

Tiger knelt on the canvas weeping as he clasped his hands in prayer. On one side Charmaine was kissing him ecstatically and Colly was hugging him on the other.

The three of them plus the two sparring partners and some new-found friends went off to nearby Caesars Palace for a celebration meal and to play Black Jack in a casino afterwards. Then they went to a nightclub to down more champagne.

Tiger was woken by the hotel phone at eight-fifteen the next morning, two hours after going to bed.

'Young man, how would you like to make three million dollars to fight Manuel Hernandez?'

'Fuck off, geezer, I'm still asleep.'

'This is Don King, young man and I would appreciate the courtesy of you refraining from using profanity when I am offering to make you a multi-millionaire. Don't you remember, we met in London recently?'

Tiger sat bolt upright.

'You sound like him, but how do I know you're really *de man*?'

'I have already arranged to meet you with Mr Coleman at precisely nine'o'clock in your hotel foyer. Just phone him in room one-one-seven to confirm. I told him I wanted to break the news personally. And don't be late. I have a meeting with Evander at ten.'

King hung up. Tiger phoned Colly but in his excitement got the number wrong. When he eventually reached his trainer, Colly confirmed the good news. So did Lonnie who was in Colly's room.

'Yep, Tiger, we've got Manuel Hernandez on the thirty-first of October at the Thomas and Mack Centre,' Colly beamed. 'It's called 'Fright Night' because it's Hallowe'en. His purse is twelve million dollars, we get three point three million, minimum.'

Colly did not hear a reply.

'Tiger, are you there?'

'Yes, rude bwoy, I'm here. I just can't believe it.'

'King approached me a week ago and said if you looked good against Drake he would get you on a Hernandez undercard. He's paid off Lance Daniels so we don't have worry about future obligations to him. King watched you on TV last night and was so impressed he now wants to match you with Hernandez. We're in the big-time, rude bwoy.'

They both laughed as Charmaine who had woken and got the gist of what was going on started smothering him with kisses again.

'Oh honey, I'm so proud of you. You've got to come on my show again. You're gonna be a big star. I love you Tiger.'

The meeting with King went smoothly. The mane of shocked grey hair made him look about seven feet tall. In trademark dark suit and chunky jewellery, he was a walking advert for all the neon and glitz of Vegas.

King had a reputation for being a dodgy dealer, but after a quick discussion over purses, TV revenues and expenses, he handed over the contract for Colly to take away to be verified by an independent lawyer.

Colly faxed the contract to his lawyer in London who within two days gave the go-ahead, providing a few minor adjustments were made first. The fight with Manuel Hernandez, the world's greatest boxer, was on!

Tiger took two weeks off to recover from the Drake exertions then threw himself into the daily regime of gym work in the afternoon and running at nine o'clock at night.

Colly reasoned that it was too hot to run in the mornings and as he was fighting at night time it made sense for Tiger to get his body used to being active around fight time. Tiger prepared like a monk and played Scrabble to keep his mind occupied. He read Steve Bunce's Boxing Greats for inspiration and Cassius sent copies of *New Nation* and *Caribbean Times* every week.

Tiger went on a nine-city tour of America with Hernandez to promote the fight. The Golden Boy was always polite and sociable but had an air of arrogance that irritated Tiger. Everywhere they went there was a strong Hispanic following for the Mexican-American. Hernandez lapped it up and Tiger was made to feel like an unwelcome gate-crasher.

Tickets for the venue were sold out within days of going on sale, but there were millions to be made from the pay-per-view audience and King, master of marketing, was not going to miss out on that. As Hernandez was the overwhelming favourite and Tiger was virtually unknown outside hardcore boxing circles, King set about playing up Tiger's chances.

In a typical verbose eulogy, at every media opportunity King talked up Tiger's chances as only he could. At a press conference he gave a virtuoso performance. Cigar in one hand, Tiger's raised hand in the other, King knew the coo.

'This Englishman is the William Shakespeare of the noble art, the Sir John Gielgud of pugilism, the Lawrence of Arabia of scintillating, unadulterated excitement. The Right Honourable William Churchill would say Tiger Crawford fights them on the beaches and in the trenches...' An embarrassed Tiger tried to pull his hand away but King held it tighter and continued the tirade.

'He has the panache, persistence and pertinence to be the paragon of pugilistic perfection for the next decade. I call him my Millennium Man. That Dome you Brits built in Greenwich should be renamed the Tiger Dome. He is the pugilist who can maintain the highest standards of the noble art in this new century. Yes, good people, the Millennium Man is as fierce as his Tiger name implies. Twice as tenacious, equally as stealthy and immeasurably more intimidating. The ruthlessness of a starving alligator, he charges like a stampeding elephant and crushes as mercilessly as a boa constrictor.'

King took a deep breath, puffed on his giant cigar and ranted on: 'No fighter in the history of the sport has emanated such perceptible hostility and reduced opponents to withering wrecks, incapable of sustaining resistance of one possessed of such mythological strength with a capacity to sustain implausible feats of human endeavour...' Another big breath as spontaneous applause broke out.

The American media corps used to King's rantings always switched off whereas the British contingent, especially the younger ones, were amused. It made for good copy and TV footage. Lincoln Crawford, one of the British Boxing Board of Control's representatives, roared with laughter and applauded King at the end of his tirade.

With King promoting Tiger's chances the media interest in the fight helped to generate over thirty million dollars in pay-per-view revenue. Tiger would get at least half a million more on top of his three-and-a-bit million when everything was totted up.

'See Colly, I told you King was cool,' said Tiger at the weigh-in the day before the fight. 'I told you he's made more black people millionaires dan anybody else. He ain't named de Don and he ain't de King for nothing.'

Tiger had to strip to his underpants to make the weight. Lonnie handed him his tracksuit and a banana to restore energy.

Hernandez weighed in at eleven stones eleven, three pounds inside the super-middleweight limit. Tiger was spot on the limit. Preparations had gone well, apart from the old ankle injury that was niggling again.

As Tiger got into the back of the stretch limo taking him back to his new hotel, a woman in a white skirt-suit, bouncing breasts struggling to stay put, climbed into the car on the other side.

Colly, sitting in the front, remonstrated, but she refused to get out.

'Don't you remember me Tiger?'

He looked up from her heaving bosom.

'Breeya! What de hell you doing here?'

'I wouldn't miss this fight for the world, baby.'

Then she leaned towards him and whispered. 'We'll celebrate like in the old days after the fight. Alright? Ged rid of Charmaine, I'll show you the works, honey.'

She pressed her ample breasts against his shoulder. He grinned.

'We'll see,' he said. 'Right now I've gotta get some food and plenty ah rest before I mash up dat Hernandez.'

'Don't forget me afterwards Tiger. I'll be waiting.'

An agitated Colly pulled her out of the car.

'Keep your fucking mind on the fight,' said Colly waving his finger. 'For fuck's sake don't let pussy sidetrack you now. You can have as much as you want after. Just keep focused. Goddit?'

Tiger smiled and nodded.

~

On the morning of the fight Tiger was awoken by a knock on the door. He knew it was seven o'clock and that it was one of the two big, black security men posted outside his hotel room by Colly. They had been there all the weeks Tiger had been staying in a suite at the Las Vegas Hilton, ensuring he didn't go out after curfew and no unauthorised females entered. Tiger tried bribing them but Colly had ensured they were both Christian family men with high morals. Plus, they were on to a big fat bonus if Tiger won. It was worth paying the premium for his own peace of mind. Lonnie approved as well.

The only time Tiger got close to breaking the curfew was when he enticed them in for the third consecutive night of Scrabble. When they were niccly settled in and seemingly off guard, Tiger made a bolt for the door. He got as far as the hotel lift to be confronted by a third hired giant. Colly had covered all eventualities. Tiger sulked back with the giant's hand on his shoulder kissing his teeth and looking like a chastised schoolboy.

Tiger turned on ESPN, the American sports channel, and waited for the fight preview.

Damn, I looked criss at the weigh-in. Even I'd be scared of those muscles. Dat Hernandez is in trouble! De lickle pussy-hole reckons he'll knock me out in six. We'll see. King's done a good job in promoting the fight. Looks like I'm gonna top four million. Don's a real breddren.

Tiger met Colly for a light breakfast of toast and honey,

bananas, orange juice and coffee and then they took a short ride to the outskirts of the city for a gentle jog, stretching exercises and long walk in the early morning sunshine. Neither said very much. It had all been said already.

The tension was only lifted when Lennox Lewis who was in town to promote the next defence of his undisputed heavyweight titles, arrived for his morning run and they exchanged pleasantries. Lennox gave Tiger some tips on how to handle the big Las Vegas atmosphere then set off for his run. Tiger really admired his professionalism and felt inspired. No way was Hernandez going to intimidate him now.

The plan was to pressure Hernandez in the early rounds, take a breather in the middle rounds by tying him up and leaning on him when Tiger's natural extra weight and strength should tell and then come on strong and try to stop him in the later rounds or win convincingly on points.

Tiger was relaxing, watching TV in his hotel room when the phone rang. Only Colly was allowed to phone him.

'Yo, Colly. Wassup?'

'Hi, Tiger, guess who?'

It was a woman's voice.

'Dat cannot be Jackie Kallen,' Tiger screamed recognising her voice instantly.

'Yes champ, it's me. I'm here with Tania Follett from Miguel's Gym. John and Steve Sims from the gym are with us too.'

He could hear them all cheering in the background: 'GO TIGER!...GO TIGER!...GO TIGER!...'

'Listen, champ,' Jackie said when the noise lowered. 'Colly made a special case for us to phone you. We don't want to break your concentration anymore, but we'll be at ringside.

283

See you at the celebration party, champ.'

'Don't worry Jackie. I'm gonna broke up de bwoy real bad. Trus' me.'

Tiger was bursting with pride. He really respected Jackie. The call was an inspiring move by Colly to motivate Tiger even more.

Tiger had lunch of tuna fish, sweetcorn, a little pasta and salad with plenty of water, then fell into an uneasy sleep. The security men woke him at six and Tiger, Colly, two sparring partners, two cornermen and a couple of Nevada State Athletic Commission officials were whisked in two stretch limos the short distance to the Thomas and Mack Centre.

Thousands of fight fans swarmed around the venue, many without tickets, there just to soak in the unique atmosphere world championship boxing generates in Las Vegas and hopeful that they might see someone who could blag them a ticket.

Tiger was escorted by a team of security men to his spacious, air-conditioned dressing room, where Colly pushed all well-wishers, media men and opportunists out.

Breeya had somehow blagged her way in and was indignant about being turned out. Apart from his boxing camp only Cassius and Tiger's dad Milton were allowed to stay in the room.

Tiger lay on a towel on a cushioned bench and rested. At eight o'clock Colly made him warm up, just before there was a knock on the door. It was one of Hernandez's trainers, sent over to watch Tiger's hands being taped up to make sure no illegal items happened to find their way inside his gloves, nor too much bandage was used.

Colly sent Cassius to do the same. Lonnie taped and bandaged Tiger's hands carefully as they were watched by Hernandez's aide and a Nevada official who signed the bandages in black marker pen when they were finished.

Twenty minutes before fight time, Tiger pulled on his jockstrap, abdominal protector, new spangled shorts sewn by his mother in the black, green and gold colours of Jamaica and his socks and boots.

Lonnie held up training pads and Tiger punched sharply on them. A film of sweat enveloped his sculptured body. As the security men arrived to take him to the ring, Colly helped Tiger put on his matching dressing gown in the colours of the Union Jack. Tiger took a gulp of water from a bottle then roared in fury as the adrenalin coursed through every fibre in his body.

Cassius hugged Tiger before everyone else took their turn. Milton was the last to get a hug. He kissed Tiger on the cheek.

'Good luck, son. I know you can do it.'

'T'anks dad. I'll make you proud.'

Tiger smiled nervously, took a deep breath and allowed himself to be bustled out by the swarm of security men.

The heat of the Thomas and Mack Centre immediately hit Tiger as he moved through the mass of people to the sound of '*No Retreat, No Surrender*'. Most of them applauded him. Only Hernandez's most faithful supporters showed hostility. Many Hispanic faces waved Mexican flags and wore sombreros.

As the challenger, Hernandez was supposed to come in first but he forfeited three hundred thousand dollars from his own purse for the psychological plus. He came bounding into the arena to the sound of a rap song a few minutes after Tiger had entered the ring, wearing a huge sombrero. King led the way, grinning like a lottery jackpot winner as he climbed through the ropes, evidently anticipating an easy night's work for Hernandez.

As Tiger limbered up he saw Cassius at ringside with Charmaine. Milton was with Iris who to the family's delight, had decided to live with her husband in Jamaica after the fight.

Also sitting ringside was Errol, the aspiring boxing writer from the Barnados children's home. Tiger had kept in touch with him and paid for Errol and his new foster father to come to the fight. Errol scribbled busily in a notepad in preparation for his first ever assignment for his local paper, the *Croydon Advertiser*. Errol's story had been featured in the *Caribbean Times* and *New Nation*. Both black newspapers had promised him work experience stints and the sports editor of the *New Nation* was going to take him to an Arsenal match with Tiger.

Richard Daley, Tiger's faithful sponsor, sat excitedly with his lovely wife June, bristling with pride. Daley had continued sponsoring Tiger even when he tested positive after the first Dale fight. 'That was the best million-pound investment I've ever made,' he repeated to June. She rolled her eyes in mock boredom, tired of hearing him bigging-up Tiger. June chatted to Samina Saeed about fashion as they waited for the big fight. Jacko Ali, the kick-boxing champion, was with a group of Asians who had forked out a fortune to get prime ringside seats.

Esther, the dentist Tiger had an early sexual experience with, had made the trip with Ralph, the estate agent who was now her husband. Sex was still boring with Ralph, but he provided a lavish lifestyle and when the mood took her she indulged in a 'bit of rough'. The last one was with a fitness trainer from the local youth club.

Al Hamilton, the Commmonwealth Sports Awards organis-er and author of the football book *Black Pearls* was there with writer Rodney Hinds and Lennox Lewis and John Fashanu. Lennox was so bombarded by autograph hunters that securi-ty men were forced to intervene to give him some peace.

Breeya had somehow blagged her way into the British press corps. The celebrity seats were occupied by mega-stars. Tiger spotted Spike Lee, Will Smith, Jack Nicholson, Sly Stallone and Halle Berry.

Tiger could see a few Union Jacks being waved by some of the hundreds of Brits who had either made the journey over or were ex-pats living in America. Hernandez still had that cheesy irritating grin.

I'll knock dat bomba-claat smile off your pretty face, sweet bwoy. Jah know.

King climbed in, waving a mini American flag in one hand and a Union Jack in the other. Only in America could some-one like him exist, as he always said. The crescendo of noise from the American-Mexican fans pierced the desert night's air.

A beaming Hernandez looked magnificent in his white shorts with red trim. Tanned and perfectly toned, he looked more like a Baywatch extra than a world champion fighter. But no-one, least of all Tiger and Colly, underestimated his unique talent to destroy.

Hernandez felt unbeatable. He was undefeated, adored by all Hispanics, was endorsing nine different billion-dollar products from cereals to fizzy drinks. There was twelve and a half million dollars in the bank accummulating interest and he was renting out properties all over Vegas, Los Angeles and Mexico City. The *LA Times* had voted him the second most eligible bachelor in America after Leonardo Di Caprio, Hernandez could get as much pussy as he wanted, whenever he wanted.

As the ring emptied and the boxers stood in their corners ready for the first bell, Tiger thought Hernandez had grown three inches and put on twenty pounds since he last saw him. His long arms looked like tentacles. As soon as the bell rang and the little bald, black American referee waved them in, Tiger's nerves disappeared, as they always did.

Tiger was surprised by Hernandez's quickness and his cold, unblinking, radar-like knack of avoiding shots. From watching hours of videos, he knew all his opponent's strengths and weaknesses but his speed was still awesome. Tiger expected an evasive opponent but this was ridiculous. It was like trying to catch a spirit.

Hernandez jabbed and moved as Tiger flailed away sending him back to his corner feeling humiliated. He could hear sections of Hernandez's supporters laughing.

'Cut him off Tiger. You've got to cut the fucker off,' pleaded Colly at the end of round one. 'He's fast but if you catch him, he'll go. He's a fucking welter, remember. You're doing well but you have to position yourself better.

'When he moves towards a corner next time, feign a right lead so he moves away from it to his right and then let a left hook go like there's no tomorrow. You'll get the fucker's respect from that.'

'You can nail him, Tiger!' Lonnie shouted.

Tiger nodded, spat out some water, took the gumshield into his mouth and walked out for the second round with the sole intent of landing that left hook. Hernandez skirted around him, jabbing at will. Tiger could hear the Americans jeering at him being outclassed and felt the anger welling up inside.

Hernandez was winning so easily he dropped his hands momentarily to sneer. Tiger saw his chance and feigned to throw his right. The American's head twitched to the right and Tiger threw the left hook with all his might.

The crowd roared.

Tiger's mind went blank.

CHAPTER 30

NO HARD FEELINGS

The next few seconds were a blur.

Tiger heard the referee yelling at him to go to a neutral corner before he could start the count.

Hernandez was sprawled on the canvas, shaking his head trying to clear it.

'Five, six!' shouted the referee holding up his fingers as Hernandez rose on groggy legs.

'Seven, eight!'

He was up at nine but clearly still stunned. The referee looked momentarily into his eyes and after what seemed an eternity waved it all over. Tiger had knocked out the best fighter in the world!

Bedlam ensued. Don King held Tiger aloft as the ring instantly bulged with people.

'Son, I knew you could do it,' King said. 'I arrived with the champion and I'm leaving with the champion.'

It had not sunk in that he was the winner until Hernandez came over to hug Tiger and wish him all the best.

'I'm proud to have lost my unbeaten record to a great champion like you,' said the American. 'I hope we can meet again, one day.'

They embraced and were prised apart by an American TV reporter wanting an interview. Tiger gave three more interviews before leaving the ring. British fans chanted the familiar: 'We love you Tiger, we do, we love you Tiger....'

It took half an hour for him to get past them and back to the dressing room where there were more interviews and an impromptu press conference. At the official press conference later, Hernandez was gracious in defeat and made no excuses.

'Tiger, you deserve to be champion. That was a magnificent shot. I wish you a long and successful career and hope one day we will have a rematch,' Hernandez said to a round of applause.

'T'anks Manuel. You're a great champ and I will give you a rematch when de time is right.'

Then he turned to the media. 'I dedicated dat fight to the memory of Stephen Lawrence, de upstanding black yout' who was murdered in Britain by racist scum in 1993 and because of British police incompetence and institutionalised racism de murderers may never be brought to justice. I will also donate a percentage of my purse to de campaign fund.' Everyone applauded.

Tiger set off for his celebration party at the Las Vegas Hilton dressed in blue Armani jeans, white T-shirt and black single-breasted Boss jacket, overwhelmed with joy. 'I just can't believe... I knocked out Hernandez...' he kept repeating. 'Dat gives me even more pleasure than beating that wort'less Dale 'Arrison. Dis is the greatest moment of my life and I dedicate it to you two, my modder and farder. God bless you.'

He kissed and hugged them again.

Charmaine kept kissing and hugging her man, much to the amusement of his parents and Cassius. Colly smiled, knocking back the Moet from a bottle as the others sipped from glasses.

Breeya was the first to grab him when Tiger entered the reception full of his friends, family and supporters. Richard

Daley pressed a bottle of champagne into his hand as he tried to extricate himself. His face mocked strangulation as she hugged him tighter.

A huge cheer erupted.

Jackie Kallen and the Miguel Gym posse cheered louder than the others. They felt this was a triumph for Brixton as much as anywhere else.

King was already there holding court and extolling Tiger's virtues. 'I knew that boy was a winner from the moment I set eyes on him,' claimed King. Tiger smiled.

'Hey sugar, this is my property,' Charmaine insisted pushing Breeya away.

'He was mine first, bitch,' growled Breeya pushing her back.

Tiger laughed as he separated the two. He waved to security men to come and escort Breeya away. As she was led away protesting, Tiger whispered to one of the security men to tell Breeya to meet him at Caesar's Palace the next night at eight as he knew Charmaine had to fly back to LA the next morning.

The party was in full swing, and Tiger was having a great time when he was tapped on the back.

'Yo, rude bwoy. No hard feelings.'

His turned round to see a grinning Junior with his arms outstretched anticipating a hug from his former best friend and partner. Flashbacks of the way Junior had cheated him out of thousands and disappeared, leaving Tiger to pick up the debts filled the champion with fury.

He grabbed Junior by the lapels of his suit jacket, pulled out his bulging wallet from a breast pocket, put it in his own then re-enacted the left hook that had felled Hernandez before calling security over again to expel the unwelcome guest.

Junior was out cold. A referee could have counted to a thousand and he would not have risen. Tiger felt as much satisfaction from that punch as the Hernandez one.

~

Exhausted and elated, Tiger slumped into bed at six-thirty the next morning, full of champagne but not too drunk to appreciate his night's work. He was barely awake when Charmaine left two hours later promising to ring him when she got home.

The hotel staff and security men outside had been instructed not to disturb him until midday, no matter what.

At one minute past twelve the phone rang. He groggily picked it up.

'Congratulations Tiger, you did well.'

'Yolanda?'

'Yes, it's me.'

'Where are you.'

'In the foyer of your hotel. Can I come up?'

'Sure.'

When she arrived Tiger opened the door and there she was as stunning as ever in a white satin slip-dress, her hair plaited in fine black strands. He was still in his red silk boxer's shorts.

'Hi Tiger. Remember me?'

'Come in, Princess.'

They stood in the middle of the room looking directly into each other's eyes as tears rolled down their faces. They embraced. He picked her up and carried her back into the bedroom.

They made love with a passion, tenderness and intensity that bettered anything either had experienced before. They remained oblivious to the phone constantly ringing and even people knocking on the door.

For both it was a fusing of spirits, an almost out-of-body experience, so luscious and precious was the experience. After months of training in spartan conditions, prohibited from any sexual contact, he had plenty of energy and semen to work out of his system. She too was mega-horny. She had not felt the hardness of a man for a long, long time.

When they had finished Yolanda rested her head on his chest and after a while she broke the silence. She pulled out the engagement ring Tiger once gave her and put it on the tip of his left index finger.

'Shall we get married?'

'We're in de right place.'

Repton Boxing Club, home of hundreds of amateur boxing champions, is proud to be associated with No Glove No Love. It's a real knockout!

Head coach Tony Burns wishes to thank all club members, past and present, for their overwhelming support.

We wish Ron Shillingford every success as a novelist and film scriptwriter and Audley Harrison good luck at the Sydney Olympics.

Repton Boxing Club,
Cheshire Street, Bethnal Green,
London E1
Tel: 020 7739 3995

CAPRIUS

HAIR
MAKE-UP
MANICURE
BEAUTY
TREATMENTS

582 KINGSLAND ROAD, LONDON E8 4AH
TELEPHONE: 0171-254 0558

LONDON

THE LONSDALE LION IS KING

LONSDALE SPORTS EQUIPMENT LIMITED

47 Beak Street, Regent Street, London W1R 3LE
Tel: 020 7437 1526 020 7437 3375 020 7434 1741
Fax: 020 7734 2094
Special orders department
24 hour answering service: 020 7434 1741

Val Walkinshaw-Browne of
Biggleswade, Bedfordshire has every
faith that 'No Glove No Love' will
be a great success.

Good luck Ron.

Val also hopes this book reaches
Dwight (Lincoln) Browne and wants
him to get in touch.

'Dwight, we love you and miss you.
Give us a call.'